A H

This is a work of fiction. Characters, locations, names and incidents are products of the author's imagination or are used fictitiously.

Copyright 2012 by L.I. Albemont
All rights reserved

Also by L.I. Albemont
The Kirk

"What do you do if the very ground is evil? If something so horrific happened here that it can never be cleansed?"

Welcome to *"The Kirk"*, the page turning new horror thriller from best-selling author L.I. Albemont.

A picturesque town with a dark history is the setting for Albemont's newest offering. Secrets lie beneath the prosaic surface of the small town of Falkirk. The bucolic beauty conceals an ancient evil that lurks in the quiet woods and lanes, an evil that feeds on murder and madness and fear.

Contagion: A Novel of The Living Dead- Book 1

A remote mountain town is isolated by a snowstorm as an ancient evil, gone pandemic, turns the residents into the living dead. Almost overnight the town becomes a snowy tomb of the roaming, hungry dead. Stranded, hiding, a small group of survivors is determined to survive. Will they be able to adjust to this hungry new world?

World Without End: A Novel of The Living Dead- Book 2

When deadly earthquakes devastate the Caribbean, an ancient disease of almost unimaginable destructive force engulfs the globe. As the earth continues to convulse and the seas encroach the dead rise with an appetite for human flesh. Survivors must learn to navigate a world in which they are now the hunted. And the hunters never sleep.

Dead Coast: A Novel of The Living Dead-Book 3

The story continues as survivors flee the infested cities, looking for a refuge from the ever-increasing, ever-hungry dead.

Table of Contents

A Haunting 1
Prologue 6
Chapter One 9
Chapter Two 16
Chapter Three 30
Chapter Four 38
Chapter Five 44
Chapter Six 53
Chapter Seven 60
Chapter Eight 68
Chapter Nine 76
Chapter Ten 83
Chapter Eleven 91
Chapter Twelve 96
Chapter Thirteen 103
Chapter Fourteen 112
Chapter Fifteen 121
Chapter Sixteen 131
Chapter Seventeen 138
Chapter Eighteen 147
Chapter Nineteen 153
Chapter Twenty 160
Chapter Twenty-One 167
Chapter Twenty-Two 172

Chapter Twenty-Three 180
Chapter Twenty-Four 188
Chapter Twenty-Five 196
Chapter Twenty-Six 207
Chapter Twenty-Seven 216
Epilogue 231
Prologue 234

> *Glendower: I can call spirits from the vasty deep.*
> *Hotspur: Why so can I; or so can any man:*
> *But will they come when you do call for them?*
> *1 Henry IV, 3,1*

Prologue

"The prisoner will stand for sentencing."

The judge looked down at her husband, who rose, standing awkwardly in handcuffs and shackles. Sarah leaned forward and clutched the back of the seat in front of her. Here each day the first week of the trial, she agonized over each charge, each witness that struck blows at his integrity and judgment. She believed in both until detailed testimony emerged of trips to Aruba with Kelly, a co-worker he had never mentioned. Kelly, tall, tanned, and what her mother would have called 'floozy blonde', cooperated with the Feds in exchange for immunity.

After that humiliating afternoon she stayed away, focusing on selling the few things she owned that the Feds had not seized. Despite that, her face appeared in newspapers and at times on local television, or so she had been told. She stopped watching television and reading the paper soon after the arrest.

She was here today to see how this ended, to see if the frozen feeling that encased her would go away. Reporters shouted at her to look their way but she hurried up the steps of the courthouse, avoiding the icy patches left by the weekend snowstorm. Wearing a black skirt and boots, black reefer coat buttoned up against the cold, she wanted the world to forget her. She looked waiflike in the slightly too large outfit and the dark sunglasses were glamorous on a small, heart-shaped face.

It felt strange to be out in public again. Her husband's financial schemes had defrauded the pension fund for city teachers and firefighters leaving them with no retirement plan and outrage had been vehement. Her husband's attorney had advised taking precautions against angry victims so she went into hiding, grocery shopping at night, never going to restaurants.

When her boss, Phil, recommended a leave of absence, she acquiesced, knowing the publicity was not good for the small property development company she had loved working for during the past three years. Two weeks ago, after she made the decision to move away, her co-workers gave her a going-away lunch. Eve and Sharon cried and everyone promised to keep in touch but she was sure she saw secret relief on Phil's face. It hurt to realize that he considered her a liability now but that was exactly what she would be until time erased the town's memory.

Sean now wore the standard issue, orange, prison jumpsuit, a painful contrast to the tailored suits he had worn throughout the trial. In spite of her determination to remain detached, her heart ached for him, imagining the humiliation he must be feeling right now. Some tiny, conjugal, sympathetic spark must still exist between them because he turned and their eyes met just as she slipped through the door and sat down in the back of the courtroom. The judge now finished reviewing the counts.

"Mr. Faust, in view of the particularly widespread and damaging nature of your crimes, this court imposes the maximum penalty of seven years for each count with each sentence to run consecutively for a total of twenty-eight years. Restitution paid from seized assets will continue. Court will be in recess until one p.m." He banged the gavel.

"All rise," the bailiff intoned.

Everyone stood. Sean and his attorney talked quietly for a few moments then the bailiff approached the table. Sean said something and the bailiff glanced at Sarah then shook his head in response. Sean looked back at her before he shuffled out, head down.

Sarah found with surprise that she was crying and sat back down, rummaging through her purse for a tissue. How could he have done this? Defrauded investors and stolen the life savings of hundreds of people, destroying their lives just as he had destroyed hers. She wiped her eyes then blew her nose and the tears stopped. Her purse sagged open and she smiled a little when a small, foldable road atlas with a highlighted route wandering down the east coast slid out. Time to go.

Chapter One

The house has Flemish curves upon its eaves;
Its doorways yearn for buckle-shoed young bloods,
Smoking clay pipes, with lace a-droop from sleeves—
Moonlight on terraces is like a story told
By sleepy link-boys 'round old sedan chairs
In days when tulip bulbs were gold.
-Carolina Chansons

"You're going to love this one. Needs a little tlc but the neighborhood is impeccable." Foster Collins of Cooper River Realty sounded genuinely enthused.

Sarah looked around. The cobblestone street was picturesque in the late afternoon light. If not for the cars parked here and there she could almost think she had gone back to colonial times. She held a flier that read:

"Historic property with established gardens. Desirable S.O.B. location only three blocks from the Battery. Don't miss out on an opportunity to own a piece of history. Shown by appointment only."

"What is an S.O.B. location?"

Foster read the flier and laughed. "Not what you're probably thinking. It means south of Broad which is traditionally a very good area of town."

"Oh."

Sarah peered through the leaves. This was the fifth house she had seen today and one of the very few that fell into her price range. Almost hidden by overgrown shrubs, the narrow structure was easy to overlook. Crumbling stone steps led directly from the street up to a small front door, and that tree…

"Do you know what kind of tree that is?"

"A rowan. It's supposed to be as old as the house."

"And how old is that?" She removed her sunglasses and looked up at the tree looming over the entrance, partially blocking the door.

"The original building permit has never been found in public records. In some historical accounts of the city, there is specific mention of a house that survived the Great Fire of 1740 serving as a smithy on this spot and based on that I would estimate it's around three-hundred-years old. But I doubt that's accurate."

A three-hundred-year-old house? Some of the homes on this street could be described as mansions. This one nestled among them like a poor relation. Double porches with peeling, vine-choked Tuscan columns adorned the left side of the dwelling. Wicker chairs stacked against the railing looked moldy with age. Obviously neglected but with good bones, the house seemed to beg pardon for its humble state. Several of the encircling trees sported green leaves even now in the deep of winter. The *plink* of a piano floated over from the red-brick house next door, reminding her of the piano she had just sold. When she thought of all the money she had flushed keeping it tuned over the years... hindsight is twenty/twenty.

This was her second day in Charleston, the city her mother had spoken of so longingly from military postings in Japan and Europe. Sarah's soldier father's career had taken them around much of the world but lovely as it was, her mother always reminisced wistfully about this southern, coastal town.

Yesterday had been Sunday and despite the rain she'd walked the cobblestone streets along with the other tourists and listened to the church bells tolling, apt in 'The Holy City' as the tour guide called it. She was already succumbing to the dilapidated charm of its shady, overgrown lanes and gated side yards in which fountains splashed unseen behind oleander and magnolia. This street was a little more tucked away than some and she hadn't come across it in yesterday's ramblings.

"Ready to see the inside?"

"Sure. You're right about the neighborhood; it's fantastic. I'm just a little worried about the repairs needed on a three-hundred-year-old house."

"There've been several renovations over the years, obviously, and some rooms are more up to date than others. I'm not saying you won't have to make some changes but you'll find that reflected in the price. I promise you, it's worth a look." He opened the quaint, arched front door to which traces of bright blue paint still clung. The foyer they stepped into was small and square with a central staircase rising to the second floor.

"The house is what is known as a 'single' and was the most common building style before the Revolution. Most of the rooms on this floor are to the right of the hallway. The first room on the right would have been called the parlor. The next room you see is wired for an overhead light so it was probably used as a dining room at some point. The tall ceilings are characteristic of Charleston houses. They allow heat to rise."

The parlor boasted a classic Adam fireplace and mantel surrounded by a beautifully paneled wall. Trash filled the dirty hearth and two grime-encrusted firedogs rested against the back bricks.

White-painted wainscoting and heavy crown-molding adorned both rooms and continued up the staircase. Two pictures, roughly the same size, hung face to the wall in the foyer. Sarah tried to turn one around and found it nailed fast. She looked at Foster who shrugged.

"Um, not sure what happened there but you can pull the nails out with a hammer and the holes should be an easy patch job. You can see that the electrical conduits run along the outside of the walls. Not everyone likes that but I find it charming and it does accentuate the age of the house. Also, I forgot to tell you that everything in the house conveys so what you see here is all yours." He made a grand, sweeping gesture as if to encompass vast riches and Sarah suppressed a laugh.

Behind the foyer, two steps led down to a small, barely functional kitchen with an old range, (only one of the electric eyes worked) green, laminate countertops, and what could truly be termed an ice box languishing off by itself near a door that led to the yard. The floor, however, was marble, gouged and scratched, but still marble. The larger, creamy squares were broken up with small, blue squares, set in a diamond pattern.

Their steps echoed on the old oak floors and the stair treads creaked when they mounted the curving staircase to the second floor. Some previous owner had carpeted the steps and the ancient, stained carpet bunched and sagged like the diseased pelt of a very old animal. The mahogany banister felt as smooth as silk under her hand.

The house's one bathroom at the top of the stairs was one of the more up-to-date rooms in the house but decorated in a horrible, seventies, brown and orange color scheme. There were two bedrooms on this floor; one, slightly larger, looked out over the overgrown garden on the side of the house. A door in the smaller one opened to a closet staircase leading to an attic crammed full of bits and pieces left behind by previous residents.

"You can see there's room for expansion. It wouldn't take much more than a little insulation and drywall to turn this into a game room or a bedroom, whatever you want. I would have all this" he gestured at the items covering most of the floor "hauled away by a professional junk removal company."

She was noncommittal. She didn't have the money to have anything professionally removed. Maybe she could sell some of the stuff on Ebay.

"Are the bedroom floors the same wood used downstairs? They look different."

"Often these old houses were built with different woods, depending on what was available. I think the floors upstairs are cherry and maybe another fruitwood. The floor downstairs is oak in all the rooms except for the kitchen, of course. The painted wainscot and that paneled wall is anyone's guess as to wood-type. Maybe you can tell from the grain if it's still visible. I don't have that level of expertise." His phone buzzed and he excused himself to take the call and went outside.

Heading for the small grime-coated attic window, Sarah accidentally kicked over a half-full duffle bag. The contents spilled across the floor. Hurriedly gathering everything up and stuffing it back in the bag, she was surprised to find a wallet containing a driver's license and credit cards. The expiration date on the license was March 1989. The bag also contained a gray, moldy toothbrush and several un-posted letters. She opened one at random.

"…and they're always here now. Yesterday, when I came home from work they were waiting, all four of them, in front of the hedge in the back. I'm leaving as soon as I can but I'm trying to get my deposit back. That bastard at the rental office is stonewalling me. I'm not crazy and I think he knows more than he's telling." She put it back in the duffle with the wallet.

Obviously an unhappy tenant. Odd that he would leave his wallet behind. She distinctly heard a child crying and she looked out of the window but saw no one. Going back down to the second floor, Sarah paced the larger of the two rooms, mentally placing furniture. The bed could be any size she wanted; she had sold the *lit matrimoniale* when she realized the extent of her husband's betrayal. There was no closet. She supposed she could have one built but it would make the room smaller. A small side-window set in a dormer had a built-in seat with drawers beneath it.

French windows led to an antiquated side porch that needed paint but would be a nice place for morning coffee. She glimpsed a plank swing moving gently back and forth underneath a giant oak and she inhaled deeply, feeling engulfed in a sea of green leaves. Sleeping in this bedroom would feel like sleeping in a tree house. The moist, fragrant air and the buzzing of invisible insects all around were soothing.

A bird flew past the railing, landed near her feet and then took off again, seeming almost comically alarmed at her presence. She heard the sound of the piano again and then a door slammed. A little girl waved to her from the porch of the house next door and Sarah waved back. She saw the realtor standing next to her ancient Volvo. She had coaxed it along most of the drive down and sent up thanks each time it started.

Outside, Foster finished his phone call. He caught glimpses of his customer at windows as she moved through the house. She had been tight-lipped from the start. Most clients would at least tell you where they were moving from but not this one. When asked she just said, "Up north" and then inquired about property tax rates. However, the north-east was in her voice and on her car tags.

"Hello?" He looked up. She called down from the side porch. "I'm going down to have a look at the basement."

The basement was gloomy, with rickety, wooden stairs. An overwhelming smell of putrefaction hit them as soon as they opened the door. They descended the steps and Foster found the source of the odor. A cat had somehow gotten in but had not been able to get back out. The desiccated, marmalade-striped body lay under the egress window. She caught just a glimpse before Foster found an old coal scoop, and took the remains outside.

"I'm so sorry about that. I usually try to pre-inspect a house before I show it but with the holidays…" He wiped his hands on his pants and trailed off, hoping she hadn't seen the body too closely.

"Poor cat. Odd that with neighbors on either side no one heard it. I can't imagine it starved to death quietly."

Foster shrugged. From the way the neck swung when he scooped it up, it was obvious that it hadn't starved to death. Someone or something had snapped its neck.

The floor was actual stone, not concrete, and housed a drainage system and sump pump since wet basements were not unusual in Charleston during a heavy rain. This one seemed drier than some she had seen. The washer and dryer connections were down here. An old, oil furnace filled most of one corner with odd cylinders and elbow joints lying scattered about. She rapped the side and a bolt fell to the floor.

"If you're interested in the house you should probably have that looked at by an HVAC company and adjust your offer accordingly."

"That's the heat right? Has the house ever had air conditioning?"

"If it did, they would have been window units that someone took with them when they left. The current owner has always rented it out and hasn't bothered to upgrade much. I don't think he has had a tenant in a while."

"How receptive would he be to a lowball offer?"

Foster thought this one over. She didn't need to know the house had been on and off their books for nearly ten years and that tenants never stayed more than a few months, if that long. If this were his house, he would jump on the first chance to get rid of it. Anyone likely to buy it would have to be from out of town and not have heard the stories and this cautious cutie was an ideal candidate. Moreover, if certain dark rumors were disregarded, it *was* a bargain.

"Make an offer if you're interested. The worst they can do is say no."

"I'll have to think about it. How soon could I take possession?"

"I would think immediately since it's empty but you never know until you ask. Do you have furniture in storage or is it en route from…?"

"I don't have a lot of furniture so I'll probably be looking for some pieces here." She sidestepped that inquiry.

"Unless you're uber rich, avoid King Street. They have some great pieces of course, but you will pay through the nose. So, would you like to sit down and write an offer?"

She laughed at his eagerness and he realized she was younger than he had first thought. Early thirties tops.

"Give me a day or so. I have some things to sort out but I promise I'll let you know by Friday. Of course, I'll need to have a home inspection company check it out."

Foster was elated. If he could close this sale, he would exceed his quota for the month and get a white elephant off the firm's books to boot. He could usually tell when someone was going to make an offer but she had a good poker face. He bent down to re-tie his shoe so she wouldn't see his excitement.

She wasn't going to tell him yet but she had already decided. This house, broken, neglected, and in need of repair, was something she could make beautiful again. This rain-drenched, green plot of land was going to be her new home.

Chapter Two

In the days and hours of Saturn thou canst perform experiments to summon souls from Hades but only of those who have died a natural death.
-*Clavicula Salomonis*

The sun shone on cobblestones still wet from an early morning rain as small, brown birds flitted from tree to tree. Sarah stood in front of the parlor window, happily surveying her new property. When the owner accepted her offer within hours two weeks ago, she asked for approval to move in early, offering to pay a nightly rate but he refused, leaving her stuck in the hotel. So after the closing yesterday evening she came straight over here with the few things she had, camping out on the floor.

She slept badly, hearing thumps in the walls and soft scratching sounds at the bedroom window. The home inspector hadn't seen any evidence of a pest problem but maybe she needed to call an exterminator anyway.

A quick shower this morning revitalized her and she decided to tackle the yard while she waited for the furniture she bought last week to arrive. A used-furniture store out on Maybank Highway yielded some bargains and she was now the proud owner of a washer and dryer, a mahogany, rice-carved, four-poster bed with matching chest and a flame-stitch fabric sofa she was told was a Chippendale reproduction.

"That fabric ain't been fashionable since nineteen eighty-five but it is sure in good shape," the proprietor, an elderly but very spry gentleman named Frederick March told her. He kept up a running commentary as he walked with her around his two-story shop that was once a feed store. "That old woman that owned it lived on Johns Island, out near the deep water in a house her daddy built for her and her sister. The sister died right after they moved in but the old woman stayed there forty years by herself. She had one of the first air conditioners on the island and she kept that place so cold- I ain't never seen furniture so well-preserved, like it was in a freezer. Now that bed, that may have come from down near Beaufort but I can't remember for sure."

She arranged to have the items delivered the day after the closing and paid in cash. Thinking about it, she now wished she had thought to buy some end tables. Her lamps were currently on the floor. At least she would have something to sit on and sleep in.

This morning, the garden called her outside and she responded eagerly, wearing old jeans, a Sox cap, one of Sean's old flannel shirts, and no makeup. Trimming back an enormous hydrangea revealed two ancient gateposts marking the beginning of a stone pathway in the yard as well as a rusting, wrought-iron fence bordering the yard closest to the street.

"Those are probably tabby you know."

She turned around. A very nicely-dressed man standing on the sidewalk in front of her house nodded to her. She must look confused because he repeated himself.

"Your gate posts there. The mortar holding the brick together is mixed tabby."

"What is tabby? Are you telling me someone killed a cat and mixed it with the mortar?"

He laughed. "Tabby is a type of construction mortar. The early settlers burned oyster shells to create lime and mixed it with local sand to make a sort of concrete that's all over historic parts of the city. It's still used sometimes but we make it with Portland cement now so it's more durable."

He smiled warmly. "I'm Noble Connelly, and I'm full of useless information about tabby posts and other subjects. My wife and I live in the white money-pit down the street and we heard a Yankee bought the house. You didn't waste any time moving in did you?"

"It's a pleasure to meet you. I'm Sarah Faust and no, there wasn't time to waste. The hotels around here do a thriving business and there was no more room for me after the eleventh. I was able to negotiate a quick closing and here I am." She removed her work gloves, reached across the post to shake his hand, and felt something sharp pierce the soft flesh of her forearm. Blood dripped onto the post and she looked in dismay at an inch long gash in her arm.

"Oh my dear, I should have warned you. Here, let me help." Noble pulled out a handkerchief (who carried handkerchiefs anymore?) and wrapped it around the cut.

"Traditionally, we cover tabby structures with plaster because the oyster shell fragments are so sharp, you see. The plaster has worn completely off these. I'm not surprised considering how old they probably are. There, I think it's stopped now."

"Thanks. I'm going in to run some water over it but again, it was a pleasure to meet you and I look forward to meeting your wife. I hope to have the garden tamed and a little more presentable soon."

"That tree is going to eat your door. Are you going to have a landscaper in or…?"

"Oh no, I like to do my own gardening." She crossed her fingers behind her back as she lied. She had never gardened in her life but she certainly could not afford a landscaper and planned to wing it and hope for the best.

"The tree is on my shortlist. I don't have a chainsaw yet so-"

"I have one. I'm on my way to my office but I'll drop by this evening and bring the chainsaw if you like."

"Really? That is so kind of you."

"It's nothing. See you later this evening." He waved and was gone.

She was touched by his kindness. On the other hand, maybe the tree was something everyone in the neighborhood wanted gone. She couldn't blame them. She started for the house to take care of her arm and remembered she didn't have any band-aids. One more thing for the list she had not started yet. Might as well do it now.

Milk
Band-aids
Coffee

Walking through the main floor, she added floor wax and window cleaner. Upstairs she wrote: bathroom cleaner, shelf paper and- she jumped back - some kind of spray to kill the millipedes that just ran under the baseboard. She started wiping down the shelves in the miniscule linen closet then made herself stop. Focus. There was so much to do and she could not keep jumping from task to task without finishing anything.

Back outside she hauled the hydrangea branches over to a corner in the back of the lot. The brick wall back here must have collapsed in the rains of the past few days. She stumbled on bricks and slipped in the mud that had spread onto the grass. Stacking the old bricks in a neat pile she heard a metallic clang.

Under a heavy clump of vines was a bronze head, somewhat sunken in the ground and still covered with mud. The large, heavy-browed skull sported ugly, twisted horns. Pan maybe? She scraped more of the mud away. It had none of the puckish charm usually associated with Pan and instead looked deformed and brutish. She dug at the ground around it, clearing away spongy, decaying, clumps of leaves and revealing goat-like legs with cloven hooves. Someone had fastened a crudely fashioned, heavy, iron collar with inverted, nasty-looking spikes around the squat neck.

Sarah instinctively reached out to try to remove it but when she touched it, it felt oddly warm. She sat back on her heels. This was a mystery but a house this old was bound to have some interesting stories surrounding it. She scraped more mud away from around the base of the figure, finding little parterres arranged in an octagonal pattern around the satyr. She stacked the debris on the growing pile in the corner, and went inside to wash her hands, feeling she deserved a coffee break. And then remembered she didn't have any coffee beans nor did she know where her grinder was. Of course.

Not wanting to have to find her phone she turned her laptop on to check the time. Almost noon. Mr. March had said she would be the first stop after lunch on the delivery schedule and not wanting to miss them; she sat on the peeling steps of the side porch and sipped a glass of water. She tried pulling up her bank account before remembering she still needed to get internet service set up. There were several wireless connections showing as available but she didn't want to vampire on to any of her neighbors' services. Bad first impression to make if they noticed somehow. She reminded herself to check on the status of her job applications as well. She had applied online to so many different companies, she had almost lost track.

Ok. Time to tackle the list of Things to do to the House. She already knew she wanted to paint the dingy, grayish stucco a warm, cream color. The red roof tiles were in good shape according to her home inspector, and the red would go beautifully with the cream. The shutters had turned out to be rotten and would have to be replaced as would several of the balusters on the porch railing.

While the kitchen was small by modern standards, lacked counter space, and had an awkward layout, she was still delighted by the marble floor. Matching, natural marble slab countertops would replace the green melamine horrors currently in place and she had already taken measurements preparing to call some stone retailers. Overall, the house was structurally sound but in need of a thorough update.

A hiss of air brakes up the street caught her attention. A white delivery truck lumbered slowly past the cars parked on the narrow street. From her viewpoint it came breathtakingly close to hitting a couple of them but it didn't hesitate and soon parked in front of her house. Two beefy-looking young men climbed down from the cab and, to her surprise, so did Mr. March.

"It's nice to see you again, Mr. March, but who's minding the store?"

He chuckled. "My daughter knows nearly as much about the business as I do and I like coming into the city. She's a charmer, my old city, and I like to check up on her from time to time. Besides, this address rang a bell for some reason and I couldn't figure out why. It'll come to me while my grandson here and his friend get your things."

The boys rolled the door of the truck up and lowered the ramp. The only difficulty was maneuvering around the tree hanging over the door but they managed to work around it. The boys had the furniture in place in no time and even hooked up the washer and dryer in the basement. She tipped them a twenty and hoped that was enough. The bed looked higher than it had in the store, maybe she should have bought the steps that went with it but seventy-five dollars was a lot of money to her right now.

"It's going to be even taller when you get the mattress and box springs on there." Almost as if he had read her mind, Mr. March entered the bedroom carrying the mahogany steps she had turned down. He set them by the bed. "I thought you'd want 'em once you saw it all set up. Most people do."

"You were right. It was going to be quite a climb."

"Well, I'll be on my way. Lots more to deliver today. I sure wish I could remember what I wanted to about this place."

She went downstairs with him, found her purse and gave him the cash for the steps. They pushed the overhanging tree branch up so they could walk out the front door.

"This will be gone the next time you make a delivery. I'm just waiting for a chainsaw."

"It's not the prettiest tree I've ever seen and I suppose you won't miss it but you don't see a whole lot of rowan trees growing this far south. I'm surprised it's gotten this big and-" He broke off and stared at the cleared bed and its bronze figure. A look of dawning recognition mixed with something else spread across his suddenly pale face.

"Young lady, are you renting this house or did you buy it? I can't recollect what you told me."

Sarah was puzzled by the expression on his face and the urgency in his voice. "I bought it yesterday and I know it doesn't look like much at the moment but I-"

"Are you one of those- what do you call 'em? House flippers? Is that what you plan on doing?"

"No, I plan to stay."

"Then may the good Lord help you." He climbed into the truck cab followed by his grandson who started the engine and began backing slowly down the street before turning around.

Sarah stood on the curb, feeling as if she had been slapped. The truck stopped and Mr. March leaned out the window and shouted.

"Whatever you do, don't cut down that tree. Trim it if you need to but take good care of it." They rumbled away, bouncing over the cobbles, again clearing the parked cars by mere inches.

A hush fell on the street. The sounds of chirping birds and the rustling leaves again predominated. What on earth had he meant by all that? The house needed work but it wasn't that bad. Maybe he thought the tree had grown into the foundation. She peered around the roots but didn't see any buckling or broken stone next to the house and the home inspector would have caught something like that anyway.

Sarah sighed, the new mattress should be here anytime and she had things she needed to get done. Inside, the house was full of little whispering sounds and she thought she smelled a lingering odor of decay from the dead cat the realtor had removed. Down in the basement the washer and dryer were a welcome sight and she started a load of whites, adding her neighbor's bloodied handkerchief. The area smelled faintly of mold; she must have imagined the other smell. Crouched in the corner like a giant, dismembered spider, the old furnace was a reminder of one of the many expensive projects awaiting her. Footsteps sounded overhead and she ran up the steps and peered around the door.

No one was in sight but the front door stood open. Puzzled, she looked out and saw the branches on the tree swaying. Nothing in the house was amiss but there wasn't that much here to harm anyway. She shut the door and seconds later someone knocked then rang the bell. She opened the door.

"That was fast! Are you Ms. Faust? Great. We've got your mattress. Just show me where it goes and we'll get you all set up." A tall young man in khaki shorts and a Spoleto t-shirt smiled down at her.

"Right up here, if you want to follow me." She led the way upstairs. "Be careful on that carpet, it's a trip hazard but I haven't had time to remove it."

Wow. The bed was high with the mattress and box springs. The steps were going to be useful. After the delivery guys left, she ran back upstairs and leaped onto the bed, luxuriating in the extra soft pillow top layer, thinking she would get a better night's sleep tonight. From this vantage point, she could see the upper branches in the trees off the porch. The swing ropes moved lazily back and forth. Getting up she walked out and looked down. Odd that the swing continued to move while the breeze had died away. A jeweled lizard darted across the railing, scurrying down the column headfirst. The dryer buzzer went off and she forgot about the swing.

Making the bed with fresh, clean sheets, she found her extra blankets and left them on the end of the bed. She still didn't have any heat in the house but it wasn't that much of a problem right now and maybe it wouldn't be until she could get an HVAC company out.

By four o'clock that afternoon, she was almost ready to call it a day. She had looked up an HVAC contractor with whom she now had an appointment for next week. Internet service installation was scheduled for tomorrow and she had a full fridge, cleaning supplies, shelf paper, band-aids, and a claw hammer. She wanted to get those pictures off the walls. She had a feeling she was dealing with plaster walls, not drywall, just because of the irregular look of the surface in places but was reasonably confident she could make whatever patches were needed.

The first one in the foyer came off easily and she turned it around eagerly to find that instead of some valuable work of art, it was a mirror, old and missing the silvering in places but not in bad shape. Why would anyone nail a mirror backwards on a wall? She knelt, propped it against the wall, and just glimpsed the reflection of a dark figure moving into her kitchen. She whirled around, heart pounding and called out "Who's there? I'm dialing the police right now." She really had no idea where her phone was, but she grabbed the hammer and walked slowly toward the kitchen. No one was there and the back door was closed and locked. Angry now, she made a full sweep of the house, almost tripping over the stupid carpet on the stairs. She found no one. Ok. What had she really seen? It must have been a reflection of something from outside because no one else was in the house. Every house had its quirks. Large trees and shrubs surrounded this one. Those were bound to cast some shadows. She still felt uneasy and her adrenalin was pumping.

Taking the hammer, she hooked it under the edge of the carpet on the top step and pulled hard. Tacks popped and the section pulled free, dust billowing. She continued all the way down, coughing in the dust, but not stopping until she reached the bottom, dragging the heavy mass over into the dining room corner. A fine grit still covered the steps but it didn't take long to vacuum it off and reveal golden oak treads in reasonably good shape. Her uneasy feeling changed to one of satisfaction as she polished them to a glowing sheen. She sat on the top step and surveyed her work happily. The doorbell rang.

"Bet you thought I'd forgotten." Her neighbor, needing only a hockey mask to complete the look of a murderer from a horror film, brandished a chainsaw then set it down next to a gas can on the steps. "There is already gas in it so you probably won't need the can but I brought it just in case. Return it anytime, no hurry." He looked past her into the foyer. The setting sun poured through the open door illuminating the curving staircase and its newly polished wood. "Someone's been busy. Did you do this yourself?"

"I did. That carpet was awful. Thanks for the chainsaw; I'll get it back to you tomorrow."

"Come over tomorrow evening for drinks, let's say around six? The old ball and chain wants to meet you but doesn't want to barge in uninvited. I have no such compunctions."

"I'll be there and thanks again."

Evening brought a new chill to the house and Sarah was grateful for the warmth the stove's single electric eye provided as she scrambled an omelet for supper. The range was so old she didn't recognize the brand name on the door. The kitchen cabinets weren't as bad as she originally thought and would probably look fine after a good sanding and a coat or two of paint. One door revealed a fold-out ironing board in perfect working order and a drawer contained a metal chute that led to who knows where.

    The beautifully paneled wall next to the back door would not need anything more than a coat of paint either. Near the baseboard she noticed a small metal plate that read "Fain Fold-Away, West 23rd Street, Norfolk, Virginia." Hmm. Feeling around, she found a concealed handle under a panel and pulled. A small bench unhinged from the wall and folded legs dropped to the floor supporting it. In the wall's center, she found two more hidden handles and unfolded a small, hinged table. A concealed breakfast nook. She laughed, delighted with the find, wondering what other surprises the house held. Sitting down, she ate her first meal in her new house and wondered when this nook was last used.

    After washing her dishes she folded everything back into the wall then, walking through the main floor, paused to admire her staircase once more. The bronze, pendant light hanging in the foyer cast sparkles of light that made the wood appear to shimmer. She reached for the light switch then stopped, feeling suddenly cold. Very clearly reflected in the mirror still propped against the wall was a dark shape. It hovered just above the floor, almost as if it wanted her to see it, before it scuttled into the kitchen and out of view. This time, she didn't bother to call out and ran into the kitchen, ready to confront whatever it was- and once again found nothing and a locked, back door. The room, chilly before, was now positively freezing and she saw her breath in the air. Leaving the lights on she ran upstairs, closed and locked the bedroom door, and, feeling about six years old, sat in the middle of her tall bed wrapped in blankets, finally falling asleep after midnight.

    She opened her eyes the next day to a morning well-advanced. After breakfast she decided last night's apparition had a logical explanation, something along the lines of "more of gravy than of grave," and she felt more in control and ready to face whatever the day brought. Or so she thought.

When the doorbell rang and she opened the door to the Fed Ex deliveryman, she was surprised and a little excited. Who didn't like getting packages? It turned out she didn't like this one. The lawyer she engaged to handle her divorce from Sean had hit a hurdle and as she read through the letter, she felt a sense of dread.

She had thought that divorcing someone for a fairly public adultery would be straightforward. It turned out not to be if the accused denied the accusation and demanded proof and that was exactly what Sean had done. The attorney enclosed a sealed envelope containing a letter that her husband had asked to be forwarded to her. She held it tightly for a few minutes before setting it aside. She didn't want to read it.

So now she had the option of pursuing the divorce on grounds of irreconcilable differences, which was what the attorney had advised in the first place, or she could try to find proof of the adultery, usually an expensive and sordid quest. Just thinking about dragging all that up made her tired. In one way she didn't care if they divorced or not. She just never wanted to see or think about him again. In another way though, there were legal ramifications involved in staying married to him.

The money she used to buy this house came from a life insurance settlement plus a legacy both of which came to her when her parents died. She and Sean had been saving that and banking most of her salary to buy a house and fortunately she had been able to prove it had nothing to do with Sean or his company when the court was evaluating their assets. A lot of her salary went to Sean's defense attorney but not all. It now dawned on her that Sean could claim half of this property as well as anything else she acquired until they were officially divorced. She had been stupid not to clear this up before she moved on. She decided she would send her attorney a quick email asking for an opinion on what she could do about that. In the meantime, she had other things to do.

The possessive feelings this house aroused were hard to explain. Maybe it was the fact that it was the first house she had ever owned or perhaps it represented a refuge from the shambles her life had become. She was trying to create order out of chaos in more ways than one. Laying the papers aside, she grabbed a roll of shelf liner.

The tiny bath upstairs had a claw foot tub, a sink attached directly to the wall, and a toilet. All were white porcelain but were badly scratched and stained. Someone had installed brown carpet (who put carpet in a bathroom?) and she thought the moldy smell probably came from that. She tried to avoid walking on it with bare feet. There was not a lot of built-in storage space in this house so even the miniscule linen closet in here was a bonus. After wiping them down, she lined the old wooden shelves with contact paper and finally put away her towels and washcloths.

Today was colder than yesterday. The fireplace worked; she just needed firewood and this was a perfect opportunity to get rid of that tree and get some heat at the same time. She retrieved the chainsaw from the basement and went outside.

A cold wind blew, swirling dead leaves around the sidewalk and yard. The poor tree seemed to hang protectively over the door and she hesitated. How could she destroy a (possibly) three-hundred year-old tree? How long did rowans live? Mr. March had told her to take care of it. It might be best to trim it and see if she could make it look a little better without cutting it down completely.

The saw felt heavier than it had yesterday, almost as if something didn't want her to lift it. She strained to maneuver it toward the limb hanging low over the door when the pressure ceased, as if a rubber band had snapped and released it. The chain hit the limb hard, immediately severing it so that it fell on her right foot. She barely kept the saw from slicing into the front door through forward momentum. Setting the saw down, she limped to the edge of the stoop and sat, massaging her foot. The tree did look better but it wept copious amounts of viscous, gray sap down the trunk. There was no way it would burn yet. She cut the fallen limb into sections, and then stacked them on the side porch to dry out.

A rustling sound in the shrubs caught her attention and she turned to see two little girls come around the corner of the house. One, slightly bigger, pulled a red painted wagon in which a smaller girl wearing glasses sat, holding tightly to a cat adorned with a plastic tiara askew around its ears. A tiny elasticized skirt fit snugly around its middle. She looked down at it with a fierce expression of love. The cat looked resigned.

"Hi. Do you live here now?" the oldest girl asked.

"I do. My name is Sarah. Do you live on this street?"

The older girl made a sweeping gesture that took in most of the street. "My Dad lives here but we only stay there sometimes."

"Let me talk, let me talk!" the littlest girl shouted. "I have to tell you something!"

"Ok, sweetheart. What is it?"

"This is my cat."

"She's beautiful." Sarah reached out to scratch her behind the ears and the cat bore it stoically.

The little girl nodded solemnly. "I love her."

"I'm sure she loves you too."

"She doesn't like the skirt," said the older girl. "She tries to claw it off and Dad said you shouldn't make her wear it."

"It's just for while she's outside. She shouldn't be naked."

"Cats can't be naked. You're stupid."

"No, I'm not! You are!" She released her stranglehold on the cat who took off like a rocket, leaving the tiara behind. She climbed out of the wagon and ran down the sidewalk, calling "Come back, kitty!" long brown curls bouncing, finally disappearing in someone's yard.

"I have to go help find her. I had a cat, too. Dad said he ran away but I think the witch got him." The child nodded as if to accentuate the truth of her words.

Sarah was taken aback. "What witch?"

"A witch used to live in your house. Sometimes she comes back."

"Witches aren't real, you know." She smiled.

"Not now but in the olden times they were." Her tone was matter-of-fact. "Bye!" she shouted over her shoulder and she was off, pulling the wagon down the sidewalk, calling for her sister.

Sarah shook her head and went inside, still smiling. Then she remembered the dead cat in the basement and her smile faded. Just a coincidence. She shuddered. The house was still freezing.

She took a quick trek down to the coffee shop and warmed up before emailing the attorney. She took another walk around the city, this time strolling the grounds around The Citadel and marveling at the huge, live oaks covered with trailing beards of gray Spanish moss. Farther down at the Battery, the sea looked choppy and gray all the way across the harbor to Mount Pleasant. Cannon from the Civil War still dotted the park here, and a brass plaque commemorated the victims of Hurricane Hugo, old and modern tragedy blending quietly beneath the call of gulls and the soft southern twilight. Willows, bare branches dangling like long, thin, brown fingers, swayed in the sea breeze.

A large white house overlooking the water was obviously hosting a celebration of some sort. Clear, sparkling lights decorated the trees and somewhere inside a band played jazz music. A full moon hung in the still blue eastern sky.

Still wandering aimlessly, she found quaint side streets, all of cobblestone, with tall, narrow, wooden-clad houses. The evening grew darker and light spilled from the fanlights that topped their doors. High-pitched, childish voices drifted from a door opened to admit a large, gray cat.

Turning her steps toward home, she walked slowly, finding the cobbles somewhat treacherous to navigate in the now dark streets. She fished the key out of her coat pocket and unlocked her front door, feeling a little thrill at the thought that this was really her house. The small rooms were still and quiet as she walked through, touching the paneling on the walls and running her hand along the curving, well-worn volute at the end of the banister. She shivered, not with cold, but with happiness that she had found a home in the city her mother had loved so.

Chapter Three

"It's a bijou, your house, I've always said so, and I can't tell you how delighted we are that you bought it and are restoring it. Did you know there's a cannonball lodged in the wall facing the Battery?" Mary-Michael stubbed out her cigarette and closed the window.

Sarah had arrived at six carrying a bottle of wine and the chainsaw. Noble was not at home, having called to say he would be delayed but to go ahead and have drinks without him. Mary-Michael had taken the opportunity to swear Sarah to secrecy and then smoke a forbidden cigarette before her husband got home.

"I just don't want him to worry about me," she confided in a soft, southern drawl. She resembled a blonde Renaissance Madonna. "On his side of the family, everyone gets cancer of some sort and dies young. On my side, we would probably never die if we didn't acquire a vice or two. My mother is seventy-five, her mother, my grandmother, is ninety-five, still drives, and she cooks for all of us at Christmas. Ok, that's my last cigarette for today. Let's open that bottle of wine and I want to hear about everything you're doing to the house."

Sarah leaned back and sipped from the exquisitely thin crystal glass. The white Italianate house looked like spun sugar on the outside with its double side porches and graceful Doric columns but the interior was a riot of vivid colors accented by heavy, cream-colored crown molding. The curving staircase soared three stories above the black-and-white checkered, marble foyer. A collie lay asleep in a patch of sunlight on the first landing. The matching, feather-stuffed sofas they sat on were well worn, comfortable, and covered with dog hair, as was most of the other furniture.

"Everything needs painting. The plumbing is fine and so is the electrical. I've already stripped the awful carpet from the stairs and it looks a hundred percent better."

"So it sounds like mostly cosmetic issues?"

"Mostly. I'm looking for countertops to match the kitchen floor and all the appliances have to be replaced eventually. But what's the story behind the cannonball?"

"Charleston was fought over from the very start of the revolution, you know. Your house took the hit during the final British assault in April of 1780. The woman living in your house at the time threw an absolute fit about it. She sued the British military commander for damages and did manage to collect some of the money."

"I'm surprised no one tried to remove the cannonball and I can't believe the realtor didn't tell me."

"I wouldn't worry about it too much. The house and cannonball made it through the 1886 earthquake intact. Probably in some other town it would have been removed a long time ago. In Charleston we tend to cherish our historical remnants, often to the point of ridiculousness, I have to admit. Have you submitted any plans to the Board of Architectural Review?"

"Not yet, but I don't plan any outside changes other than paint and new shutters. I think a soft cream color will go well with the roof and the shutters will stay black."

"That won't require the whole Board then. You should get a response within ten days or so."

"That works for me. I don't have a painter lined up yet. I'm still getting things put away and looking for a few more pieces of furniture."

"Will your husband be joining you or...?" Mary-Michael trailed off expectantly.

She knew the question would come at some point. "No husband. Or rather there soon won't be. I am in the process of a divorce."

She was spared further questions when the front door opened and Noble called out, "Hello? Does anyone have time to fix a drink for a working man? I found this beautiful woman strolling along the sidewalk so I invited her in."

The dog on the landing woke up, barked, and ran downstairs, tail thumping in excitement. Noble gave her a thorough scratching behind the ears. Walking alongside him, a frail-looking elderly woman with perfectly coiffed white hair and twinkling blue eyes smiled sweetly at them. Noble made sure she was seated comfortably before turning to kiss his wife and say hello to Sarah. Mary-Michael gave the woman a kiss on the cheek then busied herself at the small wet bar near the bookshelves.

"Sarah, I would like you to meet Nay-Nay, Mary-Michael's grandmother. Nay-Nay, Sarah just bought the stucco house down the street."

"It's so nice to meet you," Sarah said.

"Here you go, Nay-Nay, Dewar's with lemon and Noble, honey, we're out of Bombay Sapphire so you'll have to make do with Gordon's." Mary-Michael brought the drinks over.

Noble made a face but didn't refuse the drink. He took one long, thirsty swallow then whispered, "Sweetheart, Nay-Nay's parallel parking skills are not what they used to be. I just re-parked her car for her. She had half the street blocked in. Did you know she was coming over?"

"No, I didn't but my grandmother never needs to give advance notice. As for the parking, she still parks better than most of the neighbors. Sorry, Sarah, I don't mean you of course."

"Who are your people, dear?" asked Nay-Nay.

"Sarah isn't from here, Nay-Nay. Her people are from off." Noble turned to her. "If you're not born in Charleston then most natives simply refer to you as being from "off." It just means from somewhere else. Nay-Nay's people have been here since the 1600's. An early ancestor was one of the few female Caciques created in the colonies. Or was she a Landgrave? I can't remember. They're your family, Nay-Nay. You know the details better than I do."

"Lady Charlotte Farquarson Kettleby was a Cacique and owned over forty-eight thousand acres of the low country. Rumor said she caught the eye of Charles II and was rewarded for unspecified services to the Crown."

"Oh my." Sarah raised her eyebrows.

"That actually never happened. Lady Charlotte was far too young for the King to have shown any romantic interest in her but she *was* the granddaughter of Lucy Hay, a friend of the Merry Monarch's mother. The two older ladies had less than unblemished reputations, although their morals were not out of line with the times. The land and the Cacique title were a reward to the family for supporting the young King Charles during his exile in the Cromwell years."

"That's fascinating but I have no idea what a Cacique or a Landgrave does."

"They never did much of anything. Both titles were intended to be a sort of hereditary nobility for the colonies but the idea never caught on and local government assemblies never ratified the proposals. It just died away. The land grants were the meat of the matter." Nay-Nay took a sip of her drink.

"Does your family still own the property?"

Mary Michael and Noble laughed. "I wish. Noble and I could both quit our jobs, travel like we've always wanted, *and* repair the foundation under the porch."

"I can't see anything wrong with your porch."

"Upkeep on these old houses is constant. We think about selling and buying something new and less complicated from time to time. A mimosa tree had practically grown into the foundation and it was a devil of a time removing that thing. Kind of like the tree by your front door."

"I've decided to keep that tree. I trimmed it up, thanks to Noble's chainsaw."

"Take care of it, dear. It's supposed to be almost as old as the house," remarked Nay-Nay.

"You are the second person to tell me to take care of that tree. I removed that lowest branch so the door isn't blocked anymore and I'll probably leave it like that for now."

"Good. It's never a good idea to tamper with trees close to the house. Besides, they say that rowan trees are good luck for houses like yours."

"Why for houses like mine?"

An embarrassed silence fell. Mary Michael and Noble looked uncomfortable but Nay-Nay was visibly distressed.

"I should not have mentioned it but I assumed you knew. Your house is famous in Charleston."

"Famous for what? My realtor told me it's very old and was once the site of a smithy."

"Who was the realtor?"

"Foster Collins."

"Foster told you it was a smithy? He knows better. My dear, it was an apothecary shop but not your average one. Mistress Grayhame operated what was practically a little voodoo shop on the property during the sixteen and seventeen hundreds. Most of it was harmless. Love potions, creams said to make the skin whiter, the bosom larger, an eighteenth century version of the cosmetics counter. However, there were stories, probably true, of black magic, abortions procured, even human sacrifice. The tales grew so lurid that the town authorities had to step in."

"Step in how?"

"Mistress Grayhame was tried and found guilty of witchcraft."

"What did they do to her?"

"Well, to quote a letter sent by a British visitor during that spring, *The poor creature was hanged by the neck and then burnt to ashes which were scattered, her body being deemed unworthy of any sepulcher. Perchance we are all breathing her now.*" Nay-Nay recited as if from memory.

Sarah remembered the little girl saying a witch used to live in her house and felt a sinking dismay.

Sensing her distress, Mary Michael spoke up, "Sarah, the story is part history and part sensationalism. After it was all over, the city officials were ashamed of what happened and tried to hush it up, destroying documents and such. Most of what we know about it came from a cache of letters and a series of articles from the newspaper found in New York outlining some of the details. The journalist who wrote the story up back in the nineteen-twenties may have gotten inventive. We do love a little drama in Charleston. Let me get you another glass of wine, or would you like something else?"

Conversation switched to gardening and the desirability of paved driveways versus those composed of crushed shells. Sarah's own small driveway, if it could even be called that, fell into the shell category. Vines and other plants had encroached on it over the years until it was barely distinguishable from the rest of the garden but she gathered that she was fortunate to have it. Parking space was valuable in the city.

She finished her second glass of wine and consequently felt pleasantly light-headed. The evening dark had fallen without her noticing and it was time to go home. Noble stood and walked with her to the porch.

"We're just tickled that you bought the house. It's so much nicer to have a homeowner as a neighbor rather than another renter, if you know what I mean. If you need anything at all, just ask. And thank you for the wonderful wine."

Pendant moss adorning the live oaks swayed in the cold wind sweeping down the street. Streetlamps cast welcome golden light at intervals as she made her way back to her notorious house. A genuine witch had once lived here. Great. She supposed she would get used to the idea. The whole story was really more about superstitious, ignorant people fearful of anyone outside the norm than about anything evil, she told herself. Nevertheless, she felt reluctant to dwell on the story.

She forgot the whole thing when she arrived home. Her front door stood open and, as she had forgotten to leave a light on, only a deeper darkness awaited her inside.

Memory of the dark figure from the night before rushed back and she almost ran to the Connelly's to ask Noble to come over and go through the house with her. Instead, she hit a key on her phone for light and walked inside, turning on the foyer light first, then going through the whole house. Finding no one, she turned her attention to the latch on the door. It closed easily but was almost too loose in the frame. Perhaps the wood in the jamb or the door itself contracted in the cold air, making the latch less secure. Whatever the cause, she was tired of this and decided if it happened again she would call a locksmith and have it dealt with; end of story.

Her wine induced wooziness had worn off and she wasn't tired at all. Her glance fell on the second picture still nailed to the wall in the parlor and she located her hammer, carefully pried the frame from the wall, and turned it around. She wasn't surprised to find another mirror. This frame was just as elaborately carved as the other and still retained touches of gilt paint. She propped it against the fireplace, planning to hang it when she finished painting.

She took a long bath in the scratched tub and contemplated replacing it, wondering what the cost would be. The feet looked rusted but that should be fixable with a stiff metal brush and some metallic paint; it was the porcelain that was the problem. Was it possible to use spray-paint on a tub?

The old house creaked as the night grew colder and the wind picked up. A slight scent of cherries seemed to drift up from the worn, wooden floor. Wrapped in her warmest robe, she sat on the bed and surfed the internet. She found out she would have to re-glaze the tub and probably the sink too at a cost of several hundred dollars. If she did all of the interior house painting herself that should save enough money to hire a professional to do the re-glazing. Hopefully anyway.

On a whim, she typed her house address into the browser and had several hits, including Zillow and the local property assessment office but the most promising looked to be on the City of Charleston Archives website. A small line read, "Grayhame, Trial of." Sarah clicked on the link.

"Among the stories of our fair city, perhaps the happenings at 5 Rue Lane are accounted the most inexplicable. Indeed, the events that transpired on this small piece of property look like a throwback to the Dark Ages when we explore the tale of Mistress Grayhame, a Charleston businesswoman of the late seventeenth and early eighteenth century.

The trial of Mistress Grayhame was an unusual chapter in our history. Accused of and tried for witchcraft, she was the sole local fatality of the European and North American witch-hunt craze of that time.

Charges included the bewitching and torture death of the ten-year-old son of a brewer, and grave robbing. Dark tales of animals torn asunder and offered as sacrifices at crossroads, of infants boiled down for their fat to be used in candles and ointments were also among the accusations."

The article ended abruptly but a footnote indicated that more information and some original documents were available in the archives located downtown in the old courthouse. Sarah decided to go down there when she had time and see if they would allow her to look at any of their collection. She was sleepy but she needed to look up one more thing.

Typing in "Rowan trees properties of" generated many sites. She read "Long considered a tree of magical properties, the Rowan has particularly dense wood that is used for walking sticks and divining rods and is believed to help keep travelers from getting lost. The word rowan is Norse and refers to the red color of the berries and foliage but the tree has other names such as Quickbeam, Mountain Ash, Witchbane, Witchwood, and Rune tree. In folklore the tree is also said to protect against witches and other malevolent beings and is often planted in graveyards to keep the dead from rising."

She shut down the computer. She had never been superstitious and didn't believe in "things that go bump in the night" but alone in an old house on a cold night it was hard not to be a little frightened. Before she went to sleep, she did something she had not done for years. She said her prayers.

Chapter Four

"A new shipment from Italy arrived last week. We have most of it unpacked but the samples are still in the warehouse. Come back Wednesday and we should have it all set up in the showroom." The tall man in old jeans and a flannel work shirt smiled then turned away and began thumbing through a cardboard box while marking off items on a clipboard. Sarah noticed he had a fine layer of dust on his broad shoulders and some in his dark hair.

She spoke up. "Hey."

He turned back, seeming surprised that she was still there. She went on. "I spoke with Angela last week and she said I could take a look at some pieces in the warehouse today. I gave her my measurements over the phone and she said you guys have some remnants that might work for me."

"Oh, that's you. Yes, she told me. She's not here right now though."

This guy was no customer service award winner. She said patiently, "Could you show me the pieces?"

He put down the clipboard. "Yes, ma'am, I'll be happy to do that for you."

He walked out from behind the counter, opened a set of metal double doors with exaggerated courtesy and said, "After you."

She had obviously annoyed him but she really wanted to see the marble. The dusty warehouse was brightly lit and noisy. They passed by two men using a wet saw to cut a huge stone slab into sections. The piece was dark with flecks of gold and green and she could just imagine it going into some posh kitchen with vast expanses of countertops. The stone he led her to looked quite different. It was a soft, creamy white with veins of darker shades running through it.

"Both slabs are Carrara, from Italy. The piece in front has been given a honed finish and the one behind it has a more polished finish. Can you see the difference?"

She could. The front piece was slightly duller and softer looking than the shinier, more polished piece in the back.

"I like the honed piece the best. The faint blue veins running through it should match my floor. Will the honed finish stain more easily than the polished?"

"Just seal it occasionally. Do you cook a lot?"

"I plan to. How does it hold up under heat?"

"Marble starts out as a sedimentary rock and changes to metamorphic due to extreme heat and pressure. It should be fine."

"I guess that's it then. I have my measurements written down. Do I leave them with you guys and you call me when it's ready or…?"

"We'll have to come out and measure it ourselves before we cut anything. Accurate calculations are really important. Leave your phone number and I'll have Angela call you to schedule a time."

She wrote down her phone number and address on a yellow sticky note and handed it to him. He read it, looked surprised for just a second, and then stuck it on the cabinet behind him. He smiled when he said goodbye then went back to whatever he had been working on before she had interrupted him.

Soon she would have her countertops and beautiful ones at that. She was excited now about getting the cabinets ready and stopped to pick up two gallons of paint on the way home. All she had to do now was get the sanding done.

Five hours later, she was exhausted. Her eyes burned, her mouth was dry and her nose felt clogged. She was covered in dust and had an ache in the small of her back. The cabinets had so much old stain and varnish on them it was like excavating through layers of time and she still wasn't done. She removed the doors and took them outside to finish, propped them against tree trunks and then noticed the lowering clouds threatening rain. She was too tired to move them all back in right now. Sitting on the porch steps, she leaned back against the post and closed her eyes.

Leaves rustled in the rising wind and the old tree branches groaned softly. A woman, dressed in a long, brocade dress with fabric gathered at the shoulders and falling in folds down her back, sat in the swing. Small, white hands clutched the ropes as she leaned back and smiled, flirtatiously it seemed, at someone behind her. Her hair, pinned up in complicated ringlets, was very thick and dark. Sarah heard faint murmuring sounds. Opening her eyes she sat up, realizing she had dozed off and been dreaming. She rubbed her eyes. The blue and green colors and raised textures in the woman's dress had been so vivid. The swing swayed in the wind.

The rain clouds had blown out to sea and the late afternoon sun sent slanting rays into the yard, lighting the undersides of the tree leaves and creating a shimmering, green overhead canopy. The small bronze statue glowed but the iron collar was a dark blot, swallowing rather than reflecting the light.

Footsteps sounded on the sidewalk and then came into the yard. A voice called, "Hello? I knocked on the front door and didn't get an answer but I saw your-" The owner of the voice came into view. It was the salesman from the stone store. Startled, she just stared at him.

"...car. Um, hi. Someone needed to measure your countertops and, since I live out this way, they asked me to do it. Angela tried to call and didn't get an answer but since I had to come right by your house..." He trailed off, looking awkwardly uncomfortable. His eyes were very blue and there was still some dust in his hair. He looked like the kind of guy who didn't notice what he wore and probably needed to be reminded to get a haircut. Kind of yummy actually with those shoulders.

She stood up and dusted herself off. "That's fine, in fact that's great. The sooner, the better. Follow me."

Completing the measurements took only a few minutes. Her original measurements were slightly off near the sink, but only very slightly.

"Do you want an ogee edge? The slabs are still wide enough for that if you want."

"What is an ogee?"

"It's like a routed edge on a baseboard. You probably have an edge similar to what we offer somewhere in your house. Let's see-" and he strode out of the kitchen.

In the foyer, he knelt down by the door. "Right here, you see the top edge of the baseboard? That's about what it will look like."

The top of the board had a pleasant curve that ended in a straight, narrow edge.

"Or you could go with a bull nose edge if you want."

"I'll take the ogee edge. I like the idea of it echoing the shape of the baseboards. How long will it be before they're ready and you can give me a final price?"

"Angela will call you with the price and installation date."

"Great. Thanks for coming by." She opened the front door to usher him out.

"I left my tape measure and notes in the kitchen. I'll go out that way if you don't mind."

"Sure."

In the kitchen, he gathered his things and headed for the back door then paused.

"I haven't introduced myself. I'm David Staunton. Also, I guess I should tell you that I'm your neighbor." They shook hands. His was warm and calloused.

"Oh, it's nice to meet you. I'm Sarah, but you already know that, of course. Which house is yours?"

"I rent the garage apartment of the house behind you."

"The shrubbery is so thick and tall that I've never seen that house."

"Yes, the houses are close together but in Charleston we definitely landscape with privacy in mind. It was nice to meet you. Either Angela or I will get back to you soon with the price and installation date."

She watched him walk to the back hedge, lift some holly branches aside, push open a small gate, and disappear. Well, who knew there was a gate there? She waited a few minutes to be sure he was gone then walked over to inspect it. It was oddly made with a hinged, moveable gate in a rectangular enclosure. To get through, it looked as if one would have to position the gate part in the middle of the rectangle then go through the small space thus created. She played with it a few minutes then realized he could probably hear the metal clanging, and she went hurriedly back to her cabinet doors to finish the sanding.

Night fell before she was done and she turned on the porch light to sand the last one. She stacked them by the door and surveyed the now smooth wood with satisfaction. Perfect. Tomorrow she could start painting.

Back in the kitchen, she cringed at the sight of the dust covering the counters, the floor, and in the sink. She wiped down the counters and rinsed out the sink but was too tired to bother with the floor. Her footprints and David's marked the dust through the kitchen and into the foyer. She sat on the bottom step to remove her shoes- and stopped, confused. Following alongside and crisscrossing the prints from earlier, were small, child-sized footprints. Someone had walked all through the foyer and into both the dining room and parlor where the prints faded away. She tried the front door- it was locked.

Shivering, she wrapped her arms around herself and tried to think. Where had they come from? Obviously, some child, or someone with tiny feet anyway, had been in here. She thought about the two little girls with the cat from the other day. Could it have been them? She inspected the kitchen floor but didn't see any of the small prints there and she would have seen someone come out through there anyway.

She fell back on the now familiar ritual of turning on every light in the house and searching everywhere someone could possibly hide. And, of course, finding no one. Needing comfort, she gathered old newspapers, determined to start a fire, her first, in the old fireplace. Hopefully the logs would be seasoned enough to burn by now. After several attempts and numerous matches, they finally caught and soon a small fire crackled merrily in the hearth. The flames burned an unusual shade of blue. She sat back on the sofa and reflected on what she had accomplished today. The cabinets and countertops were high on her to do list and they would soon be done. It would be nice if someone were here to share these accomplishments with. The realization that she had no one to share her day with made her feel very alone.

Sudden longing for her mother welled up and she fought tears. Ten years was a long time ago but it felt like she had just lost her anew. Do we never grow out of the desire for parental love and approval? She was sure her mother would have loved this house and have been full of ideas for remodeling and decorating. She could almost hear that lilting, southern voice and feel a cool, soft hand on her hair. Every time she spoke with a native, the slow, soothing cadences of their voice evoked memories of her mother.

The fire burned low by the time she went upstairs to bed. The warmth had traveled up and her bedroom was not as icy as it was last night. Changing into her old, heavy-weight silk pajamas she got out two extra blankets and climbed into the tall bed. That sweet scent of cherries enveloped her again and she slept soundly until the birds chirping in the trees woke her.

After breakfast, she vacuumed the floors. A fine layer of dust had settled over everything. In the parlor, a foul smell suddenly engulfed her. Gagging, she pulled her shirt up to cover her nose and mouth and leaned over to check the hearth. Perhaps the fire last night had dislodged something dead in the chimney. She saw nothing except- written in the ashes, as if traced with a finger, was a message.

"*Hello.*"

Chapter Five

In such a place as this, at such an hour,
If ancestry can be in aught believed,
Descending spirits have conversed with man,
And told the secrets of the world unknown.
-*Modern British Drama*

Sarah dropped the cloth and backed away from the fireplace. Disbelief struggled with the reality of the word in front of her. She had not written it and no one else had been in the house since she started the fire. The rational part of her mind still searched for an explanation while a more primitive side of her just felt frightened.

She could not ignore this anymore. Something was wrong with this house and she needed to know more about it. She felt like calling the realtor and demanding to know why he had never mentioned the real history of the house and if he had known it was haunted when he showed it to her. The rational part of her realized how ridiculous that sounded but the angry/frightened part of her did not care.

Finding her phone and locating the number on his business card, she called Cooper River Realty. The receptionist informed her that Foster was in the office today but with a client. Would she like to leave a message? She asked for a return call.

Too angry to wait, and afraid to stay in the house, she decided to walk to the Cooper River Realty offices on Amherst Street. Outside, a blast of cold air hit her and she had to go back inside for a heavier coat. She avoided looking at the fireplace when she went past the parlor but noticed that the horrible smell from earlier was already completely gone.

Just walking through the brisk air was calming and she already felt less frightened. There were plenty of tourists out and buskers were busy performing in front of the more popular attractions. As always, the city itself charmed just by the quality of the architecture and lushness of its magnolias, crepe myrtles, and, towering over all else, live oaks. The buildings on this street all looked quite old. One, an elaborate, gray, stone building, was very large, and she stopped to read the plaque posted in front of it.

The Charleston Post Office and Courthouse, completed in 1896, is built on the site of the former town gallows. Constructed of gray granite quarried in Winnsboro, South Carolina, the building is an example of the Renaissance Revival style.

This was where the information about her house was archived. Maybe someone here would let her go through the documents. She climbed the broad stone steps under the graceful arches, and walked through the double doors.

Inside, the old building hummed with activity. Employees scurried back and forth across the red marble floors and up and down the elaborate mahogany staircase. A directory pointed her to the third floor for the Archives Department. She wandered through hallways for a while then finally found Archives at the end of a corridor near a bathroom. As soon as she opened the door the smell of old paper, leather, and just a hint of mold assailed her. Behind a tall, old fashioned, reception desk she could just glimpse a room full of very high, very full bookshelves. No one manned the desk and she rang the bell on top hesitantly. She heard a chair scrape on the floor in the back and then ponderous footsteps approaching.

Dr. Bickerstaff, for so he introduced himself, must have weighed over three hundred pounds. Immaculately attired in a tweed jacket and silk tie, with Ben Franklin half-moon glasses resting on the tip of his nose, he sailed majestically between the bookshelves, surprisingly light on his feet. Sarah could not help but notice that the fly on his pants had to be at least eighteen inches long. She supposed that once they reach a certain girth, men make the choice to either belt their trousers below the waist or find pants to accommodate that girth. Dr. Bickerstaff had made the latter choice.

"Hello, my dear. How may I help you today?" His voice was a deep, pleasant drawl.

"Hi, I'm Sarah Faust. I just bought a house on Rue and I'm researching its history. I found a little information on the city website and the article indicated that more documents were available here." Her voice squeaked on the word "here." She had not realized she was so nervous but she was, very. For some reason she feared she would not be allowed to view the documents.

"That shouldn't be a problem but I do need your house number or your parcel ID."

"Oh. Of course. It's 5 Rue Lane."

"Let me see what we have scanned into the system." He clicked away for a minute or two, frowning when he didn't find what he wanted.

"We don't have much on the computer other than property deed transactions and, as you might expect, they go way back. Looks like the house has stayed in the same family, more or less, for a long time too. We probably just have not started entering the anecdotal history yet. Give me a few moments to look in the back."

He disappeared into the stacks and she heard drawers opening and closing. In a few minutes he returned, holding an enormous leather bound folio that he placed on a table.

"These documents should really be behind glass before I let you view them but you seem like the careful type. I'm going to give you these," he handed her a pair of very thin, white cotton gloves, "and you can look through all of it. You are also welcome to take photos if you like; everything here is a matter of public record."

She turned a few of the pages and saw old deeds, copies of personal letters handwritten in graceful, spidery script, and clipped newspaper articles. This was much more information than she had expected. She asked for a few minutes to slip out and buy a camera.

An hour later and over one-hundred dollars poorer, she was back. She told herself she was taking a logical, analytical approach to this house mystery, and information was the key to resolving it. Putting the gloves back on, she photographed each page carefully then sat down to look through them again, stopping at whatever caught her eye.

As testified before Charles Ashley Esq. and Justice Matheson, and Town Council, etc.

In that the aforementioned Elizabeth Grayhame hath by rumor [sic] and testimony been long acquainted with the damnable art of Witchcraft and having been apprehended by Officers of His Majesty, did freely confess that she was a witch but declined details of her diabolical crimes and as a result being taken to the gaol and thereupon being put to the question, hath confessed and stands convicted of the following crimes.

I. That she did meet with the Devil on numerous occasions and he supplied her with a black ointment which: rubbed upon her body, did transport her through the air to a Witches' Sabbath beside the town cemetery where she and others had connection with him in the form of a Dark Man: and later danced back to back with him. [sic]

II. That she and others did violate the new grave of the infant son of The Rev. Culpeper: and did boil down said child's body, using the lighter part of the fat for tallow for candles and the thicker part in the making of more of the black ointment: which, applied to the belly and back, would take them up through the air to meet their master.

III. That her diabolical master did give to her a black powder to throw upon those she wished to harm and she did indeed bewitch several persons and cattle, as well as James Brochard's pig that did stray into her garden and trample plants therein.

She heard the floor creak behind her and looked around. Dr. Bickerstaff looked unabashed at having been caught reading over her shoulder.

"The witch hysteria at that time is difficult to understand today. Who knows what any of us would say when 'put to the question' as they were back then."

"What exactly did that mean? I've never heard of being put to the question."

"Simply put, she was tortured until she answered their questions. Did you notice the colons in the document that make no sense grammatically?"

She looked again. He was right, the punctuation made no sense. She looked up at him expectantly.

"It confused everyone in the Historical Society when we finally noticed it. Then someone thought to compare these documents to the Salem transcripts. Each colon indicates a pause in the questioning to allow for a period of torture after which the answers wrung from the victim were written down."

She shuddered, "That is one of the saddest, most horrifying things I have ever heard. Her answers were so imaginative."

"But you see, to everyone then, the Devil was very real. Church attendance was mandatory and the concept was drilled into them from infancy. Not believing in Satan would have been heresy. Demons were an accepted part of the whole spiritual hierarchy. Most everyone feared and would have shunned any contact with what they perceived as Satan but some truly did seek him out. The lust for power is certainly not confined to our own age."

"I suppose not. Still, isn't it possible these women were simply handy scapegoats when bad things happened?"

"We are ignoring one possibility."

"What's that?"

"That at least some of them really were witches."

She laughed but Dr. Bickerstaff did not. Ok then, time to go before this gets weird.

"You've been so kind to let me look through all this. I've never owned an old house before and exploring its history is fascinating." She stood and gathered her things, shrugging into her coat and patting her pocket to be sure the camera was there.

Just as she reached the door, he spoke again. "In this town we are used to living surrounded by history. Your house, like so many others here, has a strong connection to a time most people today would consider boorish and backward. The enlightenment of modern life has banished many of the shadows that plagued our ancestors but it might be instructive to remember Hamlet's instruction to Horatio. "

"'There are more things in Heaven and Earth…'"

"Exactly."

"I will. And thank you."

Outside, the town sparkled in bright sunlight and blustery cold wind. Clouds blew by overhead, pushed out to sea by a strong westerly wind. Her phone chimed. Not recognizing the number but noting the local area code, she said, "Hello?"

"Hi, Sarah? This is Angela with Stone Custom Designs. You and I discussed some countertops for your kitchen. You came in and I believe you spoke with my brother?"

"Hi, Angela. David is your brother? He was so nice to come out and measure the kitchen yesterday."

"I'm glad that wasn't an inconvenience for you. I tried to reach you by phone but couldn't. Anyway, I'm calling to let you know your countertops are cut but haven't been packed to bring out yet. We usually like for customers to come by and take a look at them one more time before we do the install. At this point we can still change the edge if you like."

"I'm in town right now but my car is back at my house. It will take me about twenty minutes to walk back and then another thirty to get to your shop. So is an hour or so from now ok?"

"No rush. We close at five."

Luckily, her car keys were in her purse so she did not have to go in the house. *Do I really dread the thought of going into my own house? The important thing is I'm going to figure out what is going on*, she told herself.

Traffic was light and she pulled into the parking lot of the stone store sooner than expected. A tall, willowy brunette who must be Angela stood behind the front counter and smiled when she walked in.

"Sarah?" Sarah nodded. "That was fast! Come into the back; I can't wait for you to see the tops. From the way David described your floors, they should be perfect for the space."

The warehouse was quieter today but no less brightly lit. Her countertops lay on top of a wheeled cart. The creamy marble shone with a soft translucence.

"You're right; they are perfect. What's the total? I'll write you a check now."

"You pay half now and then you pay the installer once they're in. We usually send two guys and it should take about three to four hours."

"Do I need to have any plumbing turned off or disconnected before then?"

"No, they'll do it and then get you back up and running when they're done." They walked back to the showroom. "David will probably be one of the installers."

"It must be nice to have your brother in business with you."

"Yes and no. This business has been in our family for five generations. I love it but David never wanted to work here. He taught history at the University before they had cutbacks last year. It's hard to have to leave a job you love. He's had a tough year in other ways too. I keep telling him it could be worse but he just growls at me."

"He was very nice yesterday and I'm really glad you guys can do this so quickly."

"Yours is a relatively small project but I think you'll find making this upgrade will have a big impact on the overall look and value of the house. Plus, it's just more fun to cook in a kitchen with quality finishes. Marble is great for rolling or kneading bread dough, too." Angela pulled up a computer screen and studied it for a moment. "So, will a Friday installation work for you? Around ten-thirty?"

"That sounds fine. It will give me time to have the cabinets painted and ready."

"Outstanding. That's everything then. Here is your total-" Angela swiveled the screen around so she could see. "So we just need a check for half that."

On the way home, she stopped to put gas in the car, trying not to think about how fast her bank account was draining. No matter how economical she tried to be, she always spent too much. As small as it was, the house was already a money pit, and she had barely started the renovations. Her job hunt was still going nowhere. She had gotten two rejection emails and one actual rejection letter but mostly she just never got any feedback at all. She was starving but drove resolutely past even the fast food restaurants, determined to eat at home, even if it was just soup.

She pulled in her driveway, turned off the engine and sat, looking at the dark silhouette of her house. The eastern sky behind it had a pink glow with tiny, silvery clouds on the horizon. A rising wind tossed the trees and bushes. Ok, it did look a little creepy with the stained, gray stucco but the rowan tree, at least, looked much neater. The stone step in front was definitely crumbling but where could she find a replacement slab that large?

After a quick meal she cleaned the kitchen. She roamed the house, looking for her laptop, finally finding it on the fireplace mantel. Wind must have blown down the chimney because the ashes in the hearth were scattered and only part of the writing was still visible. She swept the strewn ashes and now no letters were there at all. Even better.

Installing the camera software took only minutes and her photos loaded quickly. Hoping the images would be clear enough to read, she opened one at random. It was a list of previous owners and Dr. Bickerstaff was right. The house had stayed in the same family for a long time. The name Grayhame appeared repeatedly, most of the time as a surname but occasionally as a Christian name. There were some gaps in the timeline. Around 1820 or so, the name began to be spelled 'Graham' and appeared less frequently.

The images were very clear and the deeds were handwritten in elegant old script. Some of the pages would be lovely enlarged and then framed. She clicked to the next page.

This entry was much more recent than the others and was either typewritten or created on a word processor. She read on and then blinked and read the last section again. Her mother's name, Barbara Graham Sinclair, was at the bottom of the page.

For a few seconds everything around her seemed to spin. Her own middle name was Graham. Her mother always said it was a family name and one to be proud of but had never elaborated and Sarah had not been interested enough to ask questions. She and her mother and father (despite that faint air of anger and suppressed violence that often simmered in her father) had lived a somewhat rootless existence and they had been happy, mostly. Sarah knew very little about her family. Her mother had mentioned some cousins a few times but she could not remember their names.

It looked like her mother had deeded or sold the house to a Raynard G. Winslow. Sarah wondered what the G stood for. Graham maybe? Was he a distant relative? He was the last owner before she came along and bought the house. Her home. Her family home. She had so many questions. Why had her mother never told her more about her family history? No wonder she felt such an affinity for the house. It had been in her family for hundreds of years.

Her phone chimed but she silenced it when she recognized the number for Cooper River Realty. Foster was finally calling her back but she really had nothing to say to him after all. Whatever was going on here, she would figure it out. She was home.

Chapter Six

"This is the last thing I need!" Sarah stood in the foyer, holding dusty chunks of plaster and looking at her wall in dismay. Small, winding cracks radiated out from the sections where the plaster had broken away. She had been so careful when she took the frames down in order to avoid this. Her heart sank this morning when she came downstairs to find her foyer covered in dust and plaster.

She had bad dreams last night and kept waking hearing scratching sounds in the walls. During the night, a fog crept in, blanketing the neighborhood. When she woke this morning and looked out her bedroom window, the surrounding housetops appeared to float in the mist, stranded in a milky sea. Traffic sounds were deadened and even the church bells sounded muffled and distant. By ten o'clock though, the sun burned all traces of vapor away.

The countertop installers were due any time. She finished picking up the larger pieces of plaster, noticing they had strands of something that looked like thick, coarse hair sticking out of them. Creepy. She washed her hands and, shivering in the cold house, went back upstairs for a sweater. Rummaging through the chest, she touched a black, silk and cashmere sweater that Sean had brought back from one of his overseas trips. He had always told her she looked beautiful in black and, for just a minute, she held it against her cheek, remembering.

Well, the memories were somewhat tarnished now but the sweater was still soft and warm so she slipped it on. The HVAC estimate had been way beyond her means and she would just have to wait for spring to warm things up. She knew placing countertops ahead of heat and air was stupid but this was her first house and she had not known how expensive everything would be. She avoided looking at her fireplace and knew she was being cowardly but she did not want to see more messages from the mysterious beyond. There was a knock on her back door.

Three hours later, the countertops were laid and attached to the cabinets. David re-connected the sink faucets while the other installer, Dewayne cleared away all the packing material. The soft white paint on the cabinets looked clean and crisp. She finished putting the silverware and dishtowels back in the drawers.

"You know, I can't figure out what this is for." She opened the drawer door that contained the metal chute. "It's too small to be a laundry chute. I don't know where it goes."

David looked up. "Hang on a second." He finished up under the sink and came over.

"It's the hopper door for your incinerator."

"What's a hopper door?"

"It accesses a flue leading to a combustion chamber that should be in your basement. Household waste went down this chute to be incinerated. They were popular during the early nineteen hundreds. Look in the basement and see if the chamber is still there. I doubt the city allows using them anymore but you can always check."

"I never would have thought of that. Thanks."

"No problem. Different subject. I brought out some subway tile just in case you're thinking about adding a backsplash. We often install them at the same time we install the counters. I didn't think to suggest it the other day." David pulled several tiles from a cardboard box and held them against the wall.

"They look great but I can't afford them right now. Maybe soon. I haven't found a job yet."

He looked surprised. "You bought a house without a job? Someone has deep pockets."

"No. I had one pocket, not all that deep, and I saved for years to get it. I'm starting to get worried."

"What's your field?"

"Commercial real estate."

"You might have to explore other options in this economy. Goodness knows I've had to." He smiled; a somewhat bitter smile, but still... he looked nice when he smiled.

"Angela said you were at one of the local universities?"

"I taught history. My specialty is European with a focus on the Age of Enlightenment. Unfortunately when enrollment dropped, my program was not considered essential so- Hello family business."

"Have you considered relocating to another university?"

"There are a couple of things that keep me here and I wouldn't consider-"

"David, all finished up? Let's go get some lunch." Dewayne called from the porch.

"Go ahead. I'm going to run back to my place and grab a sandwich. I need my truck for later anyway."

She walked out into the back yard with him.

"What's the deal with this gate? I've never seen one like it before."

David smiled. "It's a kissing gate. There aren't a whole lot of them left in Charleston. You're lucky."

"How?"

"It's a piece of history. In colonial times and a long time afterwards there was a large village green in Charleston. The townsfolk grazed their livestock there. If you wanted a cup of milk in the morning, and didn't have a cow, you went out to the green, paid your tuppence to the person (likely a slave) herding the cow and got your un-pasteurized dairy delight."

"What does this have to do with a kissing gate?"

"They needed a way to keep the large animals grazing on the commons out of their gardens while people could still come and go. This gate was perfect. Look," he moved the gate back and forth "nothing can get through here until the person in the enclosure moves out of it so the gate can swing back again. The premise is the person who wants to go next has to kiss the person on the other side before they are allowed access. I guess they either took advantage of that or not, depending."

"So it's really about animal control and someone came up with the kissing part later."

"Well, spin-the-bottle probably had not been invented yet and teenage boys had to find some excuse to steal a kiss."

She laughed. "True. This house surprises me almost every day. Not always in a good way but it's never dull."

"Enjoy the countertops. They look really good with the floor."

"I think so too. See you later."

The yard was warm in the sunshine. Thick wisteria vines twisted up the Tuscan columns. The thorny tendrils growing on the railings already had fat buds disclosing glimpses of pink rose petals. Yesterday, she found a book on gardening in a used bookstore and had been trying to identify the plants in the garden. So far, she had discovered a row of yews, three Nellie Stevens hollies, confederate jasmine, and of course, the rowan tree (Sorbus Rosaceae). The swing hung from a live oak (Quercus Virginiana) but other trees would have to leaf out before she could label them. Small, leafy plants, as yet unidentifiable, were beginning to emerge from the ground in the parterres around the bronze statue. The almost tropical luxuriance of the garden still surprised her and the idea that her ancestor, witch or not, had planted all this made her smile. An idea, half-formed in her mind, began to grow. What if she could add a new chapter to the family history? What if she could find the true story of Elizabeth Grayhame and redeem her reputation?

Curious about the incinerator she went down to the basement to see if she could find it. The darkness down here seemed reluctant to disperse and the brick walls felt damp. Moving scattered metal pieces out of the way, she checked behind the defunct oil heater. Something stuck out from the brick wall but it was not an incinerator. It felt like metal and there were two of them but it was too dark back here to see. She went back upstairs, found a flashlight, and discovered a set of manacles, very rusted, protruding from the wall. One broke off and fell to the floor when she touched it.

What was this? Was it something to do with slavery? Someone enslaved could have been imprisoned here. She felt a suffocating sense of fear and hopelessness, as if it bled out through the wall. She tugged at the remaining manacle angrily and it pulled away from the wall, causing the old bricks to collapse in a dusty, tumbling heap that hit her feet and shins painfully. Cold, noisome air poured out from the cavity now exposed and she trained the flashlight on- a tiny human skull. She put her hand to her mouth and backed away but she could see there were more, jumbled up with a mixture of other bones. All of them child-sized.

She ran up the stairs and outside, taking deep breaths of the cold, clean air. Going back in for her phone, she called the police, hands and voice trembling, and then sat waiting on the front step, unable to stay inside the house.

The police arrived within fifteen minutes. She told the dispatcher that no one was injured and no medical assistance was needed but they sent an ambulance anyway. The officer who took her statement was kind and offered her a blanket but cold was not the reason she was shaking.

Ages passed while a forensics team took photos and then carefully bagged the tiny bones. They told her that, for now, they would regard this as a crime scene but it was unlikely to have been a recent crime. All of the bones appeared to be quite old, although they would not know for sure until they ran tests. A small crowd gathered on the sidewalk as the day grew later and people began to come home from work. The police vehicles had to move several times to let someone get through. Sarah felt exposed and moved around to the side porch. They had already told her she could go back inside but she did not want to. She kept thinking about what Mary Michael and Nay-Nay told her about the human sacrifice and abortions purported to have occurred here.

"Ms. Faust? We're all finished here. All of the remains have been removed and I think we have all we need from the scene. You'll want to have someone look at that wall eventually but I wouldn't get it repaired right away in case we need to take another look. Give it a couple of weeks if you can wait that long. We should have all the test results back by then." The officer who had been so kind smiled at her encouragingly. "You look really pale. Is there someone you want to call to come over?"

She shook her head and smiled wanly. "No, I'll be fine."

"This will probably make the news so you should prepare yourself for some phone calls at the very least. You can always refer them to the police department but we won't be saying much. I advise you not to either, and it will blow over soon enough."

"Thanks."

The streetlamps came on and the picturesque little street assumed its usual evening charm. She forced herself to go inside. The new countertops glowed but the old appliances looked worse in comparison. Still- the kitchen was improving. She had already invested so much in this house, emotionally and financially. If she walked away now, she had nowhere to go and nothing to fall back on and, in spite of everything, the house still pulled at her. She felt she had never belonged anywhere until she came here but the prospect of exonerating the Grayhame name did not seem as likely now.

She needed to understand what had happened here. Unfortunately revulsion now mixed with the fascination this house held for her and she resolutely opened the basement door and went down, determined to face her fears. The lights were still on and someone had left an empty Coke bottle on the oil furnace. The hole in the brick gaped obscenely; a wound cleaned out but not closed. She started a load of laundry, adding fabric softener, the clean, fresh smell wafting through the whole room and following her up the stairs.

She played around with the computer for a while, checking email, looking for responses to one of her many job applications. Another politely worded, generic reply informed her that the opening for which she had applied had been filled. Of course. She logged out.

Somehow, she wasn't all that surprised when she found another message in the fireplace hearth. Fainter this time as the ashes were more sparse, it read, *"Help me."* A chill having nothing to do with the temperature went up her back.

"There are more things in Heaven and Earth, Horatio, than are dreamt of in your philosophy" she quoted softly to herself as she walked out of the room and up the stairs, pausing only to be sure the front door was securely locked. She almost didn't bother; the thing she most feared was already in the house with her, and was making sure she knew it.

The sound of light, running footfalls on the floor below began before she fell asleep and followed her into her dreams.

Chapter Seven

"Hi Sarah? It's Angela with Stone Customs. I'm calling to follow up on your counter install. David tells me the kitchen looks great but I wanted to hear what you think."

Two days had passed since the countertops were installed and the kitchen, with the exception of the appliances, looked picture perfect. Keeping busy was the only way she kept her thoughts away from the grisly find in the basement. The basement door had been open each morning when she came downstairs but she pushed it closed and refused to think about it. She looked at the wall panels and the trim; the fresh, creamy paint gleamed softly in the morning light. It had been a very quiet two days with no ghostly messages from other realms, no dark apparitions darting about. She had turned the mirror to the wall.

"They're great. The marble really brightened up the kitchen and I honestly think it looks almost high-end now. I haven't used them as a work surface since I can't do a lot of baking. As of yesterday my oven won't heat up past two hundred fifty degrees." Sarah laughed.

"Sorry about your oven. Are you having it fixed or are you thinking of replacing it?"

"Angela, all of these appliances need replacing but I'm a little short on cash right now. I'm restoring this house in stages and I have to wait to finish everything."

"Yeah, I hope you don't mind but David did tell me a little about that and that's part of the reason I called. Do you have any free time this morning and feel like getting out?"

Sarah thought. The garden was still ragged, she hadn't even attempted to repair the plaster in the foyer, and she had not called anyone for estimates to fix the wall in the basement. But she would love to get out for a while.

"I can make time. Can you tell me what this is about?"

"Great! I'll be by in about forty-five minutes and I'll tell you all about it. Oh, and measure your appliances." She rang off.

Exactly forty-five minutes later, a long, white utility van pulled up in front of the house and Angela, wearing jeans and a faded Clemson sweatshirt, knocked on the door.

"You're overdressed." Sarah looked down at the blue cords and white sweater she had on. "Seriously, you should change. You don't want to ruin that sweater." Angela was insistent.

Ok, she thought. I'll play along but if she doesn't tell me where we're going, I'm backing out. A quick change into jeans and a denim jacket and she was ready.

"Where are we going?" she asked as she locked the front door.

"A house north of Broad Street has just been foreclosed. One of the bank vice-presidents wants it for his family and plans to remodel the interior in a completely contemporary style so there is a lot up for grabs. I have a little side business in architectural salvage. I pay the bank or mortgage company, whoever the owner is, a flat fee and that allows me to remove anything left in the house that hasn't been tagged. It's also a great way to pick up gently used appliances on the cheap. The former owners of this house began a kitchen renovation but didn't get it finished so the appliances they left are fairly new."

"Are you serious? What kind of appliances do they have? Stainless?"

Angela laughed as they pulled out of the narrow lane and onto the busy street. "I'm not sure but they are probably in working order. Dewayne is going to meet us there to help with the heavy stuff but we'll get as much as we can on our own. How skilled are you with a crowbar?"

"We'll find out today."

"Good enough."

The house was not far. They pulled up in front of the two-story, brick structure on another of the city's seemingly endless, shade-covered lanes. Weeds grew lush and tall in the clogged guttering and a shutter hung askew by a front window.

"How much do you know about the architecture in Charleston?" asked Angela.

"I'm learning. I think this is called a 'double.'"

"Yes, it's a simple style with a central foyer and 'twin-parlors' on either side as you walk in. These were very popular by the 1830's, especially for larger houses. Of course, the deep porticos continued to be used as they provided extra living space as well as shade. Those rams head capitals on the columns need work but this place isn't in bad shape."

Like most Charleston houses, this one had a side instead of a front yard. The huge white columns were the size of Egyptian obelisks and anchored the massive house on the overgrown lawn. Oaks with thick twisting limbs and dark green leaves towered over the large garden. Carrying a canvas sack of tools, they waded through the weedy undergrowth onto the porch where Angela produced the bank's key and pushed open the heavy, paneled door.

Dust motes sparkled in the shafts of sunlight streaming in through clean patches on the dirty windows. In the right parlor, an elaborately carved wooden mantel surrounded a cavernous fireplace. Dark bookcases with rice sheath motifs rose to the ceiling on either side. A staircase with wide, deep steps and corkscrew spindles mounted to a dusty dimness above. The entire place gave an impression of solidity and graciousness.

"Did you say you can take anything that isn't tagged?"
"Yes."
"Almost nothing is tagged."
"I know. I really should have been here yesterday but I was so busy in the shop... Anyway, they're keeping the floorboards; the refinishers are starting work the day after tomorrow. That's why I was in a hurry to get here today."

A few pieces of furniture stood here and there, all of them damaged in some way. It looked like the previous owners left behind whatever they did not want. On the dining room walls a faded mural depicted shipwreck scenes from the *Odyssey* with a forlorn Telemachus gazing sadly at his broken ship. Floor-to-ceiling silk draperies still graced the tall windows. Angela tugged gently on one of the panels and it ripped immediately, the rotted fabric falling in dusty folds to the floor. The refrigerator and other appliances in the kitchen were new and in good shape but they were black.

"I know you wanted stainless but these aren't that bad." Angela wiped grime from the smooth cook top of the stove and pulled out a tape measure. The oven and dishwasher were a fit and the refrigerator would do also.

"If I can't have stainless, I'd like white. Can you paint appliances?"

"Sure. You can buy appliance paint at a home improvement store."

Sarah smiled but privately she wondered why this woman was being so nice to her.

Angela was quick and efficient and they soon had the mantel as well as the stair spindles and banister stacked neatly in the back of the van. The bookcases were heavy mahogany and they found they could not safely lower them to the floor. Dewayne would have to get them.

The kitchen cabinets came down easily. They left them in the hallway to pick up later as they were almost out of room and wanted to leave space for the appliances.

Angela leaned against the kitchen door and wiped her face. "Oh my gosh, I'm sweating! I need to sit down for a minute."

"Me too." Sarah went out to the van, fished out two bottles of water from the cooler and gave one to Angela.

"Thanks. I'm tired. It's always this way at first when- well, you can probably tell- I'm pregnant." She placed her hands protectively on her abdomen, accentuating a faint swelling curve, not evident before under the loose sweatshirt.

"No, I had no idea. That's wonderful! Angela, you shouldn't be doing this."

"I love doing this and I did it while pregnant with my first two. It is a little harder this time though. Sarah, I should tell you I had an ulterior motive when I called you this morning. David said you have a background in commercial real estate and need a job. I have a proposition for you if you're interested."

"I'm interested."

"I need someone to step in and help manage my salvage business. I know this is different from what you did before but some of the basics are the same. Assessing properties, dealing with banks or sellers, finding the right person for the product, all of these are important in this business. And it wouldn't even have to be full-time. As you saw today, it can involve a little manual labor but if you're restoring a house, you're obviously not afraid of that." She took another drink of water and leaned back against the wall.

"I'm not but I really wish you wouldn't do any more of this today. Just tell me what needs to be done and I'll do it."

"I'm fine. It's early days yet and this little guy, or girl, is just fine too." She smiled as she spoke and her face became softly radiant. "I want a girl this time. My boys are wonderful but I think we need a little girl to smooth out their rough edges."

Sarah grew pensive. She and Sean had often talked about their "someday" children. They wanted to wait until they had a real home. Well, she had a real home now but scant chance of a child. The thought hurt and she realized anew that she had lost not only a husband, but also a chance at becoming a mother, of having a family.

"Hey, are you okay?"

"Fine. Sorry, just thinking. Look, you really shouldn't try to move those appliances so-"

They heard the front door open and Dewayne called "Hello?"

"In the kitchen, Dewayne!" Angela shouted. "So, what do you think? Are you interested enough to come down to the shop on Monday and discuss the job more formally?"

"Absolutely. What time?"

"Great! Nine works for me. We'll meet at the shop and then head to the docks so you can see the warehouse."

"Sarah, nice to see you again. Did you measure the appliances? Will they work?" Dewayne rolled a hand truck into the kitchen.

"They're the right sizes."

"Great. I'll disconnect everything and we'll get them loaded. Sarah, I'll need you to help pull them out. Angela, get out of the way. I don't want any strain on Miss Priscilla."

"Will you please stop calling her that? This baby may not be a girl and I don't want my child confused in the womb. And if she is a girl, I am not calling her Priscilla." Angela climbed the stairs, looking for a bathroom.

"This one's a girl, it has to be. You and John won't survive another hellion like the two you have now." Dewayne called after her.

"Shut up. I'm not listening to you." Her voice drifted down the stairs.

Dewayne grinned at Sarah then got to work. The oven and the fridge were easy but the dishwasher drain line leaked stale, dirty water onto the floor, sending them scrambling for something to mop it up. They finally used the downed draperies then locked up before heading back to Rue.

Three hours later, with everything installed, she and Dewayne loaded the old appliances to haul to the landfill. The tiny kitchen looked incredibly stylish, even with the black finishes. Deciding she might not paint them after all, she went upstairs to get her checkbook and came down to find Angela inspecting the foyer wall. She also noticed that the mirror was now facing outward. She quickly turned it around, resolutely not looking into it.

"Yeah, I know the wall looks bad. I have the plaster mix and I'm all set to repair it tomorrow."

"Did you notice what's in the wall?" Angela continued to peer down into the gap.

"Please don't tell me it's mice."

Angela laughed. "No. I think it's newsprint."

She looked. Some of the white dust that coated the lath had fallen off, exposing the area behind the plaster. It was covered in yellowed newsprint. She couldn't make out any of the words and got a flashlight to illuminate the aperture. Thick layers of the paper appeared to be glued to the lath and studs.

"Was it an early form of insulation? This has got to be a fire hazard."

"No idea. Maybe. Can you read any of the print?"

Sarah squinted to see. "Not really, no. There are some numbers- 1842 maybe? It might be a date."

Angela dusted her hands on her jeans. "Who knows? I'm always finding odd building materials in old houses. I think they just used whatever they had on hand. They used animal hair in the plaster mix to give it strength; you can see little tufts of it here." She ran her fingers lightly along the edge of the break.

"I wondered about that. Mystery solved." She opened her checkbook. "Now, about the appliances. How much?"

After they left, she cleaned the appliances and sat in the kitchen, reveling in the sight of them. Finally, she could do some baking. Bread was the first thing that came to mind. She found the yeast and flour and soon had a warm, beer-smelling lump in her mother's old stoneware mixing bowl. The dough came off the marble easily as she kneaded and then covered it with a dishtowel to let it finish rising. Perfect.

Hairy plaster. Kind of disgusting. The plaster mixing directions on the back of the bag did not mention hair so they must have come up with a substitute over the last two hundred years. She draped a sheet on the floor underneath the cracks, dragged the bag of plaster in from the porch and then realized she did not have a bucket in which to mix it. She had remembered everything but that.

The blustery day had turned gray. The kind of gray that promised snow in the North but she supposed that didn't happen much here. Nevertheless, she didn't want to go shopping for a bucket. She couldn't leave the bread anyway.

Showering and changing into a sweatshirt and yoga pants, she towel-dried her hair then finger-combed the tangles out. It had grown past shoulder-length but she liked it. Softer and not as professional maybe but it made her feel more feminine. She braided it into a plait then nestled down in the thick, yellow cushions on the window seat. Opening her laptop, she pulled up the images and began to read.

Chapter Eight

"The story of the very singular Mistress Grayhame of Charleston is one that begins in the colony of Virginia. What, the reader may ask, would Charleston's famous witch have to do with the more northern colony?

The first Mistress Grayhame's mother came to the New World as a 'tobacco bride', a term that begs explanation. Beginning in 1672 and continuing for several years thereafter, young women left the British Isles, including Ireland, some willingly, some not, and arrived in Virginia where they were 'purchased' for one hundred fifty pounds of tobacco by local settlers. The money was payable to the ship's captain to recompense him for the cost of the voyage. It is believed that Elizabeth's mother, deported from Ireland for crimes unspecified, became, upon arrival, the bride of one Matthew Hopkins. Little is known of their union other than that, although not otherwise a success, it did result in the birth of Elizabeth. Mistress Hopkins left her husband and, eventually, migrated down to the Carolinas, where she, and young Elizabeth, reassumed her maiden name of Grayhame."

This must be the article from the New York journalist Nay-Nay and Mary-Michael had mentioned. It appeared to go on for several pages and the digital images were very clear. She felt a sense of quiet satisfaction at having obtained all of this so quickly. Whatever was going on in this house, her house, she was on her way to figuring it out.

"It is unknown exactly when Mistress Grayhame became a landowner in Charleston but by 1682 the account books of a local tavern mention purchases of tea leaves and horse liniment from a 'Mme Gryhm, Apothecary.'

Gaining acceptance in a colonial community was crucial but not always easy to achieve. Port towns were accustomed to a somewhat transient population, but in order to stay, a useful skill was needed to prove that one would not be a burden on the parish. Elizabeth's mother seems to have had a background in folk medicine, including the use of herbs, which bought the little family a moderately good living. So good in fact, that she soon employed the services of a young Negress who arrived in Charleston by way of the West Indies. The young woman, called Katarina, does not appear to have been a slave and enjoyed the status of a free servant.

Mistress Grayhame continued to run a profitable business for the rest of her somewhat short life. Her skill with herbal cures seemed successful 'beyond ye ken' to some of the locals but no occult aspersions were ever made against her. She had lucrative dealings with the townsfolk as well as a thriving trade with the many sailors on shore leave in the port city. One of her 'cures' for baldness is worth repeating here as it shows the quest for luxuriant locks is not confined to our own age.

'If a man be afflicted with a bald pate, take newly dead bees and burn them to a powder. Mix with lemon and oil and work him a paste then anoint the afflicted one thus and all will be well with him.'

Unfortunately, curing smallpox proved beyond her abilities and she died during an outbreak around 1685. Her house and all her property passed to her daughter.

Little is known of Elizabeth's story before 1685. Town records indicate that in 1686 she was twice fined for failure to attend church services and again the next year for violating the sumptuary laws, encountering further censure when she went defiantly to her court hearing wearing the same "broidered silk dress" [sic] that prompted the fine. She must have had the means to dress well. We find mention of her by one ship's captain who complained that his sailors on leave had taken to thronging the apothecary's garden wall in hopes of catching a glimpse of the beautiful healer. She is described as having a 'queenly bearing' as well as masses of luxuriant, dark hair. We have this description of her garden from an English visitor.

'The enclosure contains divers handsome and curious plants. Espaliered fruit-trees, providing healthful and most fragrant sustenance, adorn brick and tabby walls. Medicinal plants are in no less abundance, the climate in this land being agreeable to near year-round growth and the walls shutting out any ill wind. To tread the winding paths is a pleasure to all senses as footsteps crush and release the scent of the tender leaves of mint, thyme, and lavender borders.'

In 1687, Elizabeth married ship's captain Alexander West of Holborn, England. It seems to have been a happy marriage although the Captain was often absent on voyages. In 1689, she gave birth to their first child. Four more quickly followed with their last child, a daughter, being born in early 1698.

The young couple probably struggled like all parents to feed and clothe their expanding brood. Unfortunately, in October of the same year, West's ship was lost at sea with all crew reported dead. Elizabeth's reaction to the news is not known but may be imagined by the sympathetic reader. Several local merchants tried to place liens on her property to compensate them for funds they had invested in Captain West's venture. They were unsuccessful but this may have caused ill feelings on all sides.

In 1700, she and her West Indian servant parted ways after an apparent falling out, but later events will show this may have been a contrivance. Soon after, she acquired a slave woman who came from the West African coast. Despite her marriage, she continued to use the name of Grayhame, at least in her professional life.

Tragedy struck the apothecary again in 1701. Another smallpox outbreak in that spring took the lives of Elizabeth's four oldest children. It was an age of high infant mortality but losing a child is devastating no matter how common and to lose four at once must have been nightmarish.

Smallpox announced its arrival in a variety of ways: little bodies racked by high fever, bloody urine, the dreaded 'pox' marks raising agonizingly painful pustules on peeling skin. Victims often died screaming. It was soon after this that the first reports of her late-night visits to the cemetery occur. She later testified, when 'put to the question' that she had attempted to raise the spirits of her dead children. But we are getting ahead of the story.

Charleston continued as a thriving seaport throughout the sixteen and seventeen hundreds. Ideally situated at the confluence of two rivers, the town grew and many merchants and planters waxed prosperous. The young colony experimented with tobacco and wheat but in the very last years of the seventeenth century found its staple and most profitable export. According to legend, a bag of rice, inadvertently left behind by a ship from Madagascar, was planted and thrived in the low, marshy fields. The plantation rice industry had begun.

Many planters chose to live year-round cooled by the coastal breezes of the seaport and leave their plantation fields to be worked by enslaved Africans supervised by overseers. With their rice harvest wealth, they built lovely town homes suited to the sub-tropical climate. Most were built without the help of an architect, the well-educated, aristocratic gentlemen enjoying designing their own gracious homes. For a description we may turn to Mrs. Morse Earle.

'Being generaly of Brick, the homes are most stately and high with Bricks of divers Coullers and laid in Checkers, being glazed, look very

agreable. The wood inside is covered with plasterwork most elegantly carved.' [sic]

We find little mention of Elizabeth for several years after the deaths of her children, other than notations in local business records of various herbal, medicinal purchases. However, beginning around 1702, town records and letters of the period indicate peculiar occurrences in the town and surrounding plantations.

Instances were reported of slaves refusing to work certain portions of fields, saying this land must be left for the 'Old One.' Questioning revealed little except that this 'Old One' had not always been in this land but had recently come among them and made his presence known. Overseers reported this problem to the plantation owners who ordered them, nonetheless, to plant all the usual fields. Slaves returned from these fields with broken tools and bruised, scratched arms and faces, having accomplished little or no work. In at least one instance, there were credible reports of showers of stones falling from the sky, striking and killing a slave called Minnie as well as a German overseer, Gustav Brun.

The weather also became peculiar. Random hailstorms destroyed entire fields of crops and killed livestock as well. A furious ship's captain complained of strong winds that wrecked his ship before it ever left the harbor. There were independent records of Charleston Harbor having experienced high wind gusts that damaged ships and docks.

In a horrifying instance, a young boy claimed to have come upon a grotesque scene of demon worship in a swampy thicket next to a graveyard. Returning home rather late from a visit to his cousin, he took a path through the woodland to cut some time from his journey. Surprised to see a fire burning in such a wet, dismal spot, he approached with some caution the crowd gathered there, eating and drinking. A large, goat-like beast standing upright on cloven hooves dominated the scene of masked revelers who approached the figure, warily it seemed, to kneel and kiss the creature's backside. After some time had passed (and the boy having remained hidden in frozen fear behind trees), a great pot on the fire was drained and the contents dispensed in flasks stopped with corks. The crowd then 'did make most immodest display of their bellies and other parts, rubbing them with the substance whereupon each one vanished.'

The boy fled home to his worried mother. The next day a group of searchers discovered a cooking pot among the still warm embers in the copse.

The pitiful remains of an infant lay congealed in the bottom. It was deduced the child was the recently buried son of a local clergyman. The said infant's grave was found to be opened and empty. The searchers noted the soft ground was heavily trampled with human footprints as well as impressions made by very large, cloven hooves.

The boy, one Samuel Finney, fell into an illness. He died after a week of intense suffering in which he was said to vomit iron nails and live crickets. Severe blistering and swelling of his tongue and throat added to the child's agony. His mother found certain charms pinned inside his pillow and removed them but not in time to save his life.

Less serious, more mischievous acts occurred also. Many people heard music at night all through the town. The Warboys family experienced dishes flung through the air and heard loud noises like the cracking and splintering of wood as well as scratching sounds that gave them no peace day or night.

Another household awoke to find the family cow up in the hayloft of the cow shed, lowing mournfully, unable to get down. With the help of incredulous neighbors, they devised a ramp and rescued the cow. The neighbors later said they heard maniacal laughter and distorted mumbling in languages they did not recognize.

Disappearances of items such as farm tools and even clothing became common. Strangely, the tools were often found, undamaged, high up in trees or on rooftops. A well-known parson woke one Sunday morning and found all of his personal body linen simply gone. Forced to dress without it, he arrived at the church and, along with his congregants, looked up to see his undergarments tied to the steeple and billowing in the breeze.

Odd incidents continued throughout the winter. Cemeteries were desecrated so often that watches had to be posted during the night. The weather remained unusually cold and firewood became dear as woodcutters went farther into the surrounding forests for wood. They often claimed to have seen small men in the tree branches, dressed entirely in green, grinning down at them with sharp, jagged teeth.

Dead and partially eaten livestock littered fields. Sightings of the large, goat-like creature were reported and the woodsmen often found clearings with embers still warm from bonfires and usually marked with the curious cloven-hoof prints."

Mesmerized by Elizabeth's tale Sarah had to wrench herself back to the present. The last of the daylight was gone and thunder rumbled in the distance. Tree branches outside the window swayed and she caught a flash of lightning in the direction of the Battery. Downstairs the bread had risen nicely and bulged over the sides of the bowl. She punched it down and kneaded it for a few minutes then divided it in half, placing the soft, yeasty loaves in oiled bread pans and covering them with a cloth.

Restless now she went up in the attic to see if, perhaps, some previous tenant left a bucket behind. She had yet to go through much of the stuff up here but most of what she had seen did not look very sellable. She fumbled along the rafters and eventually found the pull cord for a bare light bulb that did not illuminate much. She went back down for a flashlight, and then waded carefully through the boxes and piles. There were old blinds, curtain rods, an ancient television with a roof antenna beside it, and a cracked fish tank. Several dusty, half-empty bottles of wine stood on the floor near the one small window. The first box she opened (none of them were taped shut) held, to her delight, a crystal chandelier. She dragged the box over to the stairs and eased it carefully down into the spare room where the light was better. It was dirty but despite that, it sparkled. It would be stunning once she cleaned it up. This search just became interesting.

An hour later she still didn't have a bucket but she had found an almost complete set of china dinnerware she thought might be Spode, several large, frilly aprons, and stacks of linen napkins and tablecloths monogrammed with the letter G. Mice or rats (she hoped it was mice) had chewed several of the tablecloths. She took it all downstairs along with someone's extensive collection of paperback zombie novels. Baking the bread then leaving the linens soaking in water with just a bit of bleach, she went up to bed and spent an enjoyable hour or so lost in a zombie apocalypse before falling asleep.

~

The next day, armed with a newly purchased bucket, she tried again. The instructions said to be sure and remove all the loose plaster before beginning the repair. She gingerly prodded the wall, afraid of making it worse. Sure enough, new cracks appeared. She stopped poking and decided she would skim over it with the trowel; just enough to fill the cracks, and hope that would take care of it.

It didn't. As soon as she applied the first layer, chunks of the old plaster stuck to the trowel and pulled away from the wall. Crap. She scraped the chunks off and tried again but just continued to pick up more old plaster. This was a nightmare. The only thing she could think to do was take down more of the cracked plaster. Now she had a hole almost to the baseboard and her plaster mix was hardening in the bucket.

Sighing, she reached between the lath and the baseboard to clear out the crumbling, chalky mess. She banged her hand against something that echoed like metal. Her hand closed around a thin metal box but she couldn't pull it free. Something rattled inside as it shifted. She sat back and looked at the wall. I can't stop now; she told herself and began to pull down more plaster.

The box was slightly rusted and approximately the length of a shoebox but shallower. Latched but not locked, it opened easily and revealed four dolls, made out of what appeared to be small bones joined by rotted hempen string. Nestled in what might have been moss at one time but now resembled desiccated spiders' legs, they stared soullessly out at her. Round eyes and little slashes for mouths were dotted on each and small tufts of hair still clung on top. These were not and never had been playthings for a child, of that she was certain. They made her think of voodoo or Santeria. The bones were so small they must be fingers or toes and she feared they were human bones.

Revulsion made her instinctively close the box and put it down. Curiosity hadn't killed her but it had sure made for one giant hole in her wall. She took the bucket of hardened plaster and dumped it in the backyard, resolved to do better this time.

She made the new batch slightly thinner and it skimmed over the wall nicely. Standing a few feet away, she assessed it. It definitely showed but it's just the first coat and once it's painted... She left it to dry and had just finished cleaning her tools when the phone rang.

"Ms. Faust? This is Detective Schiller. The reports on the remains found in your home are back from the lab. The results are about what we expected."

"So they weren't recent?"

"Not by a long shot. We were able to reconstruct four almost complete skeletons, children, all of them dead for at least one hundred years, probably more. They were well preserved and were only missing-"

"The fingers?"

There was a brief silence on the other end of the line. "I was going to say hands, but yes, the phalanges and metacarpals are missing. Do you mind if I ask how you knew?"

"I think I found them."

Chapter Nine

"Hello?" An elegantly dressed Nay-Nay walked around the corner of the house, smiling. "I hope you don't mind me dropping by like this. You do remember me from the other day?"

Sarah had just returned from church. After Detective Schiller came by yesterday to pick up those gruesome dolls, she couldn't focus on anything. The thought of those tiny skeletons haunted her and she woke early this morning, listening to church bells ringing. She found a later service and offered up her own private prayers for their long-departed souls. The familiar hymns, the spoken prayers and creeds had their usual uplifting effect and she felt more at peace.

The church itself had been interesting. The pulpit hung halfway up the wall on one side of the nave and was built like a little cottage with gingerbread-style carvings. A remarkable ceiling depicted a gruesome vision of the last judgment complete with naked, despairing sinners being driven to hell by grinning, pitchfork-wielding demons. The saved ascended joyously to heaven.

"Of course I do. How wonderful to see you again."

"I was in the neighborhood and I wanted to see how things are coming with the house and to be sure I hadn't scared you off with my dark tales of yesteryear. I can't tell you how bad I felt, shocking you like that. It was never my intention."

"I know and you shouldn't feel bad. It actually startled me into digging into the history of the house a bit and it has been an interesting search. There is nowhere else I would want to live."

"Once the old house bug gets its teeth in, it can be hard to shake, I know. My sons were after me to move into one of those brand-new retirement communities out on Daniel Island but those places have no soul. I need a house that knows me and has seen me live my life. It doesn't hurt if it has seen other lives lived as well."

"I understand now better than I would have been able to two weeks ago. I found out I have a-" she broke off, hesitant to say too much. "A real connection to this place, I guess. Would you like to sit down? I just got home from church and I'm making tea if you would care for some."

Nay-Nay settled comfortably into the sagging wicker chair and kicked her shoes off.

"Church? I was just there yesterday. Tea sounds delightful. I had forgotten how lovely this garden is. It has an air of timelessness. Live oaks tower over one like a cathedral, making us realize our insignificance but sheltering us at the same time."

"And they'll be here long after we are gone. I'll be right back with the tea."

The kettle sang quickly on the new cook-top. She poured the steaming water over the tea bags then carried the mugs outside. Nay-Nay sipped the aromatic Earl Grey slowly, wrapping slightly arthritic hands around the warm porcelain. She smiled.

"Your lawn ornament. Did you put it in or was it already here? I don't recall seeing it before. That iron slave collar disfigures it."

Sarah looked at the ugly little figure and shuddered. "It was already here but had been covered up in some past landscaping renovation, I guess. That's a slave collar? I had no idea. I need to remove it. I hate the idea of perpetuating any reminders of-"

"I would remove it, too. Get rid of that and you'll have a beautiful centerpiece to your garden."

Beautiful? Nay-Nay seemed perfectly sincere. Concepts of beauty did differ but- were they even looking at the same thing? She changed the subject.

"I think the little plants coming up in the parterres might be part of an herb garden."

"Mistress Grayhame would probably have called it her kitchen garden but, considering her profession and well, other interests, it probably has some herbs that are out of the ordinary."

"The holly, the yew, and others are supposed to ward off witches and evil sorts of things. I wonder who chose those." Sarah said.

"Possibly someone else who lived here was afraid she might try to come back so they planted 'protection' for themselves. The spiked leaves of the holly represent the thorns from the crown the Roman soldiers placed on the Christ's head and the berries are drops of blood. Let's see what you have coming up in the parterres."

Nay-Nay put her mug down and led the way into the yard. She sorted through the tender green leaves.

"You'll have to dig all this ivy out if you want to keep other plants here. English ivy is very, very invasive. This little tender thing here is thyme, delicious in stews and eggs. It's also good for dandruff. And this is sage, used in bread and sausage. These over here are lemon-mint and peppermint, good for teas and freshening breath. This is henbane and this is nightshade, both deadly poison but if used in the right amount, will allow one to see spirits. Have you seen any spirits here?" She smiled up at Sarah.

Sarah laughed, and then thought of the dark form in the mirror. The little garden offered a bounty of healing, nutrition, and apparently, death and "ghost vision." Better label those last two fast, she thought. No, I'll just pull them up now and be done with it. She reached out for a good grip and then drew her hand back, exclaiming.

"What was that? It really hurt." Rubbing her right hand, she winced in pain.

"I believe those are stinging nettles, also called 'Devil's Apron' and they do burn like the dickens. Your poor hand must feel singed."

Sarah opened her mouth to agree when the sound of hooves on cobbles and a horse's loud blowing intruded. "Excuse me for a moment." She walked around the side of the house and saw a shiny, black-lacquered, open carriage stopped in the street, the blinkered, chestnut mare standing patiently.

"Ladies and Gentlemen, here at Old South Tours we like to save the best for last." The middle-aged tour guide wore dark pantaloons topped with a red sash and a voluminous white shirt. He spoke into a small microphone. "On your right is one of the most famous houses in Charleston. Dating back to the sixteen hundreds, this example of the early 'single' style house is known as the Witch House. The original owner was Mistress Grayhame whose occult career was brought to an end only after she was convicted of witchcraft and burned at the stake in 1705. Or did it end? Witnesses at the burning claimed to see an unusually large hare dart from the burned embers beneath the stake and disappear. Witches' familiars were known to take on animal form.

The diabolical brews she used on her victims grew in this very garden. Legends say Mistress Grayhame can still be seen, on moonlit nights, gathering ingredients for her poisonous concoctions."

Sarah stood still, too shocked to move. A half-dozen pairs of curious eyes stared at her and a child said, "Dad, is that the witch?" and pointed. Cameras clicked as she turned and fled to the back of the garden.

She was furious. The fact that her house was part of a ghost tour had never been disclosed to her. She paused, took a deep breath and took a moment to regain her composure before she went back to Nay-Nay.

Trying to laugh it off she said aloud, "I must have the most unethical or incompetent realtor in town. Foster can't have much repeat b-" she broke off. Nay-Nay was gone. The clip-clop of hooves and the rumble of the wheels faded away. Assuming Nay-Nay had gone to Mary-Michael's, she walked over to apologize for leaving her but no one came to the door. The house looked deserted with closed blinds and a smokeless chimney. She didn't see a car in the street. The old lady must have left right behind the tour carriage. She went back through the yard, gathered the now cold mugs and went inside.

How often did these tours run? It was still winter; they would probably run more often once the season advanced. She should have paid attention to the company logo on the carriage and she could have looked up the schedule on the internet. When she moved here, she had expected to find privacy in which to rebuild her life, not become an object of occult tourist voyeurism. She felt violated.

Washing the mugs, she left them to dry on a tea towel. The fragile china from the attic was washed and stored in the newly painted cupboards along with her monogrammed table linens. She had managed to haul the chandelier downstairs and it now rested in a corner, cleaned, polished and ready to go up in the dining room once she figured out how to wire it in.

The sense of peace she had earlier was gone and the house (the Witch House) was full of odd rustlings, almost like sighs. She thought of the slave collar on the wicked little figure in the garden. Why would anyone want to keep reminders of such a dark practice in public view? Determined to remove it, she found the hammer and went outside.

The ground, still spongy and wet from yesterday's showers, smelled fecund and fresh and squished under her shoes. She hooked the claw of the hammer on the collar and pulled but the iron was unyielding, even the rusty sections. This was going to take a saw or drill and she had neither. Frustrated, she smacked the hammer against the creature's shoulder, half expecting the arm to break off but the thick bronze was sturdy and didn't even dent. She dug around the plinth a little but a stone base went deep into the ground. Whoever put this up had meant it to last.

Giving up, she plucked a few mint leaves, chewing them and savoring the cool, sharp taste. A breeze blew through, releasing a few left-over drops of rain from the oak leaves above, cold enough to make her gasp when they hit her shoulders. She sat in the swing, twisting the ropes and then letting them unwind, getting mildly dizzy and thinking about what to wear for her interview with Angela tomorrow. Probably business casual would do it or maybe even more relaxed than that. She would play it safe with a khaki skirt, a nice sweater and flats but she thought of her black stilettos with longing. They weren't practical but she loved the way they looked. She stopped twisting the swing. She was getting *very* dizzy.

When a rabbit darted lopsidedly across the grass, she wasn't surprised. Spring came early here and the tender plants coming up in the garden tempted. What did surprise her was that it stopped and leapt into the open arms of a woman standing by the porch steps. She wore the same elaborate dress as before (how could Sarah have forgotten?) but the heavy mass of dark hair hung in ringlets around her shoulders this time, framing a pale face. When she smiled, a dimple appeared in her left cheek and the dark blue eyes almost closed, giving her a languorous look. She walked up the steps, slim, white feet bare beneath the heavy folds of the damask skirt. Sarah followed her, at a distance, onto the porch and into the kitchen. The rabbit's muzzle pulled back, revealing long, yellowed teeth. The eyes were uncomfortably knowing and so pink they almost glowed red. It nestled itself comfortably against the woman and, without warning, sank its teeth into her shoulder, drinking bright, red droplets from the creamy skin. Elizabeth (for who else could it be?) did not appear to notice. She looked around the kitchen and frowned; the room confused her for some reason. She briefly flickered out of sight then reappeared in the hallway.

  Once in the foyer she walked more confidently and entered the parlor with the fireplace. She set the rabbit down and it climbed awkwardly *up* the chimney, disappearing from sight. Kneeling by the fireplace, she tried to move the bricks in the hearth one by one, checking for something and not finding it, biting her lower lip in vexation.

  Sarah stood by the doorway, trying to hang on to some sense of reality. She knew what she was seeing was not real, not possible. If Elizabeth was aware Sarah was there; she was not interested in her. She was intent on finding something and her frustration showed. Just then, Elizabeth turned her face abruptly toward the foyer. She held her head as if she were listening to something and then left the room hurriedly, mounting the staircase, then simply vanishing halfway up.

  Sarah realized she had been holding her breath and now released it, creating puffs of vapor in the freezing air of the room. She sank down onto the sofa and shivered as the room gradually warmed. She was still so frightened that she kept looking behind her, terrified something lurked there. Her hands felt sweaty but she kept shivering, teeth chattering. The sound of hooves dragging and stomping along the floor came down the hallway.

She bolted for the stairs, preferring to take her chances upstairs with Elizabeth rather than face whatever dragged itself toward her down here. Halfway up the steps she looked down and saw red eyes embedded in a bestial face reflected in the foyer mirror. She slammed and locked her bedroom door, hands shaking as she pushed the chest against the door.

Chapter Ten

"Morning! You're early. Let me finish up with this customer and we can get started. Help yourself to coffee in my office." Angela smiled then went back to her phone conversation.

The office was down a short hallway just before a bathroom. Sarah poured a cup of the surprisingly good coffee and sat in one of the mismatched plastic chairs. The room was full of stone and tile samples, brochures, and brightly painted matchbox cars. Angela's boys must come here on occasion. Crayon drawings along with framed portraits of smiling babies decorated the walls.

Her hand shook and she set the coffee down. I need this job, she told herself. I have to pull it together. She had woken once last night to the sound of heavy, snorted breaths just outside the bedroom door. She had gotten sick then had slept heavily. Still nauseated this morning she skipped breakfast, certain it wouldn't stay down.

"Sorry about that. Business has been slow this past month then this morning I start getting all these calls. You'd think I could predict my busy times after all these years but I swear it's just random. How was your weekend?" Angela poured her own coffee then topped off Sarah's before sitting down behind the old, scratched desk.

"Mostly quiet. I did a little gardening and cleaning. Oh, and I found out my house is on a ghost tour."

Angela winced. "No one told you?" Sarah shook her head. "If it's any comfort, a lot of places are on those tours. The town is just so old; it's hard to get away from the history. We live with it all the time but I can see how that would be an unpleasant surprise."

"It's fine. I've really been looking forward to today. I brought my resume." She handed the two page document to Angela. "My references are on the last page, complete with phone numbers and email addresses."

"Great." She looked it over. "You lived abroad for a while, it looks like."

"I did. Military brat. Coming back to the States was always the plan though. I met my husband - ex-husband rather, at my first job out of school. We lived in the Northeast for seven years."

"I see that. What made you decide to move to Charleston?"

"Once we decided to divorce, I needed a change of location. My mother was from Charleston although she had been away a long time. It seemed like a good place to start over."

"What do you think now?"

"It was impulsive to move here without a job. But I think if I can find one, it will have been a good move." She felt she was standing outside of her body, watching herself perform, trying to say the right things. Maybe she was getting the flu.

"Let me tell you a little more about the job. I rent part of an old warehouse over near the docks, not far from the IMAX. I keep most of the pieces there. Lately there have been so many home foreclosures; my inventory is a little out of control. The store is open to the public of course and part of your job will be minding the store, along with some cataloguing and organizing. I need to move some product out before I take on much more. I'm not even sure what's there right now."

"My experience with cataloguing is nil."

"I have a great computer program. You just enter a description of the piece and it builds the list. You retrieve information using key words. It even generates bar code labels. Of course, I won't just dump it all on you. I'm going to be accessible. What I need is someone good with dealing with customers, including contractors, developers, and of course, home improvement junkies and the occasional antique fanatic. Are you still interested?"

"I am, Angela. Very."

"I was hoping you would be. Now let's talk salary."

Half an hour later they drove out to the docks. Fences topped by razor wire surrounded vast lots full of huge shipping containers. The wooden warehouse had a metal roof with tangled vines growing around the gutters and windows. An impressive looking, red-paneled door that didn't really go with the building opened to reveal a vast, dusty space filled with chandeliers, bookcases, stacks of wooden flooring and the like.

"I can't heat it that well but I put an electric heater behind the bar we're using for a counter. Most of the customers don't mind; they enjoy 'roughing it' while looking for a bargain. People often come here because they want something unique with history attached to it. I've tried to keep track of where everything comes from but-"

"It's been too much for you to keep up with."

"Yes! I need a break. Anyway, take a look around. I need to call this customer back then I'll come find you."

The first thing Sarah noticed was a need for better lighting. It was also quite cold. There really was a treasure trove of items here: a carved, plaster ceiling medallion that wouldn't have looked out of place in a palace, high-backed wooden church pews, several classic mantels, a mournful-looking angel statue, graceful white columns. Garden statues, some with features blunted by time and weather stared blindly into space. A pair of stone, Chinese, Foo dogs snarled in unison.

In the back near an emergency exit were stacks of doors. Some were ornate, glass constructions, others plain wood. Many of the latter were painted a bright blue color.

"What do you think?" Angela called out from somewhere behind her.

"It's an old house lover's dream in here. What's with all the blue doors?"

Angela wove her way through to her. "Oh, those. I forgot we had them. A developer bought out a bunch of folks on Johns Island and tore the old houses down. The blue is a Gullah thing. I think it brings good luck or wards off spirits or something."

"What's a Gullah?"

"Have you seen the women selling the hand-woven, sweet-grass baskets around town? They're Gullah. Most are descendants of the West African slaves that stayed in the area after the Civil War. Other than that, I don't know much about them. Those baskets are works of art though and well worth the price."

Sarah nodded but she wasn't thinking about baskets. She was thinking about her front door with the traces of blue paint. Combine that with the rowan, the hollies, and the yews, you had a real case that someone wanted a supernatural barrier around the place. But were they keeping something in or out?

"...a couple of real Foo dogs but they weren't. So if it looks Chinese, we pay extra attention. We can call in an expert if needed."

"Of course." Not wanting to admit she had been wool-gathering, Sarah faked a knowing nod.

"I guess that's it then. Any questions?"

"When would you like for me to start?"

Angela laughed. "After lunch?"

~

To celebrate her new job Sarah stopped at the grocery and bought fresh shrimp to boil and a carton of double-fudge brownie ice cream. The thought of having money coming in again was such a relief that she forgot about the events of yesterday until she pulled in the driveway.

Was she losing her mind? She didn't think so. She remembered the dress from the "dream" in the garden several days ago. Could it have been Elizabeth leaving her those messages in the fireplace? What sort of help did she want? Whatever was going on, there was something in the fireplace that related to all this.

After putting the water on for the shrimp she swept the hearth then knelt and prodded every brick. All were securely mortared in place. Sure she would regret it later; she retrieved the hammer and pounded the bricks until the mortar broke away. She pulled out the broken pieces, revealing a shallow cavity beneath. Reaching in she found a thick, leather drawstring bag. It was heavy, encrusted with soot, and so stiff she had to break the brittle leather to extract the contents.

Two leather-bound books, one quite large, the other much slimmer, slid out. If they had ever had printing on the front or spine, it was long gone now. Inside the larger book, a beautifully illustrated plate identified the book as the *Herball, or General Historie of Plants* by John Gerard. She turned the page and read the preface.

"What greater delight is there than to behold the earth apparelled with plants as with a robe of embroidered works, set with Orient pearls and garnished with great diversitie of rare and costly jewels? But these delights are in the outward senses. The principal delight is in the minde, singularly enriched with the knowledge of these visible things, setting forth to us the invisible wisdome and admirable workmanship of almighty God." [sic]

With a growing sense of enchantment she read on. Basil, according to Gerard, was good for *"those given to over-much sighing"* and *"is good for the heart ... it taketh away sorrowfulness, which commeth of melancholy and maketh a man merry and glad."* The illustrations that accompanied each plant named were precisely and beautifully drawn.

Under peony the author claimed that *"the black graines (that is the seed) to the number of fifteene taken in wine or mead is a speciall remedie for those that are troubled in the night with the disease called the Night Mare which is as though a heavy burthen were laid upon them and they were oppressed...and they are also good against melancholie dreams."* [sic]

She smiled, set the book carefully aside and took up the smaller volume. Several of the pages were stuck together and the first pages, presumably including the title page, were mostly unreadable due to water damage. The first legible passage had something to do with Moses.

"In the name of Primeumaton, which Moses named and invoked, there fell a great and severe hail throughout all the land of Egypt, destroying the vines, the trees, and the woods."

She leafed through the rest but couldn't make much sense of it. She was just able to make out what looked like *Salomonus* on one of the water-stained pages. Some of the names obviously came from the Bible but most of the contexts were not familiar.

She looked at the mess in the hearth. The bricks would have to be re-mortared which she could do herself. How hard could it be? Finding the books was worth it.

All of her prospects were brighter now that she had a job. Getting the bathtub re-glazed? Not a problem. She could start getting estimates for that and the outside painting. Taking the *Herball* with her, she strolled out to her garden and inspected the little plants in the parterres, comparing them to the illustrations in the book.

A garland of pennyroyal, according to Gerard *"made and worn about the head is of a great force against the swimming in the head, the paines and giddiness thereof."*

Thyme *"breaketh the stones in the bladder; it helpeth lethargie, frensie and madness and stayeth the vomiting of bloud."* Mint was described as *"marvelous wholesome for the stomacke…it stayeth the hicket…and was good for children's sore heads."*

The Latin plant names, further emphasizing their antiquity and timelessness, thrilled her. She rolled the names on her tongue as she touched the plants. *Pelugium, thymus, mentha.* As an apothecary, Elizabeth must have used this book often and the scribbled notes on some of the pages were probably hers or perhaps her mother's. The words were difficult and some impossible to make out. She turned the pages and found a more legible entry written next to a lovely sketch of a pennyroyal plant.

"Take ye a part of henbane mixed upon coals burnt to ash with pennyroyal. Blow it thrice where ye list saying, 'In nomine patris' and ye shall see no more the slatternly fluff on wood."

Slatternly fluff? Could that be dust? Going outside she gathered several leaves of what she was pretty sure were henbane and pennyroyal. Scooping up ashes from the hearth she mixed all three together in a sauce pan and heated it on the cook top.

Stirring it until she had a charred, powdery mess, she let it cool, then, feeling completely ridiculous, she went through the house, blowing ashes from the wooden spoon on furniture, windowsills, wainscot, the stair rail and steps, dumping the last of it on her bedroom floor and blowing it under the bed. Take that, dust bunnies. Reading the instructions again she ran back to each spot and recited *"In nomine patris."* She had probably done it in the wrong order but she could try it again later. She took the book back out to the garden and continued reading.

"Go on Thursday evening when the sun is set where thou knowest that helenium stands, then sing the Benedicite and Pater Noster and with thy knife make it stick fast and go away; go again when day and night just divide; [illegible] first to church and cross thyself and [illegible] thyself to God then pluck it and wind into chains. Then say, 'I have wreathed round the wounds the best of healing wreaths, That the baneful sores may Neither burn nor burst. Now all will be well with thee.'"[sic]

"All will be well with thee." Those were the exact words in the nonsense rhymes her mother would sing whenever she patched up Sarah's cuts or scrapes, rocking her in her arms. The wound would always be gone by morning. Her mother kept a well-organized box of dried herbs and roots and used them to make rinses, lotions, and sometimes teas. Sarah's father called it her mother's "voodoo medicine" which always made her mother laugh. In second grade she had been badly sunburned on a school field-trip. She returned to class the next day, skin back to normal after her mother bathed her in milky, fragrant water. Her teacher had commented on it.

The sun set and purple twilight descended on the garden. Closing the book she reached down to pick a few leaves of mint then stopped. In this light she wasn't entirely sure what was mint and what wasn't. Could she have accidentally eaten a leaf of henbane or nightshade yesterday and hallucinated? That would explain the lingering nausea. She clung to the explanation briefly until she thought of what she had just found beneath the hearth. No, she had to face it, something had clued her in to that be it ghost, dream or-whatever. She had experienced something real. The evidence was here in her hand.

The shrimp was ready. Angela had advised her to learn as much about southern architecture as possible and loaned her a book called *The Dwelling Houses of Charleston*. She read while she ate, not finding it as charming as the *Herball*, but undoubtedly more useful. Idly, she wondered what the *Herball* might be worth. It had to be old. She wouldn't consider selling it unless the sum was astronomical.

She put her plate in the dishwasher, straightened up and looked out into the yard. The hair on the back of her neck rose.

Chapter Eleven

Four small figures stood solemnly by the hedge, wearing stitched sacking stained with gray dirt. Their hands hung by their sides. The evening twilight was just enough to see their shapes outlined against the darkening sky. Their ages might range from ten down to two or three.

Suddenly the sound of a woman's agonized weeping echoed throughout the house. Sarah felt a sense of sadness so deep she almost couldn't breathe, and then slowly, the sounds faded away. She looked out the window again. The children were gone.

She didn't want to see this, hear this anymore. It was too much.

"Stop it!" she screamed. "Leave me alone."

There had to be a way to get these spirits away from the house. She suspected it had been tried in the past. Someone knew what those trees and shrubs were meant to do. Someone painted the door blue for protection. It hadn't worked though and her own knowledge of occult matters was non-existent. She had nothing to fight this with. Finding a priest or minister to "bless the house" seemed like such a movie cliché and she didn't know if they really did things like that anyway.

She did not want to be driven out. The affinity she had felt for the house from the beginning was still strong. It belonged to her family. Her mother might have even lived here at some point. There had to be an answer.

Upstairs she locked her bedroom door. If something had managed to come back from the dead a locked door was probably not a huge obstacle but still, it made her feel safer. The floor was a mess and she had gotten ashes on the counterpane. Great. She could just make out the swing ropes swaying gently before she closed the blinds and shut out the night.

Sarah believed in God and never doubted that a second life would follow this one. But that second life didn't involve the dead appearing to the living, remaining trapped in some sort of earthly limbo.

~

"This is the book I was telling you about." She unwrapped the slim volume from under the hearth and placed it carefully on the counter in the warehouse.

"Where did you say it came from? I forgot." Angela asked.

Not wanting to go into great detail she said, "It was in my house, with another…"

But Angela wasn't listening. She turned the pages carefully. "This looks *very* old. I've come across old books at times but I'm no expert. You should have someone look at this. If for no other reason than to find a way to preserve it. The pages are starting to crumble."

Sarah had been at the job for a week now. All that time had been spent cataloguing pieces and dealing with customers. Surprisingly, she enjoyed it. Building a database of the inventory was almost like taking courses in architecture and history. Earlier today she had explained the differences between Doric and Ionic columns to a new customer. She brought the smaller book in today because she wanted help in separating the pages and Angela, with two small children, had some experience with stuck book pages.

"Sorry, but when you said 'old book', I didn't realize you meant this old. My expertise in fixing books involves peanut butter or maple syrup related mishaps only."

"That's okay. It may not be repairable. I wonder what would happen if I put it in the microwave with a cup of warm water."

"Ask at the library or an antique shop. They might know. Oh, I forgot to tell you. My brother is coming over after lunch with some fluorescent bulbs to install. Is that tall ladder still next to the exit door?"

David showed up shortly after noon and got to work in the back. Due to a flurry of lunchtime customers, Sarah barely had time to eat the sandwich she brought from home. Most of the shoppers were browsers who didn't have a lot of questions but one, Liddy Carmody, was working with a strict timetable and knew exactly what she wanted and when.

"The good thing about dealing with the Stauntons is that you know they'll do what they say. They're one of the old families of Charleston, real solid people. So many of them are disappearing from the business life of the town. It's a shame." Liddy confided.

She confirmed her delivery time and left the store. Sarah was proud of the knowledgeable way she had handled her questions. She looked over at David to see if he had finished and found him watching her. He looked like he was trying not to laugh.

"What?"

"You have no idea what you're talking about, do you?"

"Of course I do! The classical order means the heaviest columns are always on the bottom level of the building."

"Yes but entasis does not mean the builders are trying to trick you. Entasis is used to give the illusion of a column bulging under a heavy weight."

"Same thing. Liddy knew what I was talking about. The bulge in the middle corrects a concave appearance caused by perspective. The ancient Greeks came up with it."

"I was wrong. You do know your columns. My apologies."

"Accepted. But you will have to buy me a Coke from the vending machine as a peace offering."

"Peace offering? Were we arguing?"

"No, but we came close and I forgot to bring a drink for lunch."

"Okay. One more light bulb to go and I'll get your drink."

"Don't take too long. I'm thirsty."

This is what I needed, she thought. Work to focus on and people to talk to. People who knew nothing of her recent, somewhat distasteful past. Although she had done nothing wrong, there was always guilt by association in most people's minds. Odd though, that in fleeing a new scandal, she wound up in the midst of an ancient one.

She opened up her delivery schedule for Thursday and added Liddy in the twelve to two timeframe. Right now she only offered Thursday delivery because she used the same delivery guys as the stone store. It would be nice if they could hire more delivery people. If sales continued to grow as fast this week as they had last-

"Here you are, madam. Your drink, as requested." David plunked the cold can down next to the keyboard.

"Thank you, Mr. Staunton. That will be all." She didn't look up but waved him away airily.

David walked out the door, smiling, and a little intrigued. The first day that she came into the store he had thought her pushy and no-nonsense, the quintessential Northeast coast transplant.

That evening in the garden though, had been quite different. He recalled dark-auburn hair falling around her shoulders, mouth open in a soft O of surprise, deep-blue eyes sleepy yet startled when he came around the side of the house. She quickly reassumed her business-like persona but the earlier image had stayed in his mind for a long time. Too long really. He had firmly resisted any impulse to drop by in the guise of a friendly neighbor. No time for that sort of nonsense. He shook his head as he started his car. It never ended well. At least not for him.

Sarah finished a report for Angela. It summarized inventory and then projected sales figures based on previous data. There was not a lot of history for comparison but they had to start somewhere. In her experience, new construction and remodeling picked up in the spring and she could only assume it was the same in the South.

She wished she knew more about local history. One customer had recognized a heavily carved, monogrammed door frame as one from the house where Theodosia Burr Alston, daughter of the notorious Aaron Burr, was supposed to have lived for a very brief period in the early 1800's. Theodosia set sail from Charleston in 1812 aboard the schooner, *Patriot*, on her way to see her father in New York. The ship went down at sea and no one on board was ever seen again. Sarah included the story in the catalogue but noted that it was unverified.

Angela had mentioned the Gullah people and internet searches revealed a good bit about their background and beliefs. Apparently the red rice and seafood dishes so popular in the local cuisine originated with the Gullah in Africa. The blue doors were supposed to keep evil spirits away. She had no idea if that made the doors more valuable though.

The slaves had taken on Christian beliefs and added some of their own traditions. During their church services they claimed to be possessed by the Holy Spirit during a ritual dance known as a "ring shout." They also believed that while the souls of the dead left this realm and went to heaven, the spirits (separate from the soul) often lingered on earth. Witches or "root doctors" often tried to control and use these spirits for their own purposes.

The Gullah also believed that mirrors could reflect the spirits and thus turned them to the wall in a house where someone had recently died. Newsprint, she read with a chill, was often used to paper the walls of houses to keep the spirits away. The spirits were compelled to read every word before they could approach the residents. Some Gullah even lined their shoes with newspaper for protection throughout the day.

Customers kept coming in and she was happy to finally close shop at the end of the day. The parking lot behind the building was poorly lighted and she kept looking over her shoulder as she fumbled for her car keys. The store was only a couple of miles from her house and she could have walked but everyone advised her against it as the area was a little dicey after dark.

The streets were congested tonight. She drove by crowded, brightly lit restaurants and shops. The hectic confusion died away when she turned down her little street. The house waited for her, silent and dark in the fading twilight.

Chapter Twelve

Although it didn't show in this light, the columns and porch were scraped and ready for paint. She had sanded the front door herself, removing the last traces of blue. As much as she hated to admit it, a part of her (the superstitious part) wanted to paint it blue again but she had yet to make a final decision on that.

A slight, salty breeze fluttered the leaves on the trees and mingled with the smell of mint and thyme as she walked around to the back door. She had the key in the lock when a sound behind made her freeze then turn slowly around.

A figure stood by the back hedge near the kissing gate. With a slight *clang* of metal another figure walked into view. Together they approached the porch.

Sarah hurriedly unlocked the door and turned the porch light on, illuminating the faces of the two little girls she met right after she moved into the house. The littlest sister sobbed and wiped tears away from behind her glasses. The older girl held her hand and looked troubled.

"What's wrong, darling? Where are your mom and dad?" Sarah knelt in front of them.

"My dad isn't home. My mom dropped us off but my dad wasn't there." She looked as if she were trying not to cry.

"Do you know his phone number? We can call him right now. Or we can call your mom. But first-" she went in the kitchen and grabbed a tissue and held it to the littlest girl's nose. "Blow." She did, noisily.

"Better?"

She nodded.

"Okay, what's your Dad's phone number?"

"My cat isn't here," the smaller sister interjected. "She's always here for me to feed her but she's gone. The witch got her." The last word ended in a broken-hearted wail.

"We'll find her but first let's call your dad, ok? What's his-" Sarah broke off. A tall, familiar figure came through the gate.

The girls cried, "Dad!" and ran into his open arms. Both began talking at once.

"Slow down! One at a time, okay? Lil, you first." David's voice was patient and she could tell it calmed his distraught daughters.

These were David's daughters? She didn't even know he was married, much less had two children. He seemed to have it all under control so she stood up and moved toward her door. He looked up.

"Sarah, wait a minute. Girls, I want you to wait for me over by the gate. Stay where I can see you." They moved away reluctantly.

David walked over to the porch. "I just got home from work. I hope they weren't bothering you. How long were they here?"

"Only a minute or two before you came. Of course they weren't bothering me. They were just upset. Is everything okay?"

"Fine. Without going into great detail I'll just say that my ex-wife sometimes drops Kate and Lil off without calling when she has something else she wants to do. I'm not in the habit of leaving them alone outside at night. I had no idea they would be here." He paused and motioned the girls over. "Lil, Kate, This is Ms. Faust, she works with Aunt Angela. Sarah, this" he indicated the oldest girl "is Kate and this is Lil."

"We know who she is, Dad. We know her from a long time ago," Kate said in a tone of exaggerated patience.

"Oh. Consider this a formal introduction then."

"I'm glad you came over tonight and you can come back anytime. I'll keep an eye out for the cat and let you know if I see her."

"Thanks." He turned back to his girls. "Who wants grilled cheese?" Both squealed delightedly as he lifted them onto his shoulders. He staggered through the gate and they were gone, holly branches swaying in their wake.

Hmm. No wonder he didn't want to leave town for a job. She would have never pictured him as a father until tonight; now she couldn't picture him any other way. His daughters obviously adored him. She went inside and locked the back door against the deepening night.

She thought about the way David lifted the girls up so effortlessly to his shoulders. Her father used to do that. She always felt so safe; even on that precarious perch she knew her father would never let her fall. Probably David's daughters felt the same. Lucky girls.

Darkness pressed against the house. The windows were black openings reflecting only her face back at her. She thought of something looking in, able to watch her while she could see nothing. She went through all the rooms, closing the cheap, temporary blinds. Curtains were an expense she couldn't shoulder right now.

The house had been placidly normal since the last sighting of those four, forlorn figures by the hedge. She couldn't shake the nagging feeling that she was supposed to help them but how? She felt that when she bought this house she had assumed responsibility for whatever still needed to be corrected.

Reading more of the old newspaper story over the last few days had been interesting but produced more questions than answers.

Elizabeth's mind had obviously become unhinged after her husband and children died. That was the only explanation she could come up with to account for the things she was supposed to have done. But mental illness couldn't explain everything in the story.

According to the article, *"The town continued to mark bizarre occurrences. Two children reported they were approached by a 'seemly group of women busked in satins' who offered them sweets as well as 'lengths of fine lace' to give to their mothers if they would but come a little way into the forest and help them to recover some hens they had lost. The children claimed that though they heard their words the women's lips did not move. When the children refused to go with them, a hideous screeching split the air, tree branches were blown about, the women spun like tops then vanished.*

Newborn infants disappeared from their mothers' beds never to be seen again. Elizabeth was mentioned in some of these incidents, not as the suspected agent but rather because she advised parents to place cold iron in bed with the babies. The vanishings stopped. The grateful townspeople did not appear to have questioned her knowledge in the matter."

So the good people of Charleston were content to use her skills and knowledge in some matters but she obviously crossed a line. At some point someone connected her with the ills plaguing the town. But when and how? She continued reading.

"The winter of 1703-1704 was exceptionally cold as the Little Ice Age still exerted its frigid hold on most of the Northern hemisphere. In Europe, Esquimuax paddled down from the Arctic and proceeded inland as far as the River Dee in Scotland, to the amazement of the native-"

The doorbell rang.

Mary-Michael stood on the stoop. The double-breasted, camel-hair coat and Burberry scarf looked crisp and stylish but her eyes were tired and strained. She didn't know Mary-Michael's age but she had assumed it was near her own. Tonight she raised her estimate by about five years.

"Hi! It's so nice to see you again. Come in." Sarah opened the door wider and ushered her in.

"Thanks." She unwound the scarf but kept her coat on. "It's nice to see you too, Sarah. I can only stay a minute but I wanted to ask you if our mail was delivered here by mistake. I had the Post Office put a hold on it while we were away and they were supposed to deliver it all today but it never showed."

"No, sorry. I haven't seen it. I walked over the other day but you must have still been gone. Were you out of town long?"

"Over a week. We've had…a loss. My grandmother. If you remember, you met her that first evening at our house."

"Oh no! I'm so sorry, Mary-Michael. She dropped by here on Sunday and she seemed fine. What happened?"

Mary-Michael gave her an odd look. "She had a stroke while driving. The car slammed into one of those giant oaks out on Bohicket Road but the medics told us she was probably already dead before the impact. You said you saw her on Sunday?"

"Yes, she was worried she had upset me with talk of the house's history. Of course she hadn't. I can't tell you how sorry I am."

"Sunday two weeks ago?"

"No, last Sunday."

"Sarah, you have your dates wrong. She died Wednesday before last. We buried her last Saturday."

Sarah started ticking off the days mentally. She didn't have her dates wrong at all. Nay-Nay had been here last Sunday. Mary-Michael was just confused. She decided to gloss over it.

"Was the funeral here in Charleston?"

"Yes. She was a member at St. Stephen's her whole life. Noble and I spent a few days with my mother out on Wadmalaw, going through Nay-Nay's things. I know we were lucky to have her as long as we did but I suppose I'm greedy. I wanted more time with her." Tears poured down her face and she pulled a balled-up handkerchief out of her pocket.

Sarah walked her home. Noble took charge once they got there, sending Mary-Michael up to bed.

"If I can do anything for you, anything at all, let me know," Sarah said.

"I will, and thanks for bringing her home. It was so sudden and no one had time to prepare themselves. I think that makes it harder for all of us."

"I understand completely. Several years ago, I lost my parents suddenly. You never really get over it but you do learn to go on."

It was fully dark now. The wind picked up and leaves on the trees shivered in response. A silvery, sickle moon hung over the peaceful street. Her footsteps made no sound on the cobbles and she walked home in silence, hands in her coat pockets, enjoying the cold air on her face.

It was a good night for a fire. The bundle of kindling she bought at the grocery store was well-seasoned and caught right away but she suspected it would burn up quickly. No matter. She ate her supper sitting close to the hearth, reveling in the classic beauty of the sculpted mantel highlighted by the warm, flickering firelight. The walls were now a colonial blue that contrasted nicely with the white moldings. The house was definitely diminutive but someone (her ancestors?) had embellished the little dwelling in the best of taste.

A crash on the back porch was followed by pounding on the door. She turned out the lights in the house and walked into the kitchen and looked out the window.

Nay-Nay stood on the porch. In disbelief, Sarah turned the porch light on to see better and saw she wore the same dress as last Sunday but it now had dark stains on the front. She staggered in an oddly jerky fashion as she alternated knocking on the door with pulling at the neck of her dress. Her belly was grotesquely bloated. When she turned around Sarah saw that a straight cut sliced the back of the dress from neck to hem and was held together with metal sutures.

"So cold, so-"

The swollen, blackened tongue struggled with the words as the rotting hands continued to beat on the door. The thing's eyes, just visible in the sagging, decaying face, caught hers in the window and glinted maliciously. It staggered over and pounded on the window.

Sarah ducked down, crouched on the floor and put her hands over her ears. The blows on the house intensified. She put her hands around her waist and began to pray, rocking back and forth.

"...not into temptation but deliver us from evil. For thine is the kingdom and the power and the glory, forever and ever-"

The pounding ceased abruptly but Sarah stayed where she was for a long time, terrified of seeing the dead/undead Nay-Nay again. Finally she stood, barely breathing as she edged over to the window. The porch was clear, an overturned wicker chair the only sign anything had happened.

Completely shaken and stunned, she went upstairs, climbing slowly on trembling legs. What was happening here? Was there anyone she could talk to who wouldn't think she was insane?

She pulled up obituaries online and found listed one member of St. Stephen's Church, Mrs. Emily Brochardt, aged 95, who had died suddenly and had indeed been buried last Saturday. Mary-Michael had not been confused. It was entirely possible that whatever had shown up tonight was the same thing that stopped by last Sunday. She recalled *that* Nay-Nay saying she had just been in church the day before and shuddered. Tonight's version had been decaying and clearly falling to pieces. Just thinking of that swollen, twisting tongue made her nauseated.

She remembered the Gullah tradition that souls go to heaven but spirits stay earthbound. Thinking, straining to make sense of it all, something dawned on her. The thing left after she started praying. Was that it? Was the spirit commanded by the words? Or was it just afraid of them? And who or what left the messages in the fireplace? She didn't know.

Her mother's Bible lay on top of the mahogany chest. Opening it to Psalms she read "The Lord is my rock and my fortress and my deliverer; My God, my strength in whom I will trust..." The ancient words soothed and reminded her again of her mother. She spent the rest of the evening reading verses her mother had underlined and the handwritten notes in the margins. They invoked memories of a deep and abiding faith that had never wavered and she felt safe, almost as if her mother were here with her.

Just as she was falling asleep, she thought of trying an experiment. Not sure what she hoped to discover exactly, she climbed out of bed, went downstairs to the fireplace and traced a message in the still warm ashes.

"*Who are you?*"

Chapter Thirteen

The next morning the words were stamped out, angrily it seemed, and ashy footprints led into the foyer. She photographed the prints. I should have been doing this all along, she thought. She didn't plan to show them to anyone; she simply wanted to reassure herself that she wasn't crazy.

All day at work she re-lived that horrible scene on the porch. She avoided the darker corners of the warehouse, afraid the thing might follow her here.

Distractions helped. When she wasn't dealing with customers she continued categorizing her inventory database.

She decided to do some baking and take the food over to Mary-Michael and Noble but she did not intend to say anything more about having seen Nay-Nay or whatever that had been last night. She knew firsthand how hard it is to lose someone you love to an unexpected death.

That long-ago night was still so fresh in her memory. She had just gotten back to her dorm after a disastrous date. A guy she met in Survey of European Civilization class asked her out to eat to be followed by a party at a friend's house. They had a great meal then left for the party that was already in full-swing. It was a beautiful, early-spring night. The run-down, little house vibrated with the blasting music, a keg was on the front porch and someone had already passed out on the lawn.

Just as they walked through the front door, someone, she never found out whom, staggered into them and kissed her full on the lips before she could pull away. Her date, instead of helping her just get rid of the guy, decided to take a swing at him. Her assailant was very drunk and went down easily. His drunken friends did not. Fortunately no one was seriously hurt but the evening had turned sour and she got a ride home early with someone going her way.

Back in the dorm she checked her phone and found seven missed calls from numbers she didn't recognize. She picked one of the numbers at random and called back. She was connected with a police sergeant who informed her that her parents had been severely injured in a car accident and that she should try to come as soon as possible. She was still throwing clothes into a backpack when an ER clerk called to tell her they had died.

Her world became a narrow tunnel of pain and grief out of which she could not climb. She dreamed of her mother repeatedly and often woke clutching for the hand she had just felt stroking her cheek. She so longed for just one more chance to see them, to speak to them. Her grades plummeted and if the understanding dean had not worked some administrative magic and allowed her to take the classes over during the summer she would probably have lost her scholarship.

Looking back she realized how unprepared she had been for life on her own. She met Sean not long after she graduated and got her first job. During a stint of on-the-job training she and several other new employees utilized a conference room in a building across the street from her office. She left her planner on the table in the crowded employee break room at lunch and it wasn't there when she went back to look for it. She had given it up for lost until she came in the next morning and found it on her desk. Written in bold black marker on every page were the words "Call me" and "Sean" with a phone number.

She called to thank him and he asked her out for a drink after work. They talked until midnight that first night and soon they spent every evening together. He wanted her to move in to his apartment but she resisted. That was not how she wanted their relationship to go. Comments her father made years ago about people who did that kind of thing stayed in her memory. He thought living together without marriage was irresponsible as well as immoral. Her mother would usually chime in that it was tacky as well and made holidays awkward. When she told Sean that, he laughed and asked her to marry him then. Whatever it takes, he had said, just as long as I don't have to be without you.

She first said no, things were moving too quickly but after two more months she agreed. Sean was irresistible when he wanted to be. He exuded confidence and carried others along on the wave of his enthusiasm. She was happy to be along for the ride for several golden years.

She had been swept up into his life of executive privileges and expense account dinners. Sean loved high-tech toys, vacations to exotic destinations, and Redskins football (they were fun to watch, she had to admit). Eventually she realized he loved all of it much more than he loved her but she tried to hang on, to make it work, as long as she could. It was all for nothing in the end.

The phone rang. Liddy Carmody wanted to know if they had more oak planks like the ones from the old seminary gymnasium floor. She had miscalculated the number she needed and was running a little short.

Sarah found a few of them next to the blue doors. Liddy soon pulled up with one of her carpenters to load them.

"You are a lifesaver. My client wants to keep as much of the original floor as possible and insists we don't use any new materials. I've had to pull up all the boards and even some from the closets to blend in with the pieces I've found. While I applaud his 'earth-friendly', recycling mindset, I have to tell you, it's been a challenge." She ran her fingers through her coal-black, shoulder-length hair then looked at her hands. "Do you see this? My hair is falling out!"

"But you love your job, right?" Sarah smiled at her theatrics.

"Of course I love my job! When this project is complete, I want you to come out and have a look, Sarah. I'm focusing on the interiors now while it's cold but I'm starting on the gardens in a few weeks. This will be my first historic garden restoration."

"I would love to see it. I'm working on a garden too, a little bit at a time."

"For your own house? Where do you live?"

"Downtown. In an old house south of Broad. The garden is original but neglected. I'm still figuring out the names of all the plants."

Liddy looked thoughtful. "Original, hmm. I need some classic touches for this garden. The last owner razed it flat and put in a mini-golf course for his children. Atrocious. It's like starting from scratch. I did manage to find some old photos, daguerreotypes actually, of the original garden and I plan to use those for the layout."

"I have a unique statue. No idea how old it is but I wouldn't mind selling it if I could get it out of the ground."

"Marble?"

"No, bronze and mounted on a stone plinth. I think it's a satyr, one half life-size."

"You can't get more classic than a satyr. You're sure it's not Priapus?" She frowned a little. "This family has children."

Sarah laughed. "No, it's G-rated. You're welcome to come out and take a look."

"I'll give you a call. Thanks again, Sarah. Have a great weekend."

"You too."

She had forgotten it was Friday. The tourist season, which never completely died away here, was heating up and today had been busy. Combine that with the seasonal pick-up in building and she should have plenty of business. Time to close shop for the night though.

Knowing she had to do it, she steeled herself to walk to the back of the warehouse to lock the rolling doors. The lighting was still poor back here where the stacks of old doors took up an entire dark corner. As she approached she heard a high-pitched squeaking that she couldn't account for. She thought of rats and almost turned around but then noticed a plaintive quality in the sound.

It came from the stacked doors. She went back to her desk, got the flashlight from the drawer there and carefully shined it in every nook and cranny of the stack. A sudden glimpse of a pair of golden eyes startled her into dropping the light.

Those were too big for a rat, she thought, fishing for the flashlight which had rolled away. Her hand brushed against something furry, warm, and soft. She made a quick grab and pulled out- a kitten.

Not much bigger than her hand, it spat and hissed, tiny paws batting at her ferociously.

"Where did you come from?" she asked, cuddling it close as it continued to try to rip her to shreds. "And where is your mom?"

A few more minutes of searching satisfied her that mom was not here, nor were any brothers or sisters. She found a box and deposited the furious feline inside for the drive home. It squeaked in protest the whole way.

Warming milk in the microwave and pouring it into a saucer she scooped the kitten out of the box and placed it in front of the milk. It sniffed the area briefly, stepped into the dish and began to lap enthusiastically. The little belly grew taut before it stopped and began to daintily clean its face and paws.

"What will I do with you?" she asked the kitten who ignored her completely. Tiny, pink tongue licking its tortoise-shell markings, white belly and black socks, it appeared entirely self-possessed. Finished cleaning, it yawned and began sniffing around again. She hurriedly took it outside where it scratched the sandy soil for a moment before it found the right spot. Sarah grabbed the box from the warehouse and filled it with some of the soil to use as a litter box until she could buy something better.

She debated letting it sleep in the basement. She had never had a cat before. Sean had been allergic and her mother had had an aversion to indoor animals. The basement seemed too far away, lonely, and cold. Upstairs was probably the best place for now.

Coming back into the bedroom after a shower, she found the kitten curled partly inside her shoe, asleep, head awkwardly to one side and a leg dangling just above the floor. Well, I can't leave you down there, can I?

Nestled on top of the blankets, purring like a motor, the furry little body radiated warmth. It's just for tonight, she thought drowsily. I'll buy a basket tomorrow and put it in the kitchen.

~

"Dear Ms. Faust," The letter began. "I have taken the liberty of writing you as I have information in which I believe you might have interest. Our archives have yielded a portrait of what may be one of the early owners of your house. Previously identified incorrectly as the wife of Magistrate Granholme, we now believe it to be a Mistress Grayhame, first name unknown. If you are interested in more information please feel free to contact us here at-" etc. etc. "Sincerely, Dr. Reginald Bickerstaff, PhD."

She was very interested but didn't know when she would have time to go down there. Her bathroom was a work in progress and she was up to her elbows in bleach and paint.

Further investigation had revealed that the old sink and tub were cast-iron covered in porcelain. She thought she should be able to re-coat them with a good epoxy spray-paint. This morning she cleaned each piece then sanded them with steel-wool, taping off the chrome taps and knobs. She opened the window and, hoping for the best, coated each lightly with the white paint.

The smell was overwhelming. Choking, she shut the bathroom door, then opened up the rest of the windows on this floor before retreating downstairs, taking Mr. Tumnus (she had named the kitten) with her.

Even downstairs wasn't far enough. She went out on the porch, taking deep breaths of the cold, fresh air. Mr. Tumnus came with her.

Each day saw more and more green shoots unfurling out of the ground. Early violets and lilacs bloomed in every nook and cranny of the yard, bathing it in varying shades of blue. She gathered bouquets of them for the house each evening. The fat rosebuds on the thick vines that wrapped around the columns were just beginning to bloom.

Mr. Tumnus stole quietly out onto the lawn where he crouched, stalking a squirrel. Sarah hoped he had the sense not to attack; the squirrel was almost twice his size. As she watched, the little body quivered in murderous anticipation but he stayed hidden in the grass, content to watch for now.

Back upstairs the air had cleared and the paint was dry to the touch. Both the tub and sink would need another coat but even now they shone a glossy, clean white. In contrast the brown carpet looked even more appalling. It was also sticky with paint residue. She made a snap decision to pull it up. Whatever was under there couldn't be much worse.

To her delight she found a solid floor of one-inch, black-and-white, porcelain tiles. Two were slightly cracked and the grout needed a good cleaning but it was otherwise in good shape. She dragged the carpet out to the yard, the kitten attacking her and the carpet the whole way. The growing pile in the corner of the yard was unsightly and she would have to haul it off soon. She hoped none of the neighbors could see it from their windows.

Bleach and a scrub brush worked miracles on the grout and she sat back and surveyed her work with satisfaction. Black and white was so classic in a bathroom. She should have done this weeks ago. Now she just needed to replace the worn-out, orange curtains. Black and white toile would be a nice touch.

After reading the note from Dr. Bickerstaff again, she got out her computer and started paging through the photographed documents, trying to find where she had left off reading last time. Something about "Esquimaux" in Scotland?

The trial transcripts caught her eye. The recital of Elizabeth's crimes continued.

"IV. That she did, many and sundry times, offer, for a price, to counteract spells cast by a "bad witch" with whom she had entered into this arrangement and who was paid for her services; The "accursed" families, being made easier in their minds but still dupes all the same, were led to perform boilings of various herbs whilst shutting themselves away together to endure occult ceremonies and swords being thrust up the chimneys to prevent the 'bad witch' from flying down."

Who was the "bad witch?" She sorted through the newspaper article again and found mention of the former servant from the West Indies who had acquired a reputation as one who could supply magic charms and potions. A dangerous occupation for the time and a dangerous game for the two women to engage in. It must have been very profitable for them to risk it. Perhaps Elizabeth had simply ceased to care.

"*A free woman of color, Katarina, was arrested soon after Elizabeth and tortured as well. In spite of her lowly status, her obvious intelligence comes down to us from the testimony she gave.*

'Didst thou think we had no knowledge? Our weapons were handed down from the antediluvian world by the daughters of Cain to Ham the son of Noah. We have lost much of our understanding and skill but the knowledge was there and when we were plucked from our warm lands some of us brought this knowledge with us, older than your Christianity and of the same seed. Why would we not use it?'

Katarina was described as 'proud and forward', not 'meek as one of her sex and kind should be' and the magistrates felt she deserved punishment for this as well. As we will see, the punishment they devised for her addressed her perceived character flaws as well as her crimes."

Sarah felt angry just thinking about the arrogance of those self-righteous officials condemning a woman for not being "meek." One doesn't survive in the world by meekness. Both women were on their own, trying to succeed in a male-dominated society. The unfairness of it was breathtaking.

The little book from the hearth. Had it referred to Noah or had it been Moses? She found it and went through the pages carefully. Both names were referenced throughout the book along with Adam, Solomon and many others. There were also a great many unfamiliar names identified as angels and demons.

The first completely legible paragraph stated "*Furthermore, I wish to make thee understand that God hath destined to each one of us a Spirit, which watches over us and takes care of our preservation; these are called Genii, who are elementary like us…*"

This must have been Elizabeth's book of magic, spell book or whatever things like this were called. No wonder she had kept it hidden. Had she shared this with the West Indian woman? Or was it more likely that Katarina had shared it with Elizabeth?

"*The hours of the Moon are proper for making trial of experiments relating to recovery of stolen property, for obtaining nocturnal visions, for summoning spirits in sleep, and for preparing anything relating to water.*"

The book gave very detailed, very precise instructions on what types of magic could be performed and when it would work best, complete with commands for bathing and what to wear. Even the type of weather that would aid with the efficacy of the operations was addressed.

Spirits could be summoned with certain words and rituals using the various names of God: EL, ELOHIM, EL SHADDAI. There were tips on how to deal with recalcitrant spirits who might not wish to come when summoned or with those who might be too busy to appear. Spirits could also be commanded to appear in a particular form.

"Come ye at once without any hideousness or deformity before us, come ye without monstrous appearance, in a gracious form or figure."

She closed the book and slipped it into her purse, planning to find time to talk to someone at the public library about separating the pages. She couldn't take this seriously. Yes, there was something in this house but...things like this were just not possible. Even so a small whisper in the back of her mind kept asking, "What have you seen with your own eyes?"

She shook her head and went to find her kitten.

Chapter Fourteen

"So the divorce was final just something like, six months ago. I know it's wrong to take sides in these things but when it's your brother... well, you know. Everyone in his department knew about the affair before David did. She hasn't married the guy yet. I feel sorry for him if she does."

"I can imagine how hard it must have been. It's good that he is still close enough to see his daughters. I've met them and they are pretty adorable."

"I agree. They're sweet girls and they've really been hurt and confused by all this. David moved out and just gave her the house because he didn't want the girls uprooted. They're adjusting but they don't like the boyfriend. David found that garage apartment and my mom and I did up a fantasy little-girls room to help with the transition. We wanted to be sure they would be eager to go over there when it was David's weekend to have them. We also got each of them a kitten. We may have gone a little overboard."

"That's understandable."

"I know it's not an uncommon situation but we haven't had a whole lot of divorces in our family. My gran frowns on it and we're all a little afraid of her. She is just heart-broken over David. It's almost like a death in the family."

Angela fell silent and Sarah thought about her own divorce. She had reluctantly agreed to file based on "irreconcilable differences." Her attorney had sent the final papers last week but she hadn't gone through them yet. Angela was right; it was like a death. At least there weren't any children involved in her case.

She and Angela had taken a working lunch today, eating at a rather famous seafood restaurant on Meeting Street. The walls were covered with photos of celebrities who had eaten there in the past. The char-grilled shrimp with rice and seared vegetables was wonderful. She finished her last shrimp before it got cold then said,

"Sales are picking up. Yesterday two sweet little old ladies, Mrs. Hawks and Mrs. Short, I think they're sisters, came in and bought a set of Hessian firedogs. They collect them and once they told me the history behind them, I could see why."

"What's the story? I knew they were old but I didn't know their history." Angela took a bite of her cheesecake.

"The German mercenaries the British sent over during the Revolutionary War were so hated that blacksmiths began to manufacture the firedogs in the shape of German soldiers and apparently they sold like hotcakes. I guess people wanted to kick them around or burn them in effigy?"

"There's always something in this business that I don't know. Have you been in touch with the banks this week? Are there any good houses up for salvage?"

"I have two to look at next week. One has portions that are over two hundred years old and I'm told it has a really special staircase."

"That's great. I would love to see it with you if I have the time. Have you seen much of Liddy Carmody lately?"

"Not since she picked up those last few pieces of flooring. She's probably knee-deep in her garden restoration."

"She really has a feel for these old houses and she's fanatical about authenticity. She tries to blame it on her clients but she's really the fussy one. If I could afford her, I would have hired her when I did my house."

"She may be coming over to my house to look at a garden figure I want to get rid of. If she buys it I'll pay you a commission since I met her in the store."

"No, you won't. It's your property, Sarah, and you'll be dealing with her on your own time, I assume."

"Absolutely. Ok then. Let's talk about hiring some part-time delivery guys and adding another delivery day to the schedule."

Sarah drove back to the warehouse, thinking about what Angela told her about David. Now that she had gotten past the somewhat prickly exterior, she liked him. She completely understood the humiliation that came from a spouse's public infidelity. Even now she wondered what was so wrong with her that Sean felt the need to turn to someone else for physical affection. Her confidence had been sorely shaken and she carried scars inside from it.

She glanced at her watch. She still had not visited the city archives to see the portrait Dr. Bickerstaff had written her about and she was curious. She would be driving right by the old Courthouse on her way home and if she left work a little early...

~

"Ms. Faust! I am delighted that you found time to come by. The portrait is scheduled to be cleaned next week and after that it will be in storage until we decide how we will display it. Come with me."

Dr. Bickerstaff led the way down the hallway, unlocked a door, then stepped back and ushered her inside.

An odor of age and turpentine greeted her. Wooden frames in various states of disrepair leaned against the walls. Shelves contained paraphernalia ranging from bronze and plaster busts to stuffed birds and deer heads. There was even a preserved alligator specimen. Dr. Bickerstaff began searching the shelves in the back of the room.

"It's supposed to be right here. Those interns- God bless them- don't completely understand how important it is to put everything in its proper place. Ah, here we are."

He extracted a small canvas in a simple wooden frame and placed it on a worktable.

"You can see it's somewhat darkened with age. I'm hoping the cleaners can brighten it up a little. So hard to know what type of cleaning solvent to use. Artists used a variety of pigments and although we think it's oils, we don't know for sure."

What Sarah saw was a dark-haired young woman staring serenely forward with a slight smile. Her hair was parted in the middle then pulled back in ringlets. The visible portion of her dress was made of rich fabric with puffed sleeves. She did resemble the image of the woman she had seen in her house and garden, though the eyes looked more brown than blue. The artist had painted her in profile with a background of trellised flowers and vines. The skin was olive but that might be due to the darkening of the pigments.

"Do you know who the artist was?"

"Most likely an itinerant painter. There were several who traveled around the colonies at that time, staying sometimes with well-to-do families that could afford their services. I cannot emphasize enough just how unusual it would have been for someone of this woman's social status to have had her portrait painted, if this is who I think it is. This view, profile, not full-face, was easier to produce and thus a more affordable pose. The frame" he pulled the left piece slightly "has broken away here and that's how we found this."

He indicated a small scrawl of letters on the lower left portion of the canvas. She read "bespoke for Capt. A. West."

"As you may have already discovered, one of the earliest inhabitants of your house married an English sea captain, Alexander West. I think either Captain West or his lady-love, Mistress Grayhame, commissioned the portrait. When we found this, we took another look at the original labeling and what we thought was M. Granholme may well be M. Grayhame. What you see here is the best clue we have."

"May I take photos? Just for my own use. I'm amassing quite a history on this house."

"Of course. It's delightful isn't it? Owning a bit of history."

"Most of the time, yes," she said, thinking of her occasional spectral visitors.

"Portraiture was the most important form of painting at the time. Imagine if you will, no way to have pictures of one's children and other loved ones. Of course having one's portrait painted was also a status symbol."

"I'm sure it was expensive."

"One had to have money to pay the artist, possibly room and board for him as well as leisure time enough to sit for the portrait. Most portraiture at this time would have been an idealized image representing the subject's status and wealth. This portrait is also unusual in that it shows the sitter smiling."

Sarah smiled. "Maybe she didn't have status or wealth but perhaps Captain West made her happy."

"Maybe. Whatever the case, there will be interest in this. An actual portrait of Charleston's witch." He touched the frame reverently, almost caressingly before putting it back on the shelf.

Sarah said nothing but cringed inwardly. The last thing she wanted was more interest in her house. Maybe he was wrong about the interest it would generate, but she doubted it. She took a few pictures then they left the room.

Extending her hand she said, "Dr. Bickerstaff, thanks so much for sharing this with me. I can't tell you how much you have helped me learn more about my house. I am in your debt and if there is anything I can do to repay you-"

His eyes sparkled flirtatiously (oh dear) as he took her hand and made a funny little bow. She noticed again how graceful he was for such a large man.

"It has been my pleasure. There was something about the picture that reminded me of you. The curve of the cheek and the graceful arch of the neck were especially notable."

She felt awkward and to cover her embarrassment she began fumbling through her purse for her car keys. She found them, immediately dropped them, and when she leaned over to pick them up, dumped the entire contents of her purse onto the floor. Wonderful.

"What is this?" Dr. Bickerstaff picked up the small book.

"Just an old book that I found. It's damaged and I need to talk to someone about repairing or at least preserving it."

"I have some experience with old documents. May I take a look?"

Of course he would have experience with this sort of thing. Why hadn't she thought of that before?

"That would be great, if it isn't too much trouble."

He didn't reply and she finished putting everything back in her purse. She inspected her camera. It didn't look damaged but she probably wouldn't know until she got home and tried to upload the pictures to her computer. She stood up.

Dr. Bickerstaff was paging carefully through the book. "Do you know what you have here?"

"Not really, no. I've read some of it and it looks like it has something to do with astrology and possibly witchcraft."

"This is a *grimoire* or spell book. A *Clavicula Salomonus*, to be precise."

"I don't know what that is."

"*The Key of Solomon*. It refers to King Solomon from the Bible, King David's and the infamous Bathsheba's son. Ancient occult lore purports that when Solomon asked God for wisdom that he was also given knowledge of and power over demons. Specifically he could command them to do his bidding."

"So this was written by Solomon? Really?"

"Most serious scholars will tell you no and I'm inclined to agree. However, throughout the ages many scholars felt differently and these books have been translated into almost every known language. A lot of charlatans found their own uses for the work. This book and similar works were very popular for hundreds of years. You definitely want to hang on to this and ask at the library about a way to preserve it."

Sarah thought of that statement from Katarina about the daughters of Cain.

"Dr. Bickerstaff, have you ever heard of supposed 'magic' that came from the 'daughters of Cain'?"

He looked back at the book. "If you remember your Sunday school stories, you know that Cain was the outcast son of Adam and Eve. The world's first murderer."

"Yes, as a child I used to wonder who he found to marry. I mean, there weren't supposed to be any other people in the world."

He laughed. "There are theories about that. Whoever he married, the Bible does make it clear that he had descendants. Are you familiar with the Genesis stories about the 'Sons of God' finding the 'daughters of men' fair and taking them as wives?"

He had warmed to his subject and did not wait for her to reply. "Some traditions hold that these 'daughters of men' were the descendants of Cain. Their husbands, whom many believe were Angels (sometimes called Watchers), taught them magic.

These women used the knowledge for evil purposes, adding to the corruption and decadence spreading throughout a culture that God was already preparing to annihilate. They passed the knowledge along to Noah's son Ham, who chiseled the spells onto metal and rock tablets that were unlikely to be destroyed by the Great Flood.

After the waters subsided, Ham, now an outcast cursed by his father after that unfortunate wine incident, searched the earth until he found all the engravings. He and his descendants settled in the land of Egypt and the rest of Africa, keeping the knowledge mostly within the priesthood that developed there although there is little doubt that it spread throughout all Africa to some degree."

Sarah wondered what time it was. The rest of the building was quiet and she assumed everyone else had gone home. Dr. Bickerstaff continued to expound on a topic clearly dear to his heart. She did not want to interrupt but it was getting late.

"...superpower of the ancient world. Their agricultural methods were highly advanced as were their innovative war-chariots and weaponry. Did you know ancient Egypt had no police force whatsoever? The priesthood controlled almost everything-" he paused for breath and she took her shot.

"Dr. Bickerstaff, this is fascinating but I don't want to take up any more of your time today. I did find another book in addition to this one. Would you be interested in taking a look at it?"

He gave back the *grimoire* and they agreed she would bring the *Herball* by next week. Outside, the time on the parking meter had expired but she hadn't been ticketed yet. She pulled out into traffic just as a police car pulled to the curb behind her. That was close.

The days were growing longer as well as warming up and tourists mobbed the sidewalks. Local artists exhibited their paintings in front of Marion Square and farther down near the Powder Magazine, two women sat behind a table displaying sweet-grass baskets for sale. She wondered if they were Gullah descendants and thought of Katarina's statement. Now she understood what she meant by knowledge "older than your Christianity and of the same seed." The thought of magic spells handed down by angels and brought to this country was mind-boggling.

She pulled into her driveway; the car chugged a few times before it shut down. The grass grew lush and green and the wisteria twining the columns was in full, amethyst bloom. The heady scent enveloped her even before she passed the ancient gateposts. Ladders lay against the side of the house and paint cans; rollers and extension poles were stacked on the porch. After she got the first whopping-huge estimate from a company to paint the outside of the house, it was obvious she would have to do it herself. Most of the equipment was borrowed from Dewayne or Mary-Michael and Noble. She was off tomorrow; the weather forecast looked good and she could not wait to get started.

Childish voices sounded behind the hedge. David must have his daughters this week. She felt a sudden yearning to see them but did not want to barge in. Maybe she would just walk over and say hello. Her shoes made no sound on the soft, springy grass. She leaned down to pick a few mint leaves, enjoying the fresh scent and taste. A dark form sprang out from behind the stone plinth, grabbing onto the trailing sleeve of her sweater. Needle-like claws grazed her arm.

Mr. Tumnus, one pound and six ounces of blood-thirsty ferocity, hung on to her sleeve as she took him in her arms. The girls would probably be delighted to see him.

"A kitty! Let me hold him. Please!" Kate held out her arms pleadingly as soon as Sarah emerged from the hedge.

"You have to be careful with him. His name is Mr. Tumnus. He's still a baby and he doesn't understand yet about not scratching people, ok? Let's sit down and I'll hand him to you."

The three of them sat down on the grass. Sarah scratched him behind the ears until he began purring and then carefully handed him over to the girls who held him as if he were made of fragile crystal. He was perfectly content to have his belly scratched by his new admirers. Both girls wore ballet slippers and leotards and their nails were painted with green, glitter nail polish. Their slender necks emerged like flower-stems from the leotards, their long hair confined in classic buns at the napes of their necks.

"Did you just finish ballet class?" she asked.

"No, we were supposed to go but our Mom has to go out tonight and she couldn't take us because she had to get her nails done."

Sarah wondered if this was a repeat of the other night and looked to see if there was a vehicle parked in the driveway when a voice cut into the evening stillness.

"Who the hell are you and what are you doing with my daughters?"

Chapter Fifteen

The woman standing at the edge of the garden began walking toward them and spoke again.

"Put that vermin down. It could have fleas or worms or something worse."

She came forward with a swaying, oddly predatory walk. She wore a clinging sweater with black capris. Blunt-cut blonde hair fell around her shoulders and framed a lovely face with full lips and high cheekbones. The expression on her face was far from friendly.

"I don't appreciate strange adults exposing my children to animals that might carry disease." This was directed at Sarah who got to her feet and stood, speechless at the venom in the woman's voice.

"Mom, she's not a stranger. She knows Aunt Angela." This from Lil who spoke in a pleading tone.

Sarah found her voice. "Hi, I'm Sarah Faust and I live in the house behind David. You must be Kate and Lil's mother. It's nice to meet you."

The woman stared at her then reluctantly said, "I'm Diana. You must be from out of town. There aren't a lot of locals willing to rent that house."

Her rudeness was breathtaking. "I bought it, actually. And no, I'm not from Charleston but I'm enjoying getting to know the town. Are you a native?"

"I'm from Inman, a little farther north." She practically spat the words out. "Kate, put that animal down now."

"He's asleep, Mom. See." Kate moved closer to her mother who grabbed the kitten out of her daughter's arms and tried to place it on the ground. Mr. Tumnus, rudely awakened, tried to hang on and dug his claws into Diana's wrist, drawing blood.

"Oh, I'm so sorry! He was just startled. Bad, bad kitty!" Sarah snatched him and held him close, away from the angry woman who looked as if she wanted to wring his neck.

Diana held her wrist. Lil and Kate took their mother's arm and pulled her toward the garage. "We have to clean it, Mom.

Dad has band-aids, the clear kind that don't show. Bye, Miss Sarah. Bye, Mr. Tumnus!"

The little group went up the steps that presumably led to David's apartment. Sarah went back through the hollies and the kissing-gate, keeping a tight grip on the kitten. Once inside her house, she put him down and warmed a saucer of milk in the microwave, set it on the floor and whispered "Good kitty," thinking of the look on Diana's face when she saw the blood on her arm. What a thoroughly unpleasant woman. Beautiful though, without a doubt. Maybe that was enough for men. She felt sorry for David and the girls.

For supper she tried a recipe that one of her customers had recommended. She simmered chicken with red sauce and rice until the chicken was tender enough to fall apart. It was spicy and delicious. She shared some with Mr. Tumnus.

Walking through the ground floor rooms then up the steps, she couldn't help noticing that the banister and steps she had "magically dusted" gleamed. Her bedroom floor shone too; the cherry planks had a polished depth they definitely did not have before.

~

The ladder shook more than she liked when she climbed it the next morning. She was sure she had tilted the ladder feet correctly and it should be secure but twenty feet up it did not feel it and the ground seemed very far away. Balancing the bucket on the very top, she climbed up to the step with the "Danger. Do not stand or sit above this step" warning sticker. To reach the top of the wall she would have to climb down and tilt the ladder at an even steeper angle if she obeyed the warning. She decided to take her chances on the forbidden step.

She worked slowly, taking care to avoid getting paint on the cast-iron gutters. The old stucco absorbed the paint like a sponge. Even so, by two o'clock she had all the brush and small roller work done. The big roller with the thick nap should go faster. Climbing down she critiqued her work from ground level. The light color made the dark guttering more noticeable and she liked the contrast.

The day had warmed considerably. She peeled off her sweatshirt and threw it on the lawn where Mr. Tumnus attacked it mercilessly. Leaving him to it, she poured a glass of iced tea and sat on the step, calculating how long it would take to finish. She had allotted two days but this was going faster than expected.

Lent was here and with it the usual obligation to make some sort of sacrifice in honor of the season. She had no idea what to forego. Coffee maybe? She did not have a whole lot of vices that she was aware of. She couldn't afford any. For her, apparently, virtue was one of the side effects of near-poverty. Stop it; she told herself, you are getting maudlin. Finish the painting.

She rescued her sweatshirt from the cat and was ready to pour paint into the tray when she heard the metal clang of the gate. She looked up to see Kate and Lil walking through the grass, Lil proudly cradling her ginger cat. Mr. Tumnus disappeared under the porch.

"You found her! Lil, that's wonderful. Where was she?"

But Lil turned suddenly bashful and sat down on the lawn, still keeping a tight grip on the cat. Kate sighed with exaggerated patience.

"She was here when Mom dropped us off. We don't know where she was before that but she was really hungry. We fed her already."

Unsure if the girls were alone or if David knew they were here she asked, "Was your Dad surprised?"

"He isn't here. Mom said we just had to wait a little while. So we came to tell you about Sprinkles."

"The cat's name is Sprinkles? What a pretty name."

Lil spoke up. "It's because she has those little white dots on her back. Can you see?"

Sarah exclaimed appreciatively over the markings that had given Sprinkles her name. The cat looked thin to her and she wondered where she had been. She glanced over at her painting equipment ruefully. She had a feeling she was not going to finish the house today. Oh well.

"Have you had lunch yet? I haven't and I'm hungry. Do you like peanut butter?"

"Do you have Trix cereal?" Lil asked.

"No, do you like Trix?"

"Yes. You should buy some and keep it in your house."

"I will get some the next time I go to the store. Right now let's do lunch."

The girls called and left a message on David's phone, telling him where they were. Soon the three of them sat at the kitchen table, eating sandwiches and discussing the merits of ballet versus gymnastics, (gymnastics were more fun but the costumes for ballet were prettier) and why boys were so gross (they probably didn't know any better). Everyone agreed that dads were not included in the ranks of gross boys.

While they were inside the day clouded over and grew chilly. Kate ran over and checked to see if David were home.

"No, not yet," she reported. "I found Mr. Tumnus on the porch. Is he allowed inside?"

Mr. Tumnus was duly brought in and fed. Sarah mentally searched her almost non-existent repertoire of children's activities to come up with a way to keep them busy. She remembered something she and her mother used to do.

"Let's make play dough."

"You can't make play dough, it comes from the store."

"I know a way. Let me check and see if we have the ingredients."

She rummaged through her cabinets and found everything she needed except for Kool-Aid. They could make do without it but-

"Kate, do you have any Kool-Aid at your dad's house?"

They all walked over together and Sarah waited while the girls went inside the garage apartment. She didn't feel she should go into David's home without an invitation from him. They soon emerged, triumphantly waving a blue packet.

Sarah got out a couple of the ruffled, linen aprons and wrapped them around the girls, doubling the strings and tying them in the back with big bows. They insisted she put one on

too and in a few minutes they were all mixing the flour, cream of tartar, Kool-Aid and water together in a pot on the cooktop. The gooey mixture soon took on the consistency of firm dough. Sarah dumped it on the table where the girls kneaded it into warm lumps. The resulting dough was blue and smelled deliciously of grapes. They continued to knead, enjoying the warmth on their hands. Kate and Lil were a picture, with the flounced aprons on. They looked like two little Victorian misses in old-fashioned pinafores. She grabbed the camera from her purse and snapped a couple of photos, planning to give them to Angela.

"I want to eat mine," said Lil, sniffing her portion.

"Don't eat it. Trust me on this," warned Sarah. "I know from experience it doesn't taste good."

"I'll tell Arabella but she wouldn't eat it anyway," Lil said.

"Who is Arabella?" asked Sarah.

"She's a girl Lil pretends she plays with. She's not real," Kate said, rolling her eyes.

"She is real! You're mad because she only likes me," Lil countered.

"Fine. I don't care." Kate began forming a bowl with her dough.

"Arabella is a smart girl for being careful about what she eats." Sarah tried to defuse the argument.

"She isn't careful; she can't eat because somebody sewed her lips together." Lil pressed her lips with her thumb and forefinger to demonstrate.

Kate's response was a snort of disgust. Shocked, Sarah couldn't think of a response at all. Her phone rang.

"This is David Staunton. I just got a message from this number from my daughter."

"Hi David, it's Sarah. The girls are here with me. I hope you don't mind but they came over and-"

"The message I got was garbled. They came over by themselves?"

"Yes."

"Ok. I'm on my way right now. Give me ten minutes." He sounded angry.

"There's no rush, David. We're-" but he had already hung up.

Two pairs of eyes looked at her expectantly. "Your dad is on his way to get you so let's clean up." She got plastic baggies out. "You have to put this kind of play dough in a plastic bag and keep it in the fridge when you're not playing with it. Here, Kate, you can wipe down the table and Lil, you can put the saucepan and spoons in the dishwasher."

David arrived at the back door in less than ten minutes. She could tell he was angry and embarrassed. Lil and Kate ran to him, each latching onto a leg.

"Hey! Let's give those dresses back to Ms. Faust and then I want you to go to the apartment, ok?

"They're not dresses, Dad, they're aprons." Kate sounded very superior.

"Whatever they are, they're not yours so do as I say."

They held up their arms expectantly. David and Sarah unwound the aprons and the girls were gone, bags of play dough in hand, calling for Sprinkles as they ran.

David folded the aprons and placed them on the table while she struggled to untie the knotty tangle her own apron had gotten into.

"Need help?" He asked.

She laughed and held up her arms. He unwound the strings from her waist as she turned slowly in front of him. For just a second other thoughts came into his head and he looked away in embarrassment. She stumbled over his foot and he caught her around the waist. Smiling, she looked up but the smile faded when she saw the raw, but restrained, desire in his eyes. Disconcerted, she gathered the aprons and started stuffing them back into the drawer. He spoke.

"I can't tell you how sorry I am. After I talked to you I called Angela. She said you took the day off to paint. I didn't see the voicemail until just a few minutes ago. I left a message for their mom but I don't really expect a response."

"David, honestly I enjoyed them. I don't often get a chance to be around children and this is kind of a treat for me. So don't apologize and if it will make you feel better, you can pay me back."

"How?"

"I can't think of anything right now but I will. So you've been warned. I will hit you up when you least expect it."

He smiled briefly then ran his hand through his hair. "Every morning when I wake up, I wonder, 'What will my ex-wife do today? How will she try to get back at me using the girls?' Because she always does something. Always. And she knows the quickest way to get to me is through them. I'd walk through fire for them. I used to feel that way about her, too. Before everything went all to hell."

He left. Sarah was shaken by the pain in his voice. For the first time she saw a downside to having children. It must be like having your heart walking around outside your body, vulnerable to a world you could not always protect it from.

Opening her laptop she plugged the camera in and downloaded all the pictures. Today was the first time she used it since she dropped it and she had been relieved that it worked. The first picture was of the ashy footprints from the fireplace. The image was very clear and chilling.

The pictures of the portrait from the courthouse were not as good. A shadow marred each of them, obscuring the features. The lighting in the room had not been the best. Maybe when (and if) the portrait was placed on exhibit she would get another chance.

Next came today's pictures of Lil and Kate. Their little faces looked so serious as they kneaded the dough on the pull-out table. The next image was from a slightly different angle and darker. Sarah used the tools to brighten the picture and that's when she saw it.

A pallid face stared in longingly through the glass of the kitchen door. It looked to be a child of four or five. She would have thought it a distorted reflection of one of the girl's faces or her own if not for the black thread stitches that did indeed, hold the little mouth shut. She looked back at the first photo, but the face was not in that one.

She created a file, named it "5 Rue" and dragged the pix in there. She probably wouldn't be sharing these photos with anyone.

~

Following the directions led her down Maybank Highway. She had driven a long way already and passed a tea plantation and a sign for America's oldest live oak, Angel Oak. Finally she saw the street sign for Schoolhouse Road and turned right.

She drove by an old trailer with pink, plastic flamingos in the yard and a satellite dish on the roof. The blacktop road soon yielded to a narrow, single lane of sand with a green strip down the middle. Ruts where the road had washed threatened to stop the car altogether before it evened out again. Scrub pine and palmetto dominated the landscape here. Lush weeds grew tall on either side of the road forming a living, green tunnel. She came to a fork in the road.

A white-painted, peeling signpost pointed left to Maiden Lane. She turned, still practically creeping along on the narrow lane, when she reached a clearing and a church suddenly came into view. A charming, three-storied, white clapboard building with a bell tower, a sign proclaimed it the Rockville Presbyterian Church, established in1798.

Arranged at a distance around the church, each occupying a corner and thus creating a square were four houses. All had large grounds holding ancient oaks with heavy branches sprawling across the grass. Sand and shell driveways curved to the portico of each. The particular house she had come to see backed up to the river. A wooden dock was just visible in the distance between a pair of willows.

Still driving slowly, she crunched along the driveway. Broken porch rails and loose-hanging gutters were now visible as were a rusted swing set and storage shed in the side yard. Her contact at the bank said the house had been empty for weeks. A garden wall, crazily askew and tumbled down in sections, still encircled a sadly overgrown formal garden overlooking the river.

Her contact had also told her the house had foundation problems that the owners had unsuccessfully tried to fix before giving up and walking away.

He explained, "Once the river decides to take a house there isn't much that can be done outside of a huge engineering project. Few people have the money for that. And even then, Mother Nature will win out eventually."

Almost everything about the house had seen better days. The present decrepitude, however, could not hide the fine bones of the property. Even from outside she could tell the ceilings were at least ten feet high on the main floor. Wide, tall sash windows with the classic (and expensive) nine over nine glass panes adorned the front of the house. Enormous white columns stood like mute sentinels, giving it the appearance of a Greek temple. The roof rose to a flat crown encircled with a balustrade rail.

She felt like an archaeologist exploring architectural ruins. The large, square house dwarfed everything around it, with the exception of the oaks. She climbed the wide stone stairs leading to the front door, and then knocked. The sound barely disturbed the vast stillness and no one responded.

Using the bank's key, she let herself in. The heart-of-pine, twelve-inch wide boards, felt solid beneath her steps. She had never thought of pine as a particularly durable wood but she had learned these re-claimed floors were much in demand. She had sold bundles of boards stripped from old warehouses and distilleries for premium prices. She was walking across a hefty chunk of change but felt sad that this lovely house was to be dismantled.

Matching crystal chandeliers hung in the twin parlors, dusty and web-covered. All of the furniture was gone. She took a quick look at the kitchen. It was fairly large but none of the fixtures were noteworthy except for an old soapstone sink. That would definitely sell.

Dewayne was supposed to meet her here with a truck and tools. She listened but didn't hear any vehicles outside.

She continued exploring. The central staircase was spectacular. An odd combination of fruit and plump swine carvings gamboled all the way up the mahogany banister. A classic pineapple topped the newel post. All the carvings were blunted and shiny, no doubt from years of countless hands gliding up and down.

The first room off the upstairs landing was large and looked out over the section of the lawn and garden that sloped gently down to the river. She opened a door next to a window, expecting a closet but was surprised to find a suffocatingly small, dark staircase leading down. Stepping onto the narrow first step, she peered down but saw nothing but more darkness. Without warning, the door swung shut behind her.

Chapter Sixteen

The door "knob" was one of those old-fashioned latches that latched back automatically when the door closed. She pushed and jiggled it but it held tight. A crack of daylight was visible almost all the way around the ill-fitting door so she was not in complete darkness. Still, she felt panicky in the tiny, enclosed space.

Calm down, she told herself. There has to be another end to the staircase. If I can't get out through there, I can kick this door down. It has to be really old.

She descended cautiously down the narrow steps. The passage was so tight that her shoulders brushed the side walls. She stumbled. The lower steps were strewn with- something. She kicked out and heard something thud down a few steps then stop. Going even more slowly now she edged past the objects on the steps until she was sure she was at the bottom. She felt all around the walls but could not find a door.

The darkness was total down here and it was easy to imagine spiders, rats, or something worse lurking. Turning around, she tripped and fell against the wall, hitting her shoulder hard. Annoyed now, she felt her way to the top and kicked out at the door. It rattled but held firm.

Finally, after repeated fumblings she pressed whatever caused the latch to open again and got out. She sat in the middle of the room, happy to have open space around her. She didn't feel like exploring anymore and went out to her car, found her phone and checked for messages. Dewayne wasn't going to make it but apparently David would be here soon. She heard a motor just as she finished reading the text.

David backed the utility van up to the front steps and got out, carrying a clutch of tools. She pocketed her phone and met him at the steps.

"They weren't kidding about the stairs. The banister is unique. Come and take a look." Sarah took the offered crowbar and led the way inside.

They had the chandeliers and banister down quickly. David disconnected the lines to the sink and they carried it out very carefully.

"What's upstairs? Anything decent?" David asked.

"I didn't see that much before you got here."

"Let's have a look then." He led the way up, taking care on the now completely open staircase.

She showed him the first room. He found the staircase but he barely fit inside the door so didn't go down.

"What would this be for? I went to the bottom earlier and didn't find an exit," she said.

"The ground-level exit has probably been boarded up or sealed. A back-stair like this might have been used by some owner who wanted privacy to come and go or it could be a servant's entrance." He shined a flashlight into the dark. "Someone has thrown their junk down here. Look, there's a thermos and an old broom." The light played over more rubbish, old fishing-tackle and shoes. David closed the door and they continued their explorations.

All of the bedrooms had their own fireplaces and entrances to the upper-level verandah running all along the side and back of the house.

"Do you know anything about the people who lived here? I mean, this place is amazing. They must have been important or at least wealthy." Despite her unpleasant experience earlier, Sarah found the house enchanting, especially the grounds. From their vantage point on the verandah they saw the remains of the formal knot-garden. A central statue of a horse was stained and moss-covered but the effect was more of romantic ruins than squalor.

"I do remember a story about a family out this way. It's not a pleasant one though."

"Long ago unpleasant or recent?"

"Way back in the bad old days. At least they were bad for a segment of the population; the enslaved segment. These were plantation homes; the marshy areas around all this used to be rice fields."

"The road out here was terrible. They must have kept it up better back then."

"The roads leading out here were never good but the owners usually traveled by river. Rice shipments went out that way too. Water transport was cheaper, easier, more convenient all-around."

"Let's start taking these mantels apart and after that you can tell me the unpleasant story from the bad old days."

They worked separately for a while, taking care to keep the old wood from splitting. The plaster around them crumbled but the whole house was being demolished anyway. Sarah finished hers first and called back to David that she was going to try her hand at the floorboards in the kitchen.

David smiled and shook his head. He doubted she would be able to pry up the huge old boards but had no doubt she would give it her best shot. He had already arranged for Dewayne to come out and help him with those tomorrow.

He was thinking of her more and more, unwillingly though. The other day, seeing her in the kitchen with Lil and Kate, in those oversized aprons with flour on their faces, he felt like he was looking at three children playing dress-up instead of two. Very different from that cool exterior she still exhibited most of the time.

Today she was all business, in jeans and work boots, ponytail coming out the back of a baseball cap. Angela was always commenting on what a great hire she had turned out to be. She was a hit with both the regular customers and the tourists. Sales were up. She had established herself easily with the foreclosure departments at the banks and got regular notices when an interesting property was in the pipeline. And he was glad his workaholic, pregnant sister was finally getting a little down-time.

Finishing the last mantel, he loaded everything in the van. The doors in this house were solid cypress and huge and he was not about to tackle them today. He looked for Sarah in the kitchen but didn't find her and walked into the yard.

Beyond the knot garden was a folly; an imitation of classic Greek ruins. Very fashionable in the eighteenth and early nineteenth centuries this version of a tumble-down "temple" sprawled atop a built-up mound. To access it one had to cross a hump-back bridge arching across a once-small lagoon with picturesque water lilies and reeds. Now as the river encroached it was more a river inlet with the water higher, just inches below the bridge.

Sarah stood in the middle of the bridge looking down but she must have sensed him because she looked up. Her face is like a valentine, he thought, fragile and heart-shaped. He then noticed that her eyes were large and alarmed as she put her hand up, palm facing him, as if to ward him off.

"Don't come over here. There's an alligator in the water, right under me. I don't know what to do." She spoke quietly but a little shakily.

"Just do whatever you were doing before. Alligators won't bother you."

"You don't know that."

"I'm walking over now and you'll see- he's not interested in us. There were some problems a few years ago out on Kiawah; stupid vacationers were feeding them scraps off their decks. Once 'gators get used to coming in for food, they expect it, and humans taste just fine to them. Someone did get hurt and signs went up and warnings went out and hopefully it did some good. I can just about guarantee you that no one around here has been feeding this guy. The natives know better."

He advanced as he spoke and soon stood on the bridge with her. There was indeed a good-sized alligator partly out of the water, sunning on the mud of the bank, eyes closed. Of course that didn't mean he didn't know they were here. He probably did.

"This is incredible. Are you telling me that they don't attack? This is a dangerous, prehistoric monster."

"I didn't say they never attack, just rarely. If you go out on any of the island golf courses you'll see them in lagoons under those little decorative bridges. We would rather have them around than deer. *They* cause a lot of car accidents."

Sarah looked at him and shook her head then walked quickly back to the knot garden, glancing over her shoulder at the water as she went. She saw that David was laughing at her and, annoyed, said sharply, "Are you ever going to tell me your story from the bad old days? Customers often like to know the history of a piece if possible."

His face changed and he followed her. "This is not something you want to tell customers. I'm not even sure it involves this specific house but it was in this community. It's more of a tragedy than anything although it did inspire a story of a local haunting."

"A ghost story?"

"More than that. Back around 1820 or so this whole area was heavily cultivated by rice plantation owners. They had large houses, large families, and large numbers of slaves with their own growing families. The enslaved parents were forced to work from sunrise to sunset and could not care for their own children so slaves too old or too young or feeble to work in the fields became caregivers. In this story, one slave mother had a month-old infant that, for nursing, was carried back and forth by a six-year-old girl from the quarters.

One evening the six-year-old grew tired of carrying the child and, on her way back to the quarters, took the baby out into the swamp and tossed it into the muck, headfirst. The young slave mother, returning after dark, inquired after her child. The little nurse said she had brought it back and didn't know where it was but eventually confessed. A search was made and the tiny body was found where the child said it would be."

He was right, she thought. This is not a story to tell tourists looking for a memento of the romantic Old South. It was an illustration of the horror of it instead. He continued.

"The little girl was locked in a barn for three weeks. No one seemed to know what to do with a six-year-old murderer. Finally, a speculator came along and bought the child for a hundred dollars."

"Unpleasant story is an understatement. More like epically tragic. How is this a ghost story though?"

"I'm not finished. The infant's mother committed suicide. Not long after, locals began seeing lights in the swamp. Lights swaying from side to side, like a lantern held in the hand of someone searching for something. Others reported hearing a baby crying along with a woman softly singing lullabies."

They stood in silence for a while, looking out at the river. Bull-frogs began their peculiar, guttural chorus and birds called; not pretty twittering but harsh, piercing cries. Sarah felt they stood next to a primordial jungle, where monsters lay in wait for the unwary. She turned away and walked back toward the house, just wanting to finish up and go back to the city.

"I couldn't get those boards but what about this statue? It's already leaning to one side so maybe it won't be too hard to get it out of the ground." She patted the flank of the stone horse in the center of the knot garden. Liddy Carmody might be interested in this for her garden project. She traced the carvings of the saddle and bridle, worn down from years of exposure. Broken stone stubs down by the belly must have once been stirrups. The neck arched gracefully and the lifted front leg was delicately rendered.

Something was carved on a plaque at the front of the plinth. She knelt down to read.

"By a knight of ghostes and shadowes
I summoned am to tourney.
Ten leagues beyond the wild world's end
Methinks it is no journey."

The Tom O'Bedlam quote was cut deeply into the stone but even so, showed signs of wear. She supposed this must have seemed like the end of the "wild world" to settlers at one time. A shadow fell across the stone in front of her and she looked up. David walked around the horse, assessing it.

"I'll need at least three guys and a hand-truck to load this."

"I wish I knew who the artist was. I'll just say it comes from one of the island plantations. That's true, anyway." She gestured toward the budding bulbs and other early bloomers. "It's a shame no one is going to enjoy all these flowers."

"Take some back with you if you want but they won't go completely to waste here. I'm sure the neighbors will use them to decorate the church for Easter. These little yellow daffodils mark the sight of a lot of former homes. They don't require any upkeep."

"You're right. I didn't think about the neighbors. I wonder if they all go to this church."

"It's certainly conveniently located. It was built by the plantation owners for the local community, black and white, although itinerant preachers often held separate services for the slaves. The slave population at that time was becoming more and more native-born with fewer coming in directly from Africa."

"Was Christianity forced on them?"

"Yes and no. It depended a lot on the plantation owners. Reading some of the journals and other historical accounts of the time you get the impression that some slaves didn't mind adding Jehovah and the Christ to their already lively pantheon of deities but were only nominally 'Christian.' Not in every case, of course. There were many slaves well-versed in scripture and doctrine."

Sarah thought again of the woman Katarina, accused of witchcraft along with Elizabeth Grayhame. Some of them were well-versed in even older doctrine of which their "masters" knew nothing.

"I'm going back to the warehouse. Do you want to meet me there so we can unload?"

Chapter Seventeen

A storm blew in as they drove back into town and she fought to steer through the torrents of rain lashing the car. By the time they got everything out of the van and stored in the warehouse, they were soaked and chilled.

Sarah could not stop shivering. She said goodnight to David, got back in her car and turned the heat up high. The windows fogged over on her short drive home and she had to keep wiping the windshield down. When she finally pulled into her driveway she still shook with cold. The mailman had left the lid up on her letter-box and she pulled out a soggy mess of envelopes. Lovely.

Mr. Tumnus was on the back porch, mewing loudly and hungrily. She cuddled the warm little body close while she brought him in and put out more cat food. He didn't like her drenched clothing or hair and fought to get down.

"Fine, you ungrateful animal. See if I do you any favors from now on."

Upstairs, she ran a hot bath, added bath salts, sank into the scented water and closed her eyes. She heard the cat, who had recently mastered the stairs, come in. He settled in on the fluffy white rug beside the tub and began to knead the tufts with his claws while he purred contentedly. The basket she bought for him and placed in the kitchen was mostly unused. He nestled most nights at the foot of her bed.

Today had been a good day. She enjoyed exploring the area around town but didn't get to do it often. That the people here thought living among alligators was no big deal surprised her. It felt exotic and dangerous to her and that, combined with the story David told, made her feel once again like a stranger. There were dark layers of history and experience here that were completely foreign to her. She wondered again why her mother had never spoken in detail of her family's past. Some of it was unsavory but it was still their heritage.

A few people, strangers all and most not even from Charleston, sent letters after the article about the remains found in the house appeared in the paper. Two offered to "exorcise the spirits" from the house, "satisfaction guaranteed." Another was a request to film inside the house for some sort of documentary about ghosts and haunted houses. She didn't respond to any of them. It was bad enough being on the local ghost tour circuit. Further media exposure would be a nightmare. She reached for a towel and got out of the bath, sending Mr. Tumnus fleeing.

Tomorrow she was supposed to take the *Herball* to Dr. Bickerstaff for a look. It took a while to find it. Lately, things in the house were not where she remembered leaving them. The book was on the floor near the fireplace.

Good grief, she thought, picking it up. This thing is heavy and the spine is splitting. I have to ask Dr. Bickerstaff where to get it preserved. Sitting on the sofa and balancing it on her lap she turned to a page at random.

"If a phrenticke or melancholic man's head bee anointed with oil wherein the roots and leaves (of cow parsnip) have been sodden, it helpeth him very much, and such as bee troubled with the sickness called the forgetfull evil." [sic]

Carefully leafing through the pages, she studied the precisely detailed drawings. The whole book expressed a reverence for nature and a delight in plants. She thought of the ancient pagan belief that all nature was animate and that trees and plants had power that must be respected if not worshipped. In a way, modern pharmaceuticals proved the pagans right. So many healing drugs came from trees and plants. The ability to heal is power. She closed the book and placed it on the kitchen table so she would be sure to remember to take it in the morning.

She checked her phone for messages and was surprised to find five texts, all from former co-workers and friends. While she hadn't made a complete break with her past life, distance had taken a toll on those relationships. She expected it; everyone was going in different directions with their lives and her life was here now.

The first text was from Phil, her former boss, and read, "So sorry to hear. Tough break. Are you ok?"

What tough break? All the messages were similar. Just then the phone rang in her hand. Startled, she dropped it and it stopped ringing. The screen showed a missed call from her attorney. She called back.

"Sarah? Just wanted to let you know you have my condolences." Tony, for once, sounded serious.

"I'm lost here, Tony. Condolences for what?"

"For- you don't know yet, do you? Sarah, Sean is dead."

For just a second she had the oddest feeling that she wasn't really here, that she saw the room and the ashes in the fireplace through glass. There were no sounds; no rain, she wasn't even breathing. Then everything came rushing back and she struggled to hear what he said over her own heartbeats.

"...in the cafeteria. There was a fight and several were injured but Sean was the only one killed. I know you need to think about this but I see a strong case for negligence and wrongful death. He should never have been placed in that segment of the prison population-"

Tony paused for breath and she thanked him for letting her know and hung up.

She didn't cry. She couldn't. A heaviness in her chest made her feel as if she were about to choke.

Rain continued to pound the house. A strong wind whipped the shrubs back and forth; she could just make them out through the water streaming down the windows. She poured a glass of red wine, drank it quickly and then poured another. The feeling in her chest and throat eased a little and she gradually became aware of Mr. Tumnus, winding himself in and out around her ankles. She snatched him up, holding him close for a minute, until he struggled to get down and ran into the kitchen. She followed.

He was by the back door, trying to catch the rain trickling down the outside of the door glass. Closing the window shades she put her glass in the dishwasher, reached to turn off the light and noticed the *grimoire* on the counter. She was sure she hadn't put it there.

Walking back into the hallway, looking through the little book, she felt pulled into the parlor, almost as if someone other than herself directed her steps. The book made her hand itch and she put it down, noticing a red mark on her palm that burned when she touched it. The book had fallen open to a page with lines heavily underscored and with handwritten notes in the margins.

"To obtain a certaine winde for anye fixed period of time for use by those becalmed on the seas, take ye silk, linen, or hempen cord, knotting it at intervals with three knots but onlye during a time of storm and rain. Conjure this in the name of the Ten Seraphim and by command of the demons, by all the poweres of the winds, whirlwinds, and tempests." Step-by-step directions followed.

Seized by an impulse she thought, why not? I can give this a whirl, so to speak. She found one of the monogrammed linen napkins in the kitchen and read aloud from the text.

"I conjure ye anew, and I powerfully urge ye, O demons of wind, in whatsoever part of the world ye be, that ye come promptly to accomplish our desire, enter this rag, and resist me not." She tied a knot in the napkin.

"I conjure ye Seraphim by the Two Tables of the Law, deny me not." She tied a second knot in the napkin.

"I conjure ye by the five books of Moses, submit to me." And tied the third knot. She felt a tingling in her belly, so strong she gasped.

The wind outside died down, the only sound that of water gurgling down the gutters. Her hands felt warm and they shook slightly. She put the book away, dangled the napkin in front of Mr. Tumnus (who wouldn't come near it) and got ready for bed. It was only after she had lain awake for an hour that she got up, sat in the window seat and cried; tears of bitterness and regret. She pressed her hot, swollen face against the cold, glass windowpanes and watched rivulets of rain trickle down.

Later, just before she fell asleep, she heard a soft scratching at the window but ignored it, burrowing into her pillow until sleep came at last.

~

They were downstairs. She is not sure how she knew because they made no sound but she awoke in her warm, poster-bed with an absolute certainty that someone was in the house. Her bare feet were silent on the cold stairs as she crept halfway down and sat, looking through the balusters at the impossible scene in her parlor.

She recognized Elizabeth although she appeared older. She wore a simple, blue dress with a white apron and looked tired but happy as she balanced a baby on one hip. Children surrounded her, alternately clinging to her skirt then chasing one another around the room.

The eldest child, a little girl, stood by a gate-legged table with a knife and a pair of tongs, carefully cutting a large, white cone of sugar into small, square lumps. Elizabeth watched her work, nodded approvingly then said something to which the child responded with a shake of her head.

Elizabeth moved around the room, smoothing hair, straightening ribbons, like a bird caring for its nest. In that immemorial gesture of mothers everywhere she put a hand to the forehead of a sturdy-looking little boy and frowned. She took him by the hand and led him from the room into the hallway where they both vanished. The scene in the little parlor melted away like watercolors in rain. They were gone.

Sarah, freezing, went back upstairs to bed.

~

The next morning dawned sunny and colder. She overslept and skipped breakfast, hastily packing a sandwich and yogurt for lunch. She also had to search for the book she knew she had placed in the kitchen. Both books were neatly stacked by the fireplace as if someone were showing her where they belonged.

A faint message in the fireplace read, *"I am as ye called."* She shuddered. What had she done? She photographed the words before rubbing them out and tracing, *"Go away."*

Mr. Tumnus mewed at her from the doorway. It occurred to her that she had never seen him enter this room but she had no time to ponder that as she put him outside and ran for the car.

Despite a steady stream of customers and new items to catalogue, the day dragged. David and Dewayne arrived around four with the pine floorboards from the house on Wadmalaw, more doors, (really, we need more doors?) as well as the horse statue. She decided to leave it as is, mossy and stained. It looked more interesting this way. If it didn't sell quickly she would reconsider and clean it up.

She left at four-thirty, after asking Dewayne to lock up, and drove immediately over to the old courthouse. The air, fragrant from the heliotrope growing in stone urns by the curb, had warmed. Inside, she worked her way up the stairs against the flow of people leaving for the day.

"Wrong way, lovely. Time to go home." A man, blond, with an almost military haircut, stopped a moment on the step and smiled at her.

"Not for me, not yet," she replied, continuing to press upward. The crowd thinned out considerably at the first landing. She stopped to take a breath and looked down just in time to see Dr. Bickerstaff, talking animatedly with her customers Mrs. Hawks and Mrs. Short, emerge from the elevator in the lobby below and join the departing crowd. That surprised her but perhaps it shouldn't. They all lived in the same town and shared an interest in colonial history. Anyway, drat it. She would never get back down in time to catch him.

She waited until the crowd thinned even more and made her way down the steps. Outside, she fumbled through her purse for her keys, not watching where she was going and ran smack into a broad, oxford-cloth clad back. Looking up, she recognized the man from the stairs.

"I'm so sorry. I wasn't paying attention."

He smiled down at her as if he knew her well and liked what he knew. It was a little disarming and she couldn't help but smile back.

"No harm done but you've dropped your bag." He bent down and picked up the bag containing the *Herball*. She opened it and saw the book's spine had split even more. Drat that too. She frowned.

"Is it beyond repair? Your book?" He peered into the bag.

"I hope not. That's the reason I was here. To find a way to repair it and now I've made it worse."

"Is there anything I can do to help?" He seemed to really want to know.

"Um, no. It's an old book and it has managed to hold together this long; another day or so shouldn't make a difference. Thanks, though." She found her keys and turned toward the street.

"May I tell you something?"

Surprised, she turned back. He looked a little hesitant but said, "After I saw you on the stairs I decided to wait out here to see if you would come out this way. Would you be interested in having a drink, just a drink, with me across the street at Cosimo's?" He motioned toward a sidewalk bar with little umbrella-shaded tables already starting to fill up. "I swear, I'm not a stalker or a creep and I have no criminal record other than parking tickets. I'm not married, never have been but I do approve of the institution. I'm gainfully employed and my mother would tell you-"

She laughed. "Are you asking me to meet your mother? Don't you think it might be too soon?"

He smiled again. That warm, approving smile. "Well, maybe."

~

An hour later she had learned his name was Michael Grant and he worked in the District Attorney's office as an assistant D.A. He had been born in Charleston, had three married sisters, numerous nieces and nephews, and had traveled to the northeast once, to Cooperstown, New York. That little town, with its beautiful glacier lake and the Baseball Hall of Fame, had his full approval but he had not cared for the more urban parts of the state.

"I can't really blame you. There are some sections it's just better to avoid. But everyone should see Manhattan in springtime. Especially around Easter. You can smell the incense coming out of the churches with people running in and out during their lunch hours. Sometimes you get those balmy ocean breezes and remember that it is a peninsula surrounded by the Atlantic. And New York is one of the world's great cities."

"Since you say so, I'll consider giving it another try some day. Now that you know my story, tell me yours. What made you decide to move to Charleston? I mean, I hope you live here and are not in town just for book repair purposes."

"I do, not far from here at all. I moved here after- well, I was married but I'm not anymore and I decided to move here because this is where my mother is from." It swept over her again that she truly was not married anymore and why. A sense of unreality hit her and she closed her eyes briefly. What was she doing here, talking, no, flirting (be honest) with this nice man?

"Really? What's her name?"

"Barbara Sinclair. Barbara Graham Sinclair."

He stared at her. "She died about ten years ago, right?"

"How do you know that?"

"I cannot believe this, I meet a gorgeous, interesting girl and this happens."

"How do you know my mother?"

"Sarah, I think we're related."

"What?"

"My mother had a cousin named Barbara who died ten years ago. Your parents lived abroad for a long time, right?"

"My dad was in the military."

"Oh, I didn't know that part but I do remember my mom mentioning that Barbara left and didn't come back much."

"I spent most of my growing-up years out of the country and obviously I don't know my family here. So, I have a cousin. This is definitely awkward but still… I'm glad."

They looked at each other, simultaneously raised their glasses and Michael said, "Here's to my hot new cousin."

She laughed until she thought she might choke. She finally caught her breath and said, "And to mine. You know, we're probably only third or fourth cousins."

"My mom will know. She'll want to meet you; so will everyone else. This calls for more drinks." He motioned for the waiter.

Everyone else, she thought. An extended family. She had no idea what that would be like but she was excited.

"Michael, I can't drink anymore or I won't be able to drive home."

They ordered appetizers and she peppered him with questions about her mother, (most of which he couldn't answer) his mother and the rest of his family.

"Well, the nieces and nephews are mostly still in the rug-rat stage which I think is a lot of fun but my sisters say is exhausting. They all live close by, two on Folly Beach and my baby sister, Cooper, out on Kiawah. She and her husband own an architectural firm. They're the reason I was in the courthouse. They needed some old property records verified before they start a new building project and since I work downtown I'm kind of their gopher."

"I would love to meet all of them. Give me your phone and I'll put my number in. I have to get home and feed my cat. He'll be starving."

They exchanged phone numbers and said goodbye. He startled her by kissing her lightly on the lips then giving her an exaggerated, comic wink before walking to his car. She laughed.

The time on her meter had expired but she didn't see a ticket. Lucky again. She drove with her windows down, enjoying the early evening air. Her little street was quiet and the streetlamps flickered into life just as she pulled in, as if to welcome her home.

Chapter Eighteen

"The green is the grounding wire and the red and black are the-what? I wish I had instructions for this."

"I wish you did too. This is getting heavy." Mary-Michael, drafted to help install the chandelier, had been holding it steady for ten minutes already. Most of the weight rested on the top of the ladder but not all.

"Let's put it down," suggested Sarah, climbing down the ladder.

Together, they eased the cumbersome fixture to the floor. They had thought wiring it in would be simple but the light had four differently colored wires and the box in the ceiling only had three, a green and two blacks. Sarah, armed with black electrical tape, newly-purchased end caps, and a borrowed ladder, had been so sure she could do this.

"Ok. I'm going to just go for it. What's the worst that can happen? It doesn't light up, right?"

"Sarah, have you ever heard the term 'electrical fire'?"

"I try not to let words keep me from realizing my full potential as a homeowner/handyman."

"Fine, but if anyone asks, I was against this."

"Duly noted. Let's get it up there one more time."

Thirty minutes later, Sarah, down in the basement turning the breaker back on, heard Mary-Michael shout. She rushed upstairs, expecting to see smoke if not flames.

"I can't believe it worked! It's perfect, Sarah. I really thought it was too formal for the room but now that the crown is more visible, it pulls it all together." Mary-Michael walked the perimeter of the room. "Once you get a table and chairs in place you'll be fine but in the meantime, you'd better put something underneath it so you won't hit your head every time you walk through."

The light blazed, illuminating the square but graceful little room. A few bulbs didn't work but that was an easy fix. Mary-Michael continued to look around.

"How do you keep the floors like this? I can almost see my face in them. The steps too; you must clean constantly. Did you have everything refinished when you moved in?"

"No, I think they were just in good shape (and the henbane and pennyroyal treatment didn't hurt either, she thought to herself). I can really see where the plaster needs to be touched up now. I had to use so much of it for the foyer but I think I might still have some in a bag in the basement." Sarah peered at the walls critically.

"What happened to the foyer?" Mary-Michael asked.

"Someone, I have no idea who, nailed mirrors face to the wall. I was careful but- I guess the plaster was just really old."

"I'll bet it was that last tenant. The student."

"What student?"

"Three guys rented the house almost two years ago. They all had been students at the university but I think two of them had just graduated. They complained about the house being too cold, doors opening on their own and other things. The graduates moved out and left their friend there alone. He said he was going to try and stay in the house just a few more weeks until he graduated. He didn't make it."

"What happened?" Sarah asked.

"Nervous breakdown. It was so sad. We talked to his parents when they were here packing up his things. They planned to take him home just as soon as he was released from the hospital. They were such nice people and you could tell they were heartbroken by the whole thing." Mary-Michael shrugged. "I didn't ask for details. Anyway, I have to go, Sarah. Noble will be home in an hour and we have to go-" Mary-Michael broke off and turned around looking behind her then down the hallway. "What was that? I saw something reflected in the pendants. Something black. Did you see it?"

She looked back at the light and whatever she saw there made her look behind her again. Sarah looked and saw the same dark shape reflected before in the mirrors but now reflected multiple times in the crystal pendants. *I thought you were gone. Why did you come back?*

"It must be a reflection of something passing in the street," said Mary-Michael uncertainly, looking at Sarah for confirmation. "Maybe. The trees around this house cast funny shadows sometimes. I'll walk you home. It's such a beautiful day." She had to get out of the house. If she heard those hooves skittering along the floor again she would lose her mind. She would have to take the chandelier down but she would do it on her own and find some excuse to give Mary-Michael as she was bound to notice it.

Still reluctant to go home after leaving Mary-Michael's, she took a stroll around the neighborhood. Even the sight of the tall, graceful houses surrounded by the springtide of blossoming and blooming trees and shrubs could not cheer her up. She felt so defeated. Why was it back and why did it only show in reflections? She had thought before that it only showed in the mirrors but now she knew better.

The church a couple of streets over bordered a small, picturesque graveyard containing ancient weeping-willows and yews. Treading the winding brick paths and reading the old tombstones she saw the name Graham several times and wondered if these were relatives. Of course Graham was not an uncommon name. A cat lay sprawled across a tomb, sleeping in the warmth of the afternoon sun. She walked on, past the touristy areas on into the less habited side streets and over to the Battery. The water was gray today with choppy, little waves ceaselessly lapping the base of the storm wall.

Returning home, she draped the chandelier in a sheet, trying not to look at it but making sure every pendant was covered. That would have to do for now. The house was quiet, no footsteps or scratching. She needed information so she settled into her bedroom window seat, punched the fat, yellow cushions into shape and pulled up the web. Below, tiny in the distance, Mr. Tumnus explored the lawn and surrounding shrubs.

According to the website, occultphenom.com, mirrors or other shiny surfaces could serve as portals through which spirits or demons enter the earthly realm. Sorcerers or witches could summon spirits and command them to come into physical existence using a mirror. Ok, if it was entering, it was not staying long. Or maybe it was but could only show itself for a short time?

She was being drawn deeper and deeper into something she did not know how to deal with or even completely believe in. The fact that Mary-Michael had seen something too was somewhat reassuring but put her no closer to a solution. She closed the browser and opened the documents from the courthouse again.

"*Mistress Grayhame's daughter assisted in her mother's herbal business, not unusual at all for the time. The child, who was questioned during the course of the trial, (we can only hope she was not tortured) gave testimony that her mother had given her a familiar in the form of a little ferret and told her to always keep it close and warm as it would protect her. Searches made for the creature turned up nothing more than a foul-smelling leather bucket, empty, next to the back door.*

The child was particularly adept at seeing far and finding lost or stolen objects. Indeed, it was the latter ability that brought her and her mother to the notice of authorities and thus into peril.

The town blacksmith, one John Herriot, owned a storage shed in which he kept various items brought to him and awaiting repair. The shed was broken into and several farming tools, expensive metal items, were stolen. Two farmers thus deprived of their property, demanded compensation the blacksmith could not provide and the whole matter was brought before the courts.

One of the farmers had previously applied to Mistress Grayhame for information on the whereabouts of his tools. He was told, by the little girl, that his tools were in the home of one Henry Jennings and that the Sheriff's man, Officer Norris, had accepted a bribe of two pounds not to find them.

When the wronged farmer testified thus, a search was made and the tools quickly found. Good news for the farmer but bad news for Mistress Grayhame and her daughter who now came under the scrutiny of the town officials."

Sarah sat back. So that is what tipped the scales against Elizabeth. The story continued.

"*Summarily accused and arrested, Mistress Grayhame was 'put to the question' (more horrifying than it sounds) and no doubt pressured to* name her accomplices or 'fellow witches'. The extent of her involvement (if any) in the occult activities going on around the area was never recorded if known. What we do know is that she did eventually break down and confess to consorting with a demon in an attempt, as we have noted before, to bring back her dead children. She named no accomplices. One was eventually found, the woman Katarina, but Elizabeth would never admit to any occult dealings with her.

The daughter, no doubt unintentionally, did not help her mother's case. When asked the source of her information, the child replied that she herself had no knowledge of the lost or stolen items but instead sought answers from one Robert Erpingham, a longbow archer who had died long ago during the Battle of Agincourt.

She described him as a balding man with whiskers wearing trunk hose and a padded leather jerkin over a knee-length tunic. He always appeared in response to her summons but was sometimes delayed, he said, because he dwelt such a long distance away and was often busy with other matters. She also said she had once seen him eat an entire chicken: meat, bones, and feathers.

Elizabeth, body and spirit undoubtedly broken by torture, seems to have realized her inevitable fate now and did not attempt her own defense but instead fought desperately for her daughter's life. Her pleas were moving attempts to make the authorities view the child's prognostications in a more favorable light as below.

'Not all knowledge is of the devil. We are promised that if we obey God's perfect law that in the fullness of time we will see through the mists between this world and the spirit world. Did God not say that in the last days He would pour out His spirit upon our sons and daughters and that they would dream dreams and prophesy?'

She denied her daughter had ever engaged in diabolical acts and declared her innocent of any dealings with demons. The child testified that her mother had brought her dead brothers and sisters back home 'so I should not be bereft of playmates' but declared they were not the jolly companions they once were and she seldom played with them.

I'm sure they were not jolly, thought Sarah, remembering those little, sackcloth-clad figures in the garden. In her grief,

Elizabeth must have decided to bring them back but of course she couldn't bring them back *completely*.

As for how she had brought about this return from the dead, Sarah had a hunch she would find the information, or at least some of it, in the *grimoire*. She looked and found a spell to "reduce and compel a demon to enter within a stone, locket or any object. Thus trapped the demon will do thy bidding but as they are deceitful creatures and full of guile, take great care that thy requests are simple and plain and leave no opportunity for the demon to twist thy words to its own mischievous devices."

She found one name underlined over and over again. *Malkuth*.

Chapter Nineteen

"So when you bought the house you had no idea it used to belong to family?" Constance asked, one blonde eyebrow raised questioningly.

Sarah nodded, amused at the nonplussed expression on her expressive face. Michael's mother had turned out to be a delight, enfolding Sarah in her arms and welcoming her to the family. The day after she met Michael, his mother called to tell her how happy they all were that she had "come back" to Charleston, and how excited they were that Michael had "found" her. She was immediately invited out for Sunday brunch and Michael had picked her up for the drive out to Johns Island this morning.

Michael's parents lived in a painted brick, French-style, courtyard house overlooking the salt-marshes. Framed by the dining-room windows, an ancient, cottonwood tree near the water held a flock of snowy egrets flapping their wings and grooming. Below them, an alligator sprawled on the mud bank. She finished the last of her omelet and poured another cup of Constance's delicious and very strong coffee.

"I didn't know anything about it at all. It was just one house the realtor showed me and it was within my budget. I found out about my connection to it after I bought it."

"Now that, my dear, is an amazing coincidence. It's almost like the house was waiting for you. You need to be very careful. So I assume you know by now, it's supposed to be haunted."

"Mom! Don't start." This from Cooper, Michael's sister.

"Well it is, Cooper. There's no point in not facing it." Constance countered.

"It's okay, I know. It's hard to not know since it's on a ghost tour but others have mentioned it too. I admit it was a shock at first but once I found out it had been in my family, I didn't want to leave. I never really had any roots growing up and I think I've found some here."

"Have you seen her yet?" Constance asked, her frank, brown eyes regarding Sarah steadily.

Sarah considered pretending she did not know what she referred to but finally said, "I think so."

"I always wanted to see her. I can remember as a child walking by the house, imagining I would look up and see her standing in a window. It never happened to me but over the years many others claim they saw her. Your mother was one of them. She didn't like to talk about it."

"Did my mom ever tell you exactly what she saw?"

"She didn't go into detail about it but it must have been Elizabeth. Who else? For generations, neighbors and pedestrians have reported seeing a dark-haired woman watching them from the windows."

According to Constance, she and Michael were probably fifth cousins. Over the years the Graham family had dispersed throughout the country with few remaining in the Charleston area.

"We're lucky to be here at all. When they burned Elizabeth, there was still the question of her daughter."

"But she was still a very little girl, right? A child. Surely they wouldn't harm a child."

"She would have been about five or six years old. And if they thought a child was a tool of the devil or a witch, yes, they would burn the child. There was an instance, not here but in France in which a heavily pregnant woman was burned at the stake. Her child, a boy, aborted spontaneously and fell onto the ground but was alive. The priest directed the officials to throw it back in the fire."

"Mom, this may be a bit much for little ears." Cooper picked up her three-year-old son from the floor where he played with a Tonka truck, and carried him out of the dining room, handing him over to her husband in the kitchen. Coming back in she said, "Sarah, you can probably tell that Mom is our family historian and passionate about her subject." She rolled her eyes and her mother frowned at her.

"History is important. Any intelligent person will realize the advantages of learning from the past. If nothing else it lets us know how far we've come or, in some cases, regressed."

"I don't see how that applies to our family," said Cooper. "We're here aren't we? Elizabeth's daughter survived and didn't repeat her mother's mistakes. Besides, it's just plain interesting."

"What was the issue with the daughter?" Sarah obviously already knew some of it but wanted to hear what Constance had to say.

"The child told people things she shouldn't have known. Like what was happening to love ones away traveling and where to find lost objects; small, but important things like thimbles and jewels. In one instance she told an aggrieved ale-wife that she would find a pair of treasured ear-bobs in the possession of one Mistress Byrne, a seamstress to whom the ale-wife's husband had given the jewelry. She told Master James Fen that he would not be able to get his stolen cloak back because the thief had already cut it up, made it into a kirtle and sold it."

"Did anyone try to verify her stories?"

"Yes and some awkward situations ensued." Constance smiled.

"Have you ever spoken with Dr. Bickerstaff in the city archives? He let me photograph an old newspaper article about Elizabeth and also the trial transcripts."

"No. I would love to see those."

"Give me your email address and I'll forward them to you. I took some photographs of a portrait that may or may not be Elizabeth but they didn't turn out that well. The portrait is being cleaned and restored now but it may go on exhibit eventually. I'll try to get some better photos then and I will share if you're interested."

Cooper fixed a platter of cinnamon rolls and a carafe of fresh coffee and carried it out to a terrace that gave views of the marshes. The rest of the family followed. Some of the egrets in the cottonwood tree squawked and took flight, barely clearing the murky water below. The alligator gave a deep roar and slid back into the marsh.

Sarah felt goose bumps on her arms. She would never get used to that. Michael noticed, smiled, and put his hand over hers.

"What kind of shape was the house in? Have you had to do major renovations?" Michael's dad wanted to know.

"Good shape. Most of what I've done has been cosmetic. The outside is my priority now. I have to finish the painting and the garden still needs attention. It's been a little overwhelming."

"Do it the way you eat an elephant. One bite at a time." He chuckled, amused at his own wit and Cooper shook her head. Her father finished his Bloody Mary.

"I'm glad that someone who can appreciate the house is there now and if I were you, I would ignore the haunted stuff. Any old house is bound to have a past. I would like to see it sometime. I haven't been downtown in a while."

A fretful cry came from inside the house and Michael got up, coming back with his five-month-old niece, holding her like a football. An aureole of red-gold hair surrounded a cherubic face. She sucked furiously on a pacifier and blinked at the light, burying her face in her uncle's broad chest.

"Guess who's up from her nap and needs a diaper change?" Michael handed her to Cooper who sighed and took her daughter inside.

"You know your time will come when you get married," Cooper's husband, Steve, said to Michael who shrugged.

"Probably. Right now I'm enjoying just being an uncle." His three-year-old nephew tackled him from behind and Michael picked him up, swinging him back and forth by the ankles out over the marsh while the boy screamed delightedly. Cooper, emerging with her freshly diapered daughter, looked at her upside-down son.

"He'll never take an afternoon nap now but maybe he'll sleep all night. We're in a real up-and-down phase during the night."

"It's because of the potty-training, sweetheart. It takes time."

Constance took her now smiling granddaughter in her arms and kissed her dimpled cheeks. The baby cooed softly and reached out her hands to Sarah. Surprised and pleased, she took her and cuddled her close, inhaling that indescribably fresh baby-scent. A longing rose in her and she swallowed a sudden lump in her throat. Maybe someday. Michael put his nephew down and came back to the table, grabbing a cinnamon roll.

"My apologies to all for taking Sarah away but I have some files I have to go over before tomorrow."

Sarah reluctantly handed the baby back to Constance and everyone said their goodbyes, agreeing to get together again soon. Constance walked them out and stood by Michael's car, balancing her grand daughter on one hip.

"I know how this is going to sound but I'm going to say it anyway. Has anything in the house tried to contact you?"

"Mom!" Michael looked exasperated.

"Hush or I'll turn you over my knee! Well, has it?"

Sarah thought of the messages in the ashes and the horrific impersonation of Nay-Nay.

"Maybe."

"This is important then. Sarah, don't talk to it. Don't respond to it in any way. Acknowledging it makes it stronger. Seeing Elizabeth is one thing. That's just a haunting. A haunting can only repeat something that has occurred in the past. It shouldn't be able to hurt you."

"Who else would be trying to communicate with me?"

"I think something is trapped in that house. Something very strong and very bad. You're the first family member to live in the house in several generations. Whatever is there might recognize you somehow."

"Mom, this-" Michael tried again.

"I told you to hush. Sarah, promise me you'll be careful?" Sarah nodded. "Ok, I'll stop now. Next time my other daughters will be here. They were disappointed they couldn't come today. I'm so glad Michael met you and we have the chance to get to know Barbara's daughter. I miss her. Take care, dear."

"I will and thank you for the wonderful brunch. I want all of you to feel free to come over anytime. I'll plan a brunch once the garden is done."

Michael's little Saab was fast and with the light Sunday traffic they were back in front of her house in no time.

"Thanks, Michael. That was fun. I like your family."

"Yeah, me too. I never realized how lucky I was until I began working in criminal justice and saw what some families are like. There are things very wrong with our society and it often starts at home. Marijuana, crack, and I don't even want to think about meth. Babies are exposed to that stuff before birth."

"And they're so helpless. It's hard to understand how a mother could allow it."

"Sometimes I think hardcore addicts have lost their souls. Enough about that. So, fifth cousin? What do you think?"

They both laughed. She leaned over and kissed him chastely on the cheek. "Call me, ok? If the weather is good I'll probably spend next weekend painting."

"Sounds good."

He drove away and she walked around to the back yard. Sunlight filled the small garden, reflecting in sparkles off the bronze satyr's head. Heavy-headed peonies bowed on their fragile stems, nodding sleepily in the warmth. The honey-thick smell of confederate jasmine wafted through the air as nectar-heavy bees gathered the vine's bounty. One had drunk so much it had trouble staying aloft.

She glimpsed a quick flash of fur to the side and Mr. Tumnus appeared, knocked the bee to the ground and ate it. She fully expected him to be stung but if he was, it didn't bother him.

"You are a mighty bee-slayer," she told him, picking him up and scratching him behind the ears as she walked inside.

Other than the soothing tick of the clock pendulum the house was silent. She climbed the stairs noticing that Mary-Michael was right. The wood absolutely gleamed and didn't have a speck of dust anywhere. The fragrant, cherry floor in her bedroom had a lustrous depth to it she didn't remember seeing before and like the stairs, had no dust.

A package from the Department of Correction arrived in the mail yesterday. A package that she hadn't had the courage to open. Steeling herself now to do it, she slid a knife along the flap and let the contents fall into her lap.

A watch, a wedding ring, and a picture of her, taken on their trip to St. Bart's, were Sean's entire personal effects. She couldn't remember seeing this particular watch but the ring brought back memories. They had shopped together for their wedding bands and Sean didn't like any until they found this one. It was heavy, white gold and she had the jeweler inscribe "Forever" inside it. Forever had not lasted as long as she thought it would.

Fleeing memories that threatened to choke her, she put the items away in the chest upstairs and went down to find Mr. Tumnus in the foyer just outside the parlor, hissing and spitting and making a low-pitched growling sound she had never heard him make before. The fur on his back actually stood up as he made feints toward the room but never went past the threshold.

Nothing in the room looked out of place. She picked the kitten up, taking him to the kitchen where, to her surprise, he climbed into his basket and cowered, ears back.

The day was too beautiful to stay inside; once again the garden seemed to be calling her. She found her spade and gardening gloves and went to work on the weeds near the statue. Accidentally touching it, she felt the humming vibration and quickly pulled her hand away.

Puzzled, she touched it lightly and felt the vibration again but this time she also heard scratching or clawing sounds seemingly coming from inside. The statue actually felt repulsive; unclean and slimy somehow. Something moved in her peripheral vision and she turned around and saw a little girl, gray skin turning black in patches, thread-stitched mouth struggling to move, coming toward her with hands outstretched as if pleading.

Chapter Twenty

Sarah backed away, turned, and then ran for the house. Locking the door she crouched below the windowsill, too frightened to look outside. Mr. Tumnus climbed down from his basket and sat beside her. She heard nothing for several minutes so risked a peek through the window.

No one was there. She sat down on the stone floor, exhausted. Her heart still raced and she once again struggled with a sense of unreality. She could not live like this but where could she go?

Frustrated, frightened, and angry she paced the kitchen. That statue was more than ugly; it felt evil and vibrated with some sort of power. She thought back to the name in the *grimoire*. *Malkuth*. All she could find on the internet was that it was an angel, possibly one of the fallen ones.

Elizabeth had brought something into this world that shouldn't be here and she had not been able to control it. It had brought her children back to her but, like most times when one dances with the devil, she had been tricked and cheated. The malformed satyr contained something, but what?

Suddenly she heard a loud bang and then a sound like horse's hooves only not outside; these were in the house, just down the hallway. Childish, terrified screams echoed all around her and she heard light running footfalls like before. Mr. Tumnus's ears flattened out again and he scurried back into his basket. Sarah was too frightened to move.

Invisible children ran in terror from whatever made those loud, stomping sounds. The noise continued and the screams intensified and then- they stopped.

~

"You were right. It looks like an antique this way, which I guess it should since it is one. Has Liddy seen it yet?" Angela, stopping by the warehouse the next day, was pleased with the garden figure from Wadmalaw.

"She's coming out this afternoon. I told her she has first dibs on it and we can clean it up for her or leave it as is."

"I think she'll take it as is. Who bought all the doors? I noticed the stacks have gone down a lot."

"A guy who is building a stable somewhere near Edisto and wants to use them on the stalls. He bought twenty of them so it sounds like a big project."

"I used to love to ride. My grandfather, an extremely charming and impractical man, invested heavily in thoroughbred horses. I know that some people make a fortune that way. Not my grandfather. Every time he thought he had a winner, the horse would get snake bit or the pasture would flood and their hooves would rot, always something. They had a rambling, old farmhouse out past the tea plantation and in the summer my cousins and David and I would stay there for a week at a time. I miss those days. The house is still there but one of my uncles lives in it now. David's girls go out there to ride every now and then. Neither of mine is quite old enough."

"How are the girls? I haven't seen them in a while."

"You know how angry David was the last time Diana just dropped the girls off when he wasn't there? He went back to court to try for sole, physical custody again. The judge wouldn't do it and admonished both of them to coordinate their schedules better. As if Diana is willing to coordinate anything with David. She can't stand the fact that he finally saw through her. This is all taking a toll on the girls. They're protective of their mother and Diana tells them Lord-knows-what about the situation. Lil is spending more and more time with her imaginary 'friend' when she is at David's. They're looking into counseling."

Sarah felt a jolt of guilt. How could she tell Angela or David that Lil's imaginary friend might not be something the child had invented? Something she was still not sure she believed in spite of everything she had seen and heard.

"I wish I could help. I hate that they're going through this." She felt like a hypocrite.

"Children are a lot of work and sometimes there's a lot of heartache involved. Or, as in my case right now, heartburn." She patted her now obviously-swollen belly. "I'm only seven months but I look like nine. Everyone keeps reassuring me it's a girl since

I'm carrying high but who knows? He/she wouldn't turn around during the ultra-sound."

"Hmm, sounds shy. It might be a girl."

Angela laughed. "I didn't think of that. We'll see. Heaven knows my boys could use some lessons in modesty. My husband took them camping two weekends ago and they found out they can pee outdoors. Now they are determined to do it on every occasion. Such as the church picnic last week." She shook her head. "I swear the Y chromosome is a scary mutation."

After Angela left, a wave of tourists flooded the store, looking for an authentic piece of Charleston to take home. She sold the Foo dogs and the cast-iron, gargoyle andirons, all pricy items. Everyone was interested in the horse statue and Sarah wished she hadn't put it on display yet. She really, really hoped Liddy would buy it.

Her sales added up to a very profitable afternoon. She barely had time to complete shipping arrangements on the larger items before it was time to close. As soon as she locked the main door, she heard a knock.

Liddy Carmody smiled at her through the glass side panel and she opened the door.

"Sorry! I know I'm late. I had to stay at the house until the floor refinishers left. I tried to call but my phone died. Let me take a quick peek at that horse."

Sarah could tell right away it was not what Liddy expected. She circled it twice before saying regretfully, "It's a great piece but it's not right for the space. I need something smaller."

Sarah's heart sank. I could have sold it four times this afternoon, she thought. She didn't let her disappointment show. Liddy was a great customer and the piece would sell eventually to someone.

"I'm sorry, Liddy. I so hoped it would work for you. How is the project going otherwise?"

"Behind schedule. That rainstorm the other day washed all the topsoil away just before the truck with the sod showed up. The plumbers broke some of the antique tile in the powder room and I can't find replacement tiles anywhere. So it's going about like any other project." She rolled her eyes. "What about you? Didn't you say you were working on a garden and had a statue you wanted to sell?"

"Well, I did originally but I think I might keep it." She was almost afraid to sell it now.

"At least let me look at it. I picked up a weeping fig and some clematis from the landscapers on the way here so almost all the plants will be done soon. I really need something old for this garden. You're closing anyway, right? I'll follow you home."

Liddy was insistent so she finished closing up and drove home, Liddy following in her Mercedes with the ornamental fig tree sticking up through the sunroof.

The garden glowed in the pink light of late afternoon and the little statue shone softly bronze. Wisteria vines, just burst into bloom, covered the porch rails and threatened to make their way inside the windows. She reminded herself to trim it back. Mary-Michael had advised her to get rid of it as it was so invasive but she didn't have the heart to kill it.

"Sarah, I had no idea you owned this house. You do know-"

"That it has a history? I do."

"And it doesn't bother you?"

"I've decided every house has some history, unless it's brand-new. But even those might be built on an 'ancient, Indian burial ground' or an old cemetery so- I'm dealing with it. Besides, the house used to belong to my family."

"You are related to the Grahams?"

"Yes."

"Did you inherit the house?"

"No. It was just one of the houses the realtor showed me. The statue is over here. Do you want to measure it?"

"Ok. I'm taking the hint." Liddy scrutinized the little satyr. "I don't know that it will fit in with my project. It's certainly unique. Especially that collar."

She reached out and cupped the creature's chin, drew back and exclaimed.

"It's buzzing. That felt almost like an electrical shock. Are there power lines running through the yard beneath it?"

Sarah had never thought of that. "I don't know. I'm glad you mentioned it, though. I'll call the electric company and ask if they know."

Of course. Electrical lines might be the cause of the strange vibration it gave off. Just the possibility made her feel better. It was a perfectly plausible explanation. She smiled at Liddy.

"Do you want a cup of coffee?"

Liddy looked at her watch. "How about a glass of wine instead?"

Mr. Tumnus came home just as they sat down with the bottle and two long-stemmed glasses. Bounding across the grass, he took an immediate liking to Liddy and climbed into her lap, cleaned his whiskers, then purred loudly while condescending to let her scratch his belly.

"So you obviously didn't grow up here, you don't have a southern accent. But your family are old Charlestonians and I do mean old. As in before the Revolution old. I guess you know most of the story by now." Liddy sipped her wine.

"I've found some information on the house and a family member told me more. My mother never, ever talked about the more sensational side of our family history."

"She must have had a reason. Maybe it embarrassed her? I know that some of my aunts and uncles didn't want to talk about our past. I think parents didn't want to inflict the bad memories of the old slavery days on their children. It's a shame really; a lot of history was lost that way. Have you ever heard of the South Carolina cowboys?"

"No."

"Some of my enslaved ancestors handled, on horseback, the large herds of cattle that grew out of the original stock sent from England and other places. The cowboys sometimes deserted, falling in with the local Indian tribes and others from Florida fleeing north from the Spanish down there."

"So you know your family history? Do you have family close by?"

"Oh my goodness, yes. I have aunts, uncles and cousins all over town and beyond. I grew up in a big old house close to Bohicket marina and my husband and I just restored a house not too far from my parents. Have you seen Delmont's Restaurant down on Market? My family owns that as well as a chain of grocery stores. All my aunts are great cooks and so is my mother. I can barely boil water so I studied architecture and design and it seems to be working out." She spoke the last sentence with a mixture of pride and satisfaction.

Sarah said, "Doing something you love and earning a living at the same time must be gratifying. Even though I was never really interested in history and architecture before I think I've caught the old house bug. Living in a piece of history is satisfying in ways I never thought about. Well, usually. Last week was an expensive week. I had to have a section of a basement wall rebuilt and it was not a cheap repair." She winced at the memory of the check she had written.

"I know. Sometimes the amount of work and money required to keep the original features intact is incredible. As long as my clients don't mind paying for it, I will go above and beyond but it's hard. There are days when I would be happy to weave sweet-grass baskets and sell them on the side of the road. Some of my aunts used to have stands for that."

"Really! Is your family Gullah then?" Sarah was surprised.

"I know. I don't look it, do I? We definitely have Gullah and European ancestry though mixed with native Catawba blood. People always assume we are Italian but we're much more interesting than that. One of my great-uncles was what used to be called a 'root doctor.' He was a horticulture expert and you should have seen his herb garden. I remember as a child wanting to play in there because it was so lush and green and smelled like heaven but my aunt was always afraid I would trample the plants and she made sure I stayed out. She was probably right."

"What does a root doctor do?"

"He mostly treated people for minor illnesses. Sometimes people claimed they had been 'cursed' by someone and my uncle would give them a juju bag full of herbs to wear around their neck. He always knew the best times to plant and harvest crops too. Oh, and he used to line his shoes with folded-up newspaper. It kept the evil spirits away."

"This house has newsprint plastered to the inside of the walls."

"Wow, someone really tried to fortify this house against the spirits, didn't they? The rowan tree, the hollies and yews... they pulled out all the stops."

"I don't think it worked that well."

They were silent for a moment, listening to the comfortable sounds of the kitten purring and the wind rustling the leaves. The skies looked like rain was imminent.

Liddy spoke. "So what are you going to do about the children?"

Chapter Twenty-One

Startled and wary, Sarah asked, "What children?"

"Don't try to tell me you haven't seen them. I'm looking at them right now."

Sarah looked behind her and there they were, all four, standing by the hedge. Mr. Tumnus woke and ran under the porch.

"I can't do anything about them, Liddy. I think they came with the house." Her laugh sounded borderline hysterical but she couldn't control it.

"You have to help them. They won't go away until you do something."

"If I knew of a way to help them go away, believe me, I would have already done it. What do you know about them?"

"I know they're frightened and want their mother. They don't understand why they're here."

"I think their mother did this to them but I can't help them. How do you know what they're thinking?"

"Sarah, they're just children, of course they want their mother. These are shades, you know, like the shades Homer mentions in the *Odyssey*. They're not strong enough to leave on their own once they've been summoned. Something is holding them here. What do you know about their mother?"

"I think their mother is one of the original owners of the house, Elizabeth, the one burned as a witch. I found something, a book, and it's full of charms, spells, and even prayers for dealing with demons and spirits. I know she admitted to consorting with a demon in order to raise her children from the dead. There is a name that seems to be important, *Malkuth*."

"I have no idea what or who that is. If their mother called up a demon to bring them back, it may be that the same demon is keeping them here. I know what I said earlier about power lines in the ground but I have to tell you- these beings or demons or whatever you call them are often the same as the vegetative, fertility gods and goddesses of legend and myth. I can't help but notice how lush the growth around the statue is."

"The herbs are really potent too. Oh my goodness, do you realize how crazy this whole conversation sounds?"

Liddy said, "Yes, I do. Imagine a woman crazed enough by her children's deaths to go to such lengths to bring them back. Satan really is a roaring lion stalking us, just like the Bible says. He waits for our grief and despair and uses our weakness to enter into our lives and destroy us and all that we love. What she did goes against the will of God; she suffered for it, and these children still suffer. This needs to be put right."

Sarah glanced back at the hedge. The figures were gone. Mr. Tumnus came padding silently back and entwined himself around her ankles.

"I keep getting messages traced in the fireplace ashes. For a while I thought it might be the spirit of Elizabeth or the children but now I think it's something else."

"They are not human and because of that they have difficulty communicating with us. Sometimes things from the other side can only show themselves in certain ways. They leave messages or appear in reflections. Whatever it is, it's probably trying to trick you. It will try to either frighten you or gain your sympathy. Don't talk to it. If you talk to it, it gets stronger. They'll often try to take on the persona or even the appearance of someone you know if they can get enough clues from you. I suppose it's possible that it is holding the children captive. If you can find out what it is, maybe you can banish it and free the children."

"I'm in totally over my head here, you know."

"I don't know that much about it either. I'm probably a little more comfortable talking about it because of my family background. My grandmother used to say that if we could see, really see, just how many spirits are around us every day, we would go crazy. The air is thick with them. May I see the book you were talking about?"

The book was beside the fireplace again. Coming back outside, she handed it to Liddy then poured both of them another glass of wine. She idly swirled the dark red liquid in her glass while Liddy paged through the book.

"I think I found it." Liddy frowned in concentration.

"Found what?"

"A charm to summon a demon to carry out commands."

"Please don't say it aloud."

"It's more complicated than that. You have to consecrate a circle in a certain way. Here, read it."

"Come ye, then, without delay, without noise, and without rage, before us, without any deformity or hideousness from wherein ye are, from all mountains, valleys, streams, and ponds. Come ye, come ye, ye Angels of Darkness; come hither before me within this circle and be ye ready to perform and complete all that I command ye."

Sarah looked up. "I found a similar one the other day. How would I reverse it and make it go away? Say it backwards?"

"I have an idea about that. You may not need to do anything at all other than remove that iron collar. Look," she flipped back a few pages, "this says these spirits fear iron. Perhaps, what was her name again? Oh right, Elizabeth, called it to come into the satyr and then bound it with that slave collar. You take the collar off, this thing is gone and, voila, you have no more haunted anything hanging around."

"Are you sure? You can't really know that."

"No, but what can it hurt? Iron is a bugaboo in many cultures for some reason. The Jews were not allowed to use it on-site when they built the temple in Jerusalem. In Africa, mothers often put iron bracelets and bells on their children to keep evil, illness-causing spirits away. It's an idea worth pursuing."

"Elizabeth advised parents to place iron in bed with their babies to keep them from being stolen. Maybe you're right." Sarah had a sense of dawning hope that all this could be made right and just end. "But if I release it, there is no way to know what it will do."

"Maybe not but you do know what it is doing now."

She did unfortunately, not just to her but also to David's daughter.

Liddy stood. "I have to drop these plants off at the project so they'll be ready for the grounds crew in the morning. Call the electric company and see if any lines run near that statue; just to cover all of our bases. Don't do anything else until I talk to my uncle to see what he thinks. He'll know what's best. I'll call you, ok?"

Liddy drove away, the green, fig-tree leaves jutting out of the sunroof and fluttering like a botanical banner in the wind. Carrying the wine glasses in, she almost tripped over Mr. Tumnus who didn't want her out of his sight this evening. She poured cat food in his dish and gave him fresh water.

The house was quiet. A gentle, misting rain had begun and made soft, pattering sounds on the roof. She looked out at her garden and saw a rabbit scurry across the lawn and disappear into the hollies. It looked unusually large but that was probably due to the distorting effect of the old-fashioned, individually-crafted glass panes. Her dining room looked bizarre with the chandelier wrapped in a sheet but she didn't feel like taking it down. She was angry that this spirit or whatever it was would not stay away. Maybe Liddy was right and it was trapped here. If she could set it free and send it away… she felt a release of tension in her shoulders just at the thought of all of this ending.

With a sense of well-being she had not felt in a long time, she decided to clean house. Her mother used to say an intense session of dusting and mopping was better than therapy. The bathroom was a quick clean now with the moldy carpet gone. She had not yet found floor tile to replace the cracked ones but they were barely noticeable. The newly-restored finishes on the sink and tub shone.

There wasn't much to do in the dining-room and she glanced out the windows. The day grew darker now and the street lamps were already on, golden pools of light illuminating the cobbles shining in the rain. An errant burst of wind twirled a bunch of dead leaves into a brown, twisting column that collapsed against a yew.

Descending the steps into the garden she hurriedly cut an armful of white peonies, arranged them in a deep bowl and placed it on the kitchen table. The garden contained a thick bed of pinks and reds too but only the whites sent their sweet, delicate scent drifting throughout the house. The odd thing about the flowers was that no matter how many blooms she cut, they were always back the next day, spilling luxuriantly across the beds.

The same with the herbs, the few she felt she recognized well enough to safely use. She had seen Mr. Tumnus eating the small green leaves occasionally and he seemed to know what he was doing. He never suffered any ill-effects.

A few days ago, the small tree in the side-yard burst into pink, frothy blossoms. She was now almost certain it was a cherry and planned to attempt jelly making if the fruit survived the birds.

Down in the basement she started a load of laundry then inspected her newly-repaired brick wall. The patch definitely showed as the new bricks did not completely match the old. The mason told her he could rebuild the entire wall and blend the new bricks with the old that way but the cost would have more than doubled. He assured her that the wall was not load-bearing and the house should not have suffered any structural damage because of the collapse.

Turning to leave, she glimpsed, through the egress window, the hem of a white garment and a pair of little, bare feet walking slowly across the lawn, toward the house.

Chapter Twenty-Two

She backed away from the window and ran up the stairs. Fighting an impulse to run screaming from the house, she closed the basement door behind her and stood with her back against it, looking and listening. Very faintly, she heard footsteps on the porch, a child's voice, and what sounded like laughter. Relieved, she went outside in time to see Lil, wearing a white nightgown, step from a chair onto the porch rail and begin to walk across it. Swaying, and then recapturing her balance, she reached one of the wisteria-covered posts and clutched it with both hands. Turning and laughing she said triumphantly, "Do you see? I told you I could make it all the way. I can..." She trailed off. Looking down she saw Sarah standing by the door.

"Where's Arabella?" She sounded confused and a little peeved.

Sarah walked over, plucked Lil from the wet rail and set her down. "What were you doing up there? That rail is eight feet off the ground. If you fell from there you could be hurt. Don't ever do that again!"

"Arabella does it all the time."

"Lil, listen to me. Arabella is not real. You shouldn't talk to her or pay her any attention because-"

"I know. They all died." Lil said matter-of-factly. "Both of her brothers and her sister died at almost the same time she did. They have to stay here because of their mother but she's gone now and they're afraid of the other thing."

"What other thing?"

"The thing that lives with you. It likes to hurt them."

"How does it hurt them?"

"It bites them and burns them and...other things."

"Does Arabella tell you this?"

"She *thinks* it to me."

"Lil, please promise me you won't talk to Arabella anymore. It isn't safe."

"If I don't talk to her, she pinches me, hard."

The kissing-gate *clanged* and David, face unreadable, strode toward them across the wet grass. Lil ran to her father. He picked her up, said something in a low voice to which she nodded. He put her down and she began walking toward the gate. David came over to the porch.

"Hi." He ran his hand across his chin distractedly and attempted a smile.

"David. She was on the porch rail. It's slippery and she could have really gotten hurt."

He bowed his head briefly and took a deep breath. "I don't know what to say. She has had this imaginary friend since the divorce and she blames some of what she does on this 'friend'. It wasn't so bad at first but it's become dangerous. Last week I found her in the street at two o'clock in the morning. 'Arabella' wanted to play. I thought she would grow out of it but it's getting worse. We meet with a counselor next week."

"Has it been happening since the divorce or since you moved to the apartment?"

He seemed surprised. "Good question. It might have started after I moved here. I have to tell you though, it's been a difficult year or two and I'm not sure exactly when it began."

"Does she ever see the friend anywhere else?" She knew she was prying but she needed to know.

He frowned and she thought she might have asked one question too many until he said slowly, "I don't think so but I'll ask her and Kate. I never thought of that."

"If it helps any, I promise I'll keep an eye out for her when I'm home."

"Thanks." To her surprise he reached out and brushed back the hair at her temple then handed her the curling tendril of Spanish moss pulled from her damp hair.

"Oh um, I should get back inside. I've obviously been outside too long if moss is growing on me. Good night, David."

He watched over his shoulder as she retreated indoors. He had wanted to touch her hair since he first saw her. It was as soft as he had imagined it would be. Now he wanted to kiss the curve of her cheek where it… stop now, he told himself as he walked slowly back home.

~

Sarah slowly went through the house, locking all the doors and thinking about David. For just a second she had thought he was going to kiss her and she didn't know how she felt about that. His mouth looked firm and intoxicatingly masculine and it had been so long since- well, since romance had any place in her life.

She didn't need it. It would be too complicated anyway. Working together, plus an ex-wife… it was too much to work out. She needed friends a lot more than she needed a boyfriend.

In the kitchen, Mr. Tumnus stood on the table, lapping water from the bowl of peonies. He stepped on the edge of the bowl and water poured onto the table and floor. He jumped back from the spreading pool and she grabbed a cloth from the counter and felt a breeze encircle her, gently lifting strands of her hair up off her shoulders. Suddenly a howling wind blew through the room, knocking the bowl of flowers from the table and whipping the curtains against the window panes. The kitten scrambled to stay on the table and she caught him just before he fell. The bowl shattered when it hit the floor and flowers scattered everywhere. The stemware hanging from the rack beneath the cupboard broke and covered the counter-top with slivers of crystal. Her hair blew into her eyes and she couldn't see. The wind continued for several minutes then abruptly stopped.

Brushing back her hair and looking down at the cloth in her hand, she realized this was the linen napkin she had used a few nights ago when she made her ridiculous attempt to capture the wind. She had inadvertently loosened one of the three knots.

Her hand trembled as she oh-so-carefully placed the napkin in a drawer, closing it firmly. She should never have played around with that book. Wearily she picked up the broken glass and mopped the floor.

Mr. Tumnus did not protest when she picked him up and took him upstairs with her. Her arm bled from where he had scratched it when she pulled him from the table. She settled into the window seat with him and her laptop. Scratching him behind the ears until he sounded like a tiny motor, she pulled up the newspaper article and resumed reading.

"*Mistress Grayhame did manage to save her daughter's life. The magistrates and the local clergy decided it was enough to have the child re-baptized and taken in by a local 'Godly' family. Although all of her mother's property was confiscated at the time of the execution, as an adult she successfully petitioned the town council and received some of it, most notably the house, back. She continued her mother's business as a successful apothecary. Town officials were embarrassed by the entire episode by then and it is believed that most of the trial records were either destroyed or amended around the time of the girl's petition.*

A different fate befell the free-woman Katarina. Instead of her life, she lost her freedom and was sold into slavery, the money being used to defray her court costs. As for the others supposed to have participated in the occult activities in the area, they were never successfully identified."

The article ended there. The daughter's name was never given and when Sarah checked the property records she found several gaps in the owner timeline in the 1700's. None of those named were women.

Questions remained. When was the statue placed in the garden? Who lined the walls of the house with newsprint? It must have been long after Elizabeth died, judging by the date on the paper. Someone was still trying to ward off spirits at that date. Constance said that the ghost of a dark-haired woman still appeared to passersby, including Sarah's mother.

Leaving Mr. Tumnus in the window seat she went downstairs and walked the house restlessly. She put the clothes in the dryer then checked the parlor fireplace ashes for another message but found nothing.

The paneled fireplace wall was one area she had not painted yet. The rectangular, beautifully symmetrical white panels drew the eye up and emphasized the height of the ceiling. To her, the wall represented the classic ideals of the Age of Enlightenment and made the room one of the most beautiful in the house.

Looking at it now she decided to sand and get it ready for paint. The panel to the immediate left of the hearth was especially smoke-blackened. Finding her fine grit sandpaper she sanded it hard, heard a click and the panel sprang away from the wall, leaving an open crack about four inches wide and three feet tall. Opening it all the way revealed a wood-encased, rectangular space with narrow slits in the right side. It was empty.

She remembered touring, near Stratford-on-Avon, Anne Hathaway's cottage which had a very similar box called an airing cupboard. It was used for drying clothing and sometimes to keep stored linens from mildewing using the heat of the fireplace next to it.

This was a perfect hiding place for the linen napkin. If what she had read about that particular incantation was correct, the last two knots should produce even stronger winds but she certainly did not want to test it. She wondered what would happen if she burned it but was afraid to try.

Opening the kitchen drawer, she gently poked it with one finger. The remaining knots were intact. Even so, she carried it like a grenade and was relieved to shut it up safely inside the cupboard. She considered sealing the panel closed somehow but decided that might be taking caution too far. Especially if Liddy's uncle knew how to deal with all this. Knowing she was placing a lot of hope in an elderly man she had never heard of before today, she felt tentatively optimistic anyway. She spent the rest of the evening happily sanding the fireplace wall, only going to bed when her hands cramped in exhaustion.

~

"Do you think it's too much? It's a small room but it's the only one suitable for a nursery. I want us all on the same floor. The boys' room is only slightly bigger and the bunk beds barely fit in there."

The two women backed away and contemplated the round crib, a peach-colored skirt spread out around it like the folds of a ball gown. Angela had placed it in the middle of the room directly under a securely anchored, crystal chandelier.

"No, I love it. I would put a dimmer switch on the light though; that way it can be sort of a sparkly night-light. You can even hang toys, animal shapes, whatever you want from the arms and have a super-posh crib mobile too. It's fit for a princess, Angela, are you sure...?" Sarah trailed off and raised an eyebrow inquiringly.

"That it's a girl? Reasonably. I'm carrying so high that two of my ribs are broken."

Sarah gasped. "What? Are you serious? What did the doctor say?"

"Not much to say. They hurt but they will heal. The worst of this is waking up in the night feeling like I'm suffocating. I try to sleep sitting up in bed but I always slide down at some point."

Something crashed on the floor below. She looked at Angela who shook her head.

"No, I only investigate if the sound is followed by screaming. That usually means someone is hurt or out for revenge, or both. Of course they might have been knocked unconscious but that hasn't happened yet."

The sound of laughter drifted up the stairs. Angela had taken the last few days off to get things ready for the baby. Dark circles ringed her normally bright-blue eyes and her face looked thinner. Sarah was worried about her.

Angela's house was a narrow, three-story, brick structure that started life as the slave quarters for a grand, antebellum residence long vanished in a fire. Due to legal wrangling over inheritance and zoning issues, the empty lot had never been rebuilt on. She and her husband had jumped at the opportunity to own a house in the city with extensive grounds. They then embarked on an ambitious remodeling project that resulted in bright, airy rooms with high ceilings embraced by deep, wrap-around porches outside. Old brick pathways wound through the maze-like shrubberies at the back of the property, creating shaded, green, hide-and-seek play areas.

"I'm thinking a French blue on the walls and dark-blue curtains because this room gets the afternoon sun. The rocking chair will go by the fireplace and that, with the changing table, is really all I have room for."

"You're not painting it yourself? Good. Who is going to be with you after the baby is born?"

"My dad, possibly my mother but she is also going to work in the shop some while I'm out. I'm taking six weeks off. This is going to be hard on everyone but- what else can I do? David is up to his neck with the shop and the girls. Lil is getting worse. Two nights ago she climbed out the bedroom window onto the roof. She is deadly serious about this imaginary friend. You can see the frustration in her little face when we don't go along with her. It breaks my heart to see her go through this. If it were up to me I probably would pretend with her a little bit. But the therapist says no because this 'friend' is leading her into danger."

Sarah cringed at that news and hoped Angela did not notice. They finished going over the expense and sales reports that Sarah had brought out for Angela to approve before taking them to the accountant. They said their goodbyes.

She drove slowly back to the docks, car window down, enjoying the smell of the sea air and all the spring blooms and immediately felt guilty. Right now a little girl knew that her family thought something was wrong with her or at the very least that she was lying. Sarah wondered why the spirits didn't appear to everyone. Was it a way of isolating their victim and making them feel lonely, frightened, and crazy? In this case she wondered if something else was directing the Arabella spirit.

In the warehouse she checked the office voicemail to see if Liddy had called here. Nothing. It had been over a week now since they talked and she almost wondered if she had imagined the whole conversation. Liddy's commonsense and "let's get this done" approach had been like balm to her troubled mind.

When she called, the electric company had looked at their maps and then sent a tech out. There were no power lines running near the satyr.

Making a snap decision she dialed Liddy's cell. The call went straight to voicemail. She did not leave a message.

The warehouse was moderately busy that afternoon. A man building a house on Seabrook Island came in looking for period light fixtures and wound up buying most of the salvaged pine floorboards from the Wadmalaw plantation house to go in his kitchen. He wanted the cypress doors as well but the builder had already completed the inside framing and they wouldn't fit the openings without a lot of ripping out and reframing.

"This house has already run way over cost and I can't afford any more change orders. We sat down last night and looked at the numbers and it wasn't pretty. So I'm saving money buying these used pieces, right?"

"I can't tell you that but I'm sure you'll be happy with them. Wide boards like this aren't that easy to find anymore and are really in demand. They're fairly soft too, so they're a little more forgiving than other surfaces. When you drop something on tile it's almost always going to shatter. Pine also has a natural resin that makes it somewhat moisture resistant and you really want that in a kitchen."

They made arrangements for his builder to pick the boards up next week and Sarah went into the back to tag them as sold. Although inventory wasn't really low yet, it was moving out a lot faster these past few days.

That was her last sale of the day and she flipped the Closed sign over with a sense of relief. She had a feeling her days were just going to get busier and busier. The hours of operation here were already somewhat irregular since she often had to assess properties and help with salvage. It might be time to hire someone to help mind the store. She needed to put some numbers together on that and see if it was practical, but not tonight.

She got stuck behind one of the horse and carriage tours and stayed well back; the horses relieved themselves anytime and anywhere they pleased. Grateful when it didn't turn down her street she bounced slowly over the cobbles to her house where she found a truck parked in her driveway.

Chapter Twenty-Three

Mystified, she pulled in at the curb and approached the house with caution. She let herself in through the front door, walking slowly through the silent, peony-scented rooms. Laughter sounded from the back-yard and she heard a familiar masculine voice.

David stood halfway up a ladder propped against the back of her house, rolling paint on the wall. Kate and Lil both held paintbrushes and appeared to be painting the window trim. She opened the door and the girls looked up.

"Miss Sarah! We're painting your house for a surprise!" The girls ran up on the porch, jumping up and down in their excitement. Sarah noticed their brushes did not have any paint on them. "Are you surprised?"

"Yes! I didn't know anyone was even here. Let me look at what you did." They took her hands and led her into the yard.

"Did you know your house had this weird bulge in the wall? Look." David gestured up toward an area already painted.

"I knew. It's a cannonball. How long have you been here? You have it almost done."

"We started right after lunch, didn't we, girls?"

"We have to clean the wood with the brushes first then our dad paints it. We worked really hard. Do you see my sweat?" Lil pointed to her face and Sarah leaned down and kissed her tiny (and perfectly dry) forehead.

"I do. You did such a good job and the house looks beautiful."

It really did. The creamy paint contrasted with the red roof tiles. The newly clipped shrubs and trees seemed to embrace the house now instead of obscuring it. It would never be one of the grand residences of Charleston but its lesser charm suited her just fine.

The girls led her around the house to point out everything they had done. Apparently wasps had started a nest under one window and David had scraped it off before painting. Here, they pointed out, Mr. Tumnus and Sprinkles had gotten into a hissing and spitting fight that ended with both disappearing into opposite sections of the hedge. By the time they circumnavigated the house and arrived back where they started, David had finished painting and was washing his paint tray with the garden hose.

"David, Kate, and Lil, I don't know how to thank you. What if I ordered pizza for all of us?"

Forty-five minutes later they were settled into the sagging wicker seats, looking out over the garden, eating and talking about whatever the girls wanted. Could they have a wedding for Sprinkles and Mr. Tumnus and would she mind if they put a bowtie on Mr. Tumnus? Sarah explained that cats did not usually marry and wouldn't like to dress up for it even if they did. Was it okay to pray to Santa Claus? Apparently their Sunday school teacher did not think it was a good idea. David agreed and said that prayers, in general, should be addressed to God.

Sarah watched Lil's face, thinking that some of her little-girl bounce and confidence had disappeared. At times she stumbled over words and seemed to lose her train of thought halfway through a sentence. When this happened David reached out and covered her hand with his. Kate was much more patient with her than usual. It pierced Sarah to the heart and guilt gnawed at her.

Sprinkles returned, padding silently across the lawn, just before the sun went down. Kate and Lil went down into the cool grass to meet her. Sarah thought they walked with an unusual grace and looked like garden fairies in the softening light. Their hair was a soft, golden brown, no doubt the mingling of their mother's blonde and David's very dark, almost black hair.

"You didn't have to do it, you know. I planned to do it this weekend."

"Well, it's still not completely finished. I didn't get the window trim."

"I can get that. How did you get the paint? I thought I left it in the kitchen."

"Your front door was unlocked and not on the latch. I locked it for you. Things do get stolen around Charleston from time to time. You should be more careful."

"My carelessness paid off this time." So that little issue was starting again. She hid her disquiet. "I haven't seen much of you lately. Things busy in the stone store?"

"Yes, and that's a problem. Especially now. I just received a job offer from the history department at Charleston Southern. I don't know how to turn it down. Amazingly, they offered me the chair."

"Really? David, that's exciting. Aren't those positions usually filled from within?"

"They have a new president who wants to shake things up. He read one of my papers about the Renaissance and Deism and loved it."

"So the Renaissance related to Deism how?"

"The Renaissance was a major factor in introducing a secular world view. Once Europeans knew about the philosophy, literature, plays, etc. of the ancients, that Pandora's Box was not going to close. Deism was an amalgam of Christianity and ancient philosophy from the classical period in Greece. Or so I contend. It's not an original idea but I did introduce some points no one had brought up before."

"So, when do you start?"

"Sarah, I haven't named a start date. I haven't even talked to Angela about this yet. She's exhausted and the baby is only weeks away."

"Tell me how I can help. What if I just opened the salvage warehouse in the afternoon and pitched in at the stone store in the morning?"

"I appreciate the offer and I'll pass it along. The next few months are going to be rough on everybody. But I think we'll be ok. My parents are going to help out and they're old hands of course."

They fell silent and watched the girls. Kate made a clover chain and dragged it through the grass in front of the cat who arched her back and pounced on it repeatedly. The sounds of birds and crickets filled the evening air. Church bells rang in the distance, the sound reassuring and familiar.

"Some places still do it every hour." Sarah remarked.

"Do what every hour?" David asked.

"Ring the church bells. In some small European towns the *Angelus* called people to prayer in the morning, noon, and then again in the evening in others. People used to pray a lot more than they seem to now."

"We don't believe in the supernatural like we used to."

Sarah caught a flash of a white ruffle of cloth and bare gray legs flickering just out of sight around the corner of the house. She felt a moment of blind panic and wished for a way to get everyone out of here.

"Miss Sarah, may I use your bathroom?" Lil had climbed the steps quietly in bare feet.

"Of course. It's right up the stairs at the top." She replied distractedly.

"Thank you!" she called as she ran into the house.

"It's time we left," said David, sensing her attention had shifted. "Now you can do something fun this weekend instead of painting."

"Actually, I have no idea what to do with myself now." She glanced surreptitiously toward the corner of the house and saw nothing. How about an exorcism? That would make an interesting weekend. She felt a hysterical desire to laugh.

Kate, still sitting in the grass, looked up and screamed. She shouted, "Get down, Lil! Dad, make her stop!"

David and Sarah ran into the yard and saw Lil balanced on the upper porch rail, arms wide for balance and taking careful steps as she walked toward a wisteria-covered column. She nodded and smiled as if in response to invisible encouragement.

David ran for the house, shouting for Lil to stay still. Sarah stood and watched, almost afraid to breathe as if that might make the child lose her balance. She saw, at the upper range of her peripheral vision, a white-clad figure, arms and legs splayed like a lizard, scramble up the side of the house. Just before it disappeared onto the roof, it turned and through gray, shredded lips now ripped free of their stitching, it grinned. Not like a child but as something unspeakably evil and impossibly ancient.

Lil swayed then righted herself as David came through the door from the bedroom and reached for her, just missing as she turned, so gracefully on her tiny, bare feet, and fell. The little figure lay on the green lawn, crumpled and silent while her sister screamed and screamed.

~

The hospital waiting room was cold and smelled like stale coffee and rubbing alcohol. Sarah sat with one arm around Kate and the other holding Lil's twisted and bent glasses. They waited for someone to come out with an update. David had ridden over in the ambulance and Sarah followed with Kate in her car. The rest of the family had already been called.

The automatic doors swooshed open and Angela, her husband, and the boys hurried in, looking around worriedly until they saw Sarah and Kate.

"Have they told you anything?" asked Angela, her face pale and pinched with worry and fear. Kate ran to her and buried her face in her aunt's side. Angela stroked her hair.

"Not yet. They let David stay while they examined her and ran tests. We should hear something soon." Sarah's voice shook and she had trouble controlling it. All of this was her fault.

"But she was breathing, right? Could she move on her own?"

"She was unconscious but she was breathing. She was bleeding, just a little, from her mouth."

"Oh please, God." Angela sank into a plastic chair and pulled Kate up beside her.

The doors opened again and two EMT's came through pushing a stretcher on wheels. Diana, wearing a short, black skirt and heels, came through right behind them, accompanied by a man in a sweater vest and khakis. He held her hand but fumbled in his pocket for his phone which emitted a muffled buzz.

Diana's eyes narrowed at the sight of everyone clustered together in a group. She clearly felt nervous about approaching them and spoke Kate's name softly. Kate burst into tears and reached for her mother.

"Where is she?" Diana demanded, taking Kate into her arms.

"Still being examined, we think," said John, placing an arm around Angela who found his hand and held tight. Only then did she look up at Diana.

"David is with her. We don't know anything yet."

"How did it happen? David's voicemail only said that she had fallen and wasn't conscious."

"I don't have any more information than you do, Diana. We just got here."

Sarah sat in silence. She had a feeling she would not be a welcome participant in the conversation. Diana had already shot her a hostile, questioning look which she ignored.

Diana stalked over to the admissions desk and waited impatiently behind a mother who held a crying baby.

"My name is Diana Staunton and my daughter Lil was just brought in by ambulance. I need to be back there with her."

The tired-looking clerk checked her computer. "Only one person at a time can go back with the patient and it looks like her father is already there. I can call back and let him know you are here so you can take turns if you like. Just a moment."

Diana fumed. The boyfriend tried to sneak a look at his phone but she saw him and frowned. He hastily shoved it back in his pocket.

The clerk spoke to someone briefly then hung up the phone. "Mrs. Staunton, the admitting physician is coming out to talk to you."

Angela and John heard this and went over to the desk. The doctor emerged through the double doors accompanied by David. Both looked grim.

"How is she? I need to see her." Diana's voice broke on the last word and she began to cry. The boyfriend patted her shoulder awkwardly.

"Tell me, please," she said, blotting her cheek with her palm.

"Mrs. Staunton, your daughter has some very serious injuries. We know for sure that she has a broken collarbone and scapula and preliminary tests indicate possible internal injuries. We are putting her through MRI right now and this will tell us more."

"I want to see her," Diana again insisted.

"Come with me. There's a window that looks into the lab. You can see her through that while the tests are run." He ushered Diana back with him through the swinging doors.

"Hello, David. It's been a while." The boyfriend held out his hand.

"You can't seriously expect me to be happy to see you again, Craig." David turned to Angela who wrapped her arms around him. Craig, not at all abashed, retired to a chair and pulled out his phone.

"Has she said anything? Does she know where she is?" Angela asked.

David helped his sister back to a chair. "She hasn't woken up. They don't suspect head injuries but they're checking of course. Her pupils respond to light. She's bleeding internally and they want to find out from where if they need to go in." Kate climbed into his lap and he held her tight, resting his chin on top of her head.

"I saw her, Dad. I saw Arabella," Kate whispered to David, who suddenly stiffened and turned her around to face him.

"Did Lil see Arabella, too? Tonight?" David asked.

"I don't know. She didn't talk much about her to me anymore because I made fun of her. I was mean to her..." She began to cry again and David held her close.

Minutes later, Diana came out and made straight for David.

"They're reading the results now and then they want to see both of us. What the hell, David? Can't you keep her safe for one afternoon?"

"Mom, you shouldn't swear," Kate said tearfully.

Diana sat down a couple of seats away and glared at Sarah. Craig took the seat next to Diana, winking at Kate who turned away.

"Why are you always showing up? Are you some sort of family member by proxy?" Diana addressed Sarah.

Sarah opened her mouth to respond when Angela said, "Give it a rest, Diana. Just be nice."

Two white-coated doctors came through the doors and David and Diana both stood, huddling for a quiet conversation that lasted only minutes. Diana then went back with the doctors while David updated everyone.

"They don't know. The bleeding is intermittent and they now think they might get a better picture with x-rays. Once they're finished admitting her she'll be in a room where they allow more than one visitor at a time." He looked at Angela. "You guys need to go home and get some rest. Is it ok if Kate goes to your house, just until Mom or Dad can pick her up? They're on their way."

"Of course, you know you don't have to ask." Angela took Kate's hand and held it tightly.

Sarah handed Lil's glasses to David and said goodbye. There was nothing she could help with here. The night air was warm from the black asphalt parking lot giving back the heat of the day. Sarah watched Craig fold himself into a black Porsche Boxster and take off with a roar and squeal of tires. She tried to call Liddy again with no success. This time she left a message. "Liddy, please, please call me. Something bad has happened and I need to do something before anyone else gets hurt. It doesn't matter what time you get this, call me."

She was almost home when she remembered there was something she had to get first. Making a U-turn she headed for the hardware store.

Chapter Twenty-Four

The collar didn't come off easily. After an hour of sawing she had done more incidental damage to the bronze satyr than to the iron collar. She took a break only to get a drink of water and call Angela for an update on Lil whose condition was unchanged. She looked at her hands. Blisters had formed and popped and oozed watery blood. Running them under a cool tap, she wrapped them in gauze and put her gardening gloves back on.

After another hour she had sawed completely through one section. Pulling, straining she tried to bend it enough to get it off the neck. No luck. The darkness in the garden was now deep and crickets and cicadas kept up a cacophonous symphony. She picked up the hacksaw again.

When both sections finally fell to the ground one of the inverted spikes hit her foot hard and she bit her lip to keep from crying out. Feeling around in the lush vegetation she found both pieces and carried them to the big, outside trash container. She didn't want them in her house.

She considered decapitating the statue for good measure but her hands wouldn't cooperate anymore tonight and she gingerly pulled off her gloves and unwound the bloody gauze. Exhausted, she sat on the ground with her back against the plinth and let her hands sink into the cool herbs at her sides. The only sounds now were those of distant traffic; even the crickets had stopped calling. She still felt a faint vibration or buzz coming from the little figure but it didn't seem as strong as before. Despite her worry about Lil she felt a little better. At least she was fighting this thing. Time would tell if it worked.

Mr. Tumnus waited for her at the back door. She wondered where he had been all evening. He ran in ahead of her, checked out his empty food dish and twined around her ankles until she filled the bowl.

Later, in the shower, she noted that her hands were completely healed. No peeling skin, no blood. It must have been the herbs. She couldn't deny there was something magical about them and that something was infusing them with additional strength but what?

After an hour or so prowling the internet she had some ideas. Opinions varied on the creatures named in the little *grimoire*. What Elizabeth summoned might have been a powerful, high-ranking demon. This type of demon was accompanied by lesser demons who often took the form of familiars or imps. Some said these demons were former angels who joined Lucifer in his unsuccessful rebellion against God. They were cast out of heaven and fell for nine days before they reached earth and had been here ever since, making appearances in a wide variety of folklore and legends. Others contended these beings were trapped in the Abyss as punishment and could only come out if summoned.

In Celtic lore familiars were sometimes fairies, creatures that pre-dated Christianity and who fled from that religion when it came to their land. Having power over animals, sometimes children and often the weather, they were placated mostly by small gifts of food or drink. Whatever they were, they had the ability to enter into the physical, human world. They also feared iron.

An Irish ditty attributed to "The Little People" seemed to at least suggest a link between the rebellious angels and the faerie folk.

Not of the seed of Adam are we,
Nor is Abraham our father;
But of the seed of the Proud Angel,
Driven forth from Heaven

She read late into the night with the phone on the pillow beside her, still hoping for a call from Liddy. The phone, however, remained silent and she fell asleep sitting up with her computer in her lap.

~

Heavy *thuds* on the roof followed by shrieking car alarms woke her. Putting the computer aside, she climbed out of bed and stumbled over to the window, wincing each time another blow hit the house. The sound seemed to come from everywhere and she heard glass break in the bathroom.

It was still dark out. Alarms and barking dogs resounded. She pulled on some jeans and found her shoes.

Downstairs she flipped the switch for the porch light but it didn't come on. Nothing else did either. The street lamps were out all along the street. The pounding on the house lessened and car alarms began to die away.

Fumbling through the kitchen drawers she found a flashlight and used it to inspect the bathroom. One of the window panes had broken, scattering glass all over the floor and sink. She swept it all up as much as possible in the dark. She searched the house for Mr. Tumnus but wherever he was, he refused to come out, even when she called.

The hits to the house stopped and she ventured out onto the side porch and found it covered in golf-ball-sized chunks of ice. She heard people talking, exclaiming over something, and then, oddly, horns and flutes playing wildly somewhere in the distance. She listened as the sound slowly faded. She looked toward where she knew her car was parked in the street but could not see if it was damaged. It was still too dark.

According to her phone, it was just after four in the morning. She had only been asleep for three hours. Until daylight came or the electricity came back on there was nothing she could do so she went back to bed, waking again in daylight to the sound of chainsaws. Mr. Tumnus greeted her in the kitchen and she let him out into the garden.

The sun was high by the time she dressed in jeans and old leather boots and went outside to survey the damage. The sky was brilliantly blue and the air smelled fresh and clean. To her dismay, the windshield of her car was cracked and she had several new dents in the hood. David's truck, still in her driveway, had fared better with just a dent or two on the roof of the cab. A tree at the end of the street had gone down, blocking the entrance to the lane. Two men with chainsaws were slicing the limbs into logs and she heard more chainsaws in the distance.

The power was still out. She went into the garden and found she didn't have a lot of damage other than some small tree branches scattered around. The entire lawn was covered in downed leaves though. The satyr looked the same, except for the missing collar. The herbs in the parterres were wilted with edges turning brown. She began raking the leaves into a soggy pile and found a surprise.

Underneath the leaves, scattered throughout the garden, were small, smooth stones. Searching, she found them everywhere; on the porches, in the gutters and on the street. She saw Noble walking her way, looking at the rocks he held in his hand with a bemused look on his face.

"Have you seen these yet?" he asked, holding them out to her. "They're all over the yard and they, or the hail, demolished my car. I've never heard anything like last night."

"Neither have I. Did you guys have a lot of damage? I lost a window upstairs."

"That big window at the landing shattered. I'm glad no one was near when it happened or they might have been killed. Other than that we're ok. I'll bet we've all got roof damage though. Mary-Michael is on the phone trying to get a window repair company out. They'll probably just put us on their list. You wouldn't happen to have any good-sized pieces of plywood lying around anywhere?"

"Sorry, Noble, I don't. Have you heard anything about when the electricity might be back on?"

"The guy that lives behind us said that a sub-station was practically pulverized last night. It might be awhile."

Sarah shrugged. "Could be worse. Let me know if you need anything."

"Will do. Same here."

She swept the bathroom floor again, finding several glass slivers she had missed in the dark. Checking her phone she found a voicemail from Liddy! She called it immediately but the message was garbled. The only words she could make out were "not to" and "worse." Not exactly encouraging. Calling back just took her to Liddy's voicemail again. She clenched the phone in frustration then dialed Angela.

"Angela, it's Sarah. How is she?"

"Not good and I can only talk for a minute. My battery is almost dead. David needs to come by for the truck. Is your street passable?"

"There's a tree blocking the Rue entrance and I don't know about Argyle Street. You said 'not good.' Is she worse?"

"They found some more problems. I'm going to have to let David tell you when he comes for the truck. You aren't going anywhere, are you?"

"My windshield is broken and it may take a while to get it repaired. Let me know if there is anything I can help with later."

There was no response, just dead air. Angela's phone must have died.

Resuming raking her soggy garden she kept finding more stones and started tossing them under the porch. They looked like granite, something found more often on the beaches in Massachusetts than here where the beaches were sandier.

The lilacs and peonies lay flat on the ground, their delicate petals shredded. Her cherry tree was practically stripped of leaves. All of her raking revealed something else as well.

Crossing the yard were prints, very large hoof-prints. She followed them. They circled the house, left deeply indented, muddy prints on the sidewalk, and then disappeared on the street cobbles near the lamp post. She walked all the way down the street and back up again, looking for more prints but didn't find any. Just as she passed between the tabby gate posts leading to her garden, she glimpsed a large, brown rabbit near the yews. It stayed still for just a moment, long enough for her to see that it had a deformity; a twisted left foot that looked more like a bird's claw than a rabbit's foot. Then it disappeared under the shrubs.

The bright morning seemed to darken and the grinding, buzzing of the chainsaws faded away. Looking up at the bedroom window she saw a familiar, dark-haired figure gazing down at the street.

It took all the courage she possessed to walk into the house. She felt as if she had a fever. Silence greeted her. Once again, she inspected the house and found nothing. She folded two garbage bags and taped them over the broken pane in the bathroom window. Someone knocked on the front door.

David stood on the front stoop, looking exhausted. He shook his head when she invited him in.

"I just talked to the guys down the street. They should have the road cleared in about another thirty minutes or so. I wanted to let you know I'll be taking the truck as soon as they finish."

"How did you get here? You didn't walk from the hospital?"

"No, Dewayne dropped me off. There's been a lot of damage around town but most of the streets are still passable."

"At least come in and have something to eat. Everything in the fridge is still cold. Do you have time to tell me how she is?" Sarah had never seen anyone look so tired.

He came inside and sat down at her little kitchen table. She started to pour him a bowl of cereal, then reconsidered. That wasn't much of a meal and she didn't know when he had last eaten. She cut four thick slices of bread from a loaf and made two sandwiches piled high with thin-sliced turkey, provolone cheese, lettuce, and tomato. He ate everything and drank two glasses of iced tea.

She loaded a platter with Pepperidge Farm chocolate cookies and they went into the parlor. Looking out at the street she saw a car drive out so they must have finished with the tree. David sat on the sofa and talked while she held Mr. Tumnus and listened.

"She's not any better. Were you still there when they said they needed x-rays? Apparently they didn't want to say anything yet but what they were really trying to do was confirm what the MRI showed."

"What is it?" she asked.

"They found things in her stomach. Nails, and ink pens, a skeleton key. I don't know where she would even get something like that. She has bruises too, all along her back and stomach."

Sarah remembered Lil telling her that Arabella pinched her and she opened her mouth to tell him then reconsidered. David would think she was crazy. The important thing was that Lil was away from this house and the shade Arabella couldn't get to her anymore. Then she thought of those hoof prints leading out of the yard to the street.

"The hospital called in a social worker because they suspect abuse. For now we only have supervised visitation with her. I get to see her again today at four p.m."

"That is ridiculous! They think you did this?"

"They think either I did it or her mother. I have to tell you, for all of my ex-wife's faults, I don't think she would do something like this. Lil must have swallowed those things, but why? It sounds almost physically impossible. As for the bruises, I have no idea. I'm terrified they'll try to take Kate away. I don't know how they do these things but it's the logical next step, isn't it?"

David leaned back against the arm of the sofa and closed his eyes. Mr. Tumnus tried to get down. He still did not like this room. She took him to the back door and let him out. When she returned, David had fallen asleep.

She found a quilt. He was so tall she couldn't cover him up completely. There was really no point in waking him until it was time to go back to the hospital. He grabbed her hand and held it to his cheek briefly and mumbled something she couldn't understand. In his sleep he looked younger and the lines on his forehead were smoothed out. His eyebrows were dark and very straight. She traced the stubble along his jaw line briefly then made herself stop.

The air inside the house felt heavy, almost as if she moved through water. Chainsaws still sounded distantly and their monotonous buzz was strangely soothing. A van sporting a local window repair company logo drove by.

If the electricity did not come back on soon she would lose all the food in the fridge. She needed ice but didn't want to risk driving her car. That windshield crack was wide and spider-webbed out enough to make it difficult to see. She left David a note and went out on foot to find bagged ice.

Chapter Twenty-Five

Evidently she wasn't the only one who had had this idea. The few stores open, and within walking distance, were out of ice; there wasn't even any dry-ice. There were downed trees everywhere and green leaves covered the sidewalks and streets. The crowds of tourists were definitely thinner and they milled about aimlessly, most looking somewhat un-groomed. Restaurants were closed but a few street vendors did a booming business (cash only).

Down near the Battery a horse-drawn carriage tour operator was still in service, the driver in the process of loading a group into the glossy, red carriage. The gray horse stood patiently, occasionally swishing his tail and tossing his head to disperse hovering flies. A father, holding his infant son, brought the child over to see the horse that blinked placidly when the child's chubby fist grazed his nose.

The driver climbed aboard, shook the reins and clicked his tongue, signaling the horse to move. In the process of lifting his front leg, the horse stopped, put his leg down and refused to go. The driver flicked the reins again and at this the horse's eyes rolled wildly and he actually backed up a step or two, causing the seated passengers to exclaim questioningly. A woman shouted "Look!" and pointed out to sea.

In the distance, hovering just above the gray waves, a roiling fog uncoiled itself as it approached land. The wind that drove it whipped around and reached land first, bringing with it a stench of creatures long-dead and rotting.

The horse reacted to the smell by backing up farther, tipping the front of the carriage up. He seemed ashamed of his behavior and the muscles in his withers and flanks twitched as he struggled to overcome his terror of what approached. The driver spoke sharply and raised his whip. The horse lurched forward onto the sidewalk, turned sharply left and swung the carriage forward, overturning it against the wall. The passengers not crushed were flung into the sea and the oncoming fog. Their screams joined the shriek of the wind. The horse lay on its side in the traces, foreleg twisted at an unnatural angle, unable to get up.

The fog slowed once it reached land, sending curling tendrils of mist into Battery Park. A small crowd gathered around the overturned carriage and Sarah lost sight of them in the thickening mist. She ran to the sea wall, looking for a way down. No longer visible, shrouded in fog, people called for help from below. Sirens sounded, coming closer until two police cruisers rounded the corner, followed quickly by fire trucks. The firemen immediately sent down rescue ropes and got to work. There was nothing she could help with here and she turned toward home.

A shady, brick-paved lane just past Broad Street beckoned as a possible shortcut. She thought she saw the distant steeple of St. John's beyond the roof tops and her house was just south of the church. Wanting to outpace the fog but not sure why really, she entered the narrow street.

The houses here were neglected with peeling paint and weeds growing up through porches. This was too run-down even for student housing. An old woman in a stained nightgown stood just inside a broken-down fence, smoking a pipe and peering through squinted eyes into the street. Two vacant-faced children sitting in the dirt of the front garden stared at Sarah as she walked past. The combined smell of garbage and sewers hung in the air. She walked faster.

This was a mistake. She should never have come this way. Overhanging willow branches brushed against her head. Something scurried along the gutter ahead. She caught a glimpse of a furred body with a repulsive, naked tail. She stopped, wondering whether she ought to go back and find another way home, when she heard the distinctive sound of hooves on pavement.

Surely carriage tours would not come down this street. It was hardly an area to show off to tourists. She heard a whistling sound above and looked up. Leering, malevolent, brown eyes in a nut-brown face looked down at her from among the leaves then disappeared, leaving the branches swaying. Another face appeared ahead of her then vanished. The whistling sounds came again from farther away then stopped.

The fog swirled around her feet and looking back she could no longer see where she had just been. Pressing on she prayed this was not a dead end and that she would soon emerge on a street near the church. From there she was less than five minutes from her house. She heard more scurrying, scraping sounds in the mist around her and she ran, not sure if she heard the hooves again or her heart pounding in her ears.

She came bolting out into Calhoun Street, awkwardly dodging a passing cyclist and startling a family sitting on a bench and eating ice cream cones. Normalcy teetered on the edge of the bizarre and she knew she probably looked crazed. She slowed down and made an effort to smooth her hair. Glancing back she saw the fog creeping into the crowded street and she hurried home.

David was gone. The quilt was folded neatly and laid across the arm of the sofa. She opened the back door to admit a hungry Mr. Tumnus then fixed her own lunch. While she ate the day grew darker and colder. The fog had finally reached her street.

Marooned in an opaque white sea, Sarah paced the side porch. Visibility barely extended past the sidewalk. She needed to talk to Liddy but none of her calls would go through. A weather alert advised against travel due to extremely hazardous driving conditions caused by the fog. Charleston International Airport cancelled all outbound and inbound flights until further notice. The information, even though she had no plans to fly anywhere, made her feel trapped and restless.

Tea. She needed a warm, soothing glass of tea. Chamomile preferably. She searched her cabinets for the tea kettle then remembered. The power was still out. She had chamomile in the garden, though and she could at least gather some leaves and hope the electricity would come on soon.

Mr. Tumnus was by the back door ready to be turned out. Finding the flashlight she went out and plucked a handful of the wilted leaves. She chewed a few, finding them unexpectedly bitter. The mist swirled around her and she had an impression of hidden creatures moving within the white mass. That was ridiculous but still.... She went upstairs and wrapped up in her comforter in the middle of the big bed, overcome by drowsiness and trying to get warm.

She opened her eyes to almost total darkness. The street lamps were not on, of course, and the surrounding houses were just as dark as hers. Having no idea how long she had slept, she stumbled downstairs and eventually found her phone. Three hours? A bittersweet, dry taste in her mouth recalled the tea leaves and she wondered just how strong they were. Her head felt heavy.

The flashlight was still on the kitchen counter and she rummaged through cabinets until she found candles and her single oil lamp. Amazing how comforting light was.

Suddenly she heard music, that wild, weird mingling of pipes and horns emitting silvery notes distant at first and then drawing nearer. She paused, then obeying some instinct she blew out the lamp. She didn't want whoever or whatever was out there to see her. Feeling helpless, she crouched in the dark like a frightened child hiding under the bedclothes, hoping the bogeyman would pass her by. The music grew louder then stopped.

Faint, rustling sounds outside grew to scratching on the walls and windows, something seeking a way in. She heard voices but they spoke in a language she didn't understand. The agonized yowl of a cat just outside the door pierced the other sounds and she went cold in terror but to her shame stayed where she was. Her feet simply refused to move.

The sounds died abruptly and there was a dull thud against the kitchen door. Trembling, she tried to stand but couldn't. She crawled to the kitchen and opened the door.

Mr. Tumnus lay brokenly on the porch floor. The fur on his little back still stood up in ridges. She picked up the limp body and laid it in a rocker before closing the door.

~

The next morning the fog still held fast. Outside, everything was eerily silent and she wondered if power had been restored anywhere. She glanced at the rocker on the porch, and then looked away. She did not own a shovel. The acrid smell of cigarette smoke drifted her way and she walked over to Mary-Michael's, finding her in the side garden, hiding behind a magnolia.

"Oh my gosh, Sarah! You scared the hell out of me." Mary-Michael picked up the cigarette she had just thrown on the ground. "I thought you were Noble."

She puffed on the now damp cigarette, trying to get it going again but it was too wet. Sighing, she pulled another one from the pack.

Despite everything, Sarah almost laughed. "Sorry, Mary-Michael. I just want to borrow a shovel, if you guys have one."

"We do, somewhere. Hang on a second and let me finish this one." She lit her cigarette. "You're not going to garden in this mess, are you?"

"No. Something-" she tried to speak around the lump of grief that was suddenly in her throat, "Something got my cat last night. I need to bury him."

"Oh no! I'm so, so sorry. Don't dig the grave yourself, I'll send Noble over to do it later. He went out to find an open grocery store. Do you have any idea what might have gotten your cat? Did you see anything?"

"No, I didn't see anything." It was technically true. "Did you guys hear anything unusual last night?"

"Do you mean that music someone had blasting half the night? Yes, and I'd complain if I knew who was doing it. What a waste of batteries. That was obnoxious."

Sarah wasn't sure they were talking about the same thing and let it drop. She insisted she needed to dig the grave herself and they finally found a shovel leaning against the wooden storage shed.

The soil in the garden was damp and friable and digging the grave didn't take long. It didn't have to be that big anyway.

The little body had stiffened but began to relax again by the time she finished. She laid him gently in the soft ground.

She was going to have to get out in spite of her cracked windshield, if only to charge her phone with the car charger. The mist had not dissipated at all; if anything, it was thicker. The guy at the auto glass repair company had laughed when she asked if he could come out today. He put her on the list for Friday.

Pulling out slowly, she drove to the end of the block, then hesitated. She could barely see the stop sign. Hopefully no one would drive fast in this mess. She said a quick prayer and rolled out into the street, deciding on the spur of the moment to go to the hospital and check on Lil's condition. Maybe David or Angela would be there.

She drove through a shadowy, misty landscape. Visibility was still almost nil. The fog drifted thick in some spots then lifted in others. Occasional pedestrians came into view then faded away like ghosts as she passed. The tree branches hung low and heavy with moisture that dripped sporadically onto her windshield. She passed a utility crew working on underground lines right before she turned into the hospital parking lot.

The hospital appeared to have some power restored or maybe they were running on generators. The automatic doors had to be pushed open but the lighting inside seemed much as usual and most of the chairs in the waiting room were full. The ER clerk referred her to hospital admissions, which was up one floor. In the office there, she found an energetic young man with blond dreadlocks. He kept flipping them back while he looked up the name and read the accompanying notes. His expression became guarded.

"Looks like Miss Staunton has supervised visits only. Are you an aunt or…?"

"I'm a friend of the family. I'm not asking to see her; I just want to know if she is any better."

"Her condition is unchanged. I can't tell you more than that unless you're family. Sorry."

"I understand."

Turning away she made her way to the stairs. Just as she reached the bottom, the door opened and David walked into the stairwell.

"Are you leaving?" David wore jeans with an expensive-looking, starched, Brooks Brothers button-down and shiny brown loafers without socks. He noticed her looking.

"Yeah, I know. I'm running out of clean, ironed clothes. I've started wearing things hanging in the back of the closet from the dry-cleaners. I wasn't prepared for a power outage this long. If it doesn't come back soon, I'll be wearing some of my wool suits. Thanks for the sandwiches and the nap by the way. Did you come to check on Lil?"

"They told me she's the same."

"She still hasn't woken up but they don't know why. No head injuries other than that she bit her tongue when she fell. They're still considering surgery to remove those objects from her stomach. If they're causing the internal bleeding they need to come out and I don't know why they're hesitating."

Still talking, they climbed the stairs to the second floor, passed admissions and walked down a poorly lighted hallway. Only some of the lights in the ceiling seemed to be working. A sturdy-looking woman wearing an ankle-length, cotton dress, and sandals with socks, waited outside room 207. She nodded to David who seemed to know her already.

"Mr. Staunton, I still have a few things we need to go over and a few more release forms for you to sign." She extracted a folder from a bulging bag. "This will allow the hospital to release test results to Child Protective Services and this," she handed him two forms, "is your request that your insurance recognize us as temporary guardians."

David handed them back to her. "Get a judge to send me a court order telling me that he has taken custody from me and I will. Until then, let's hear no more about guardianship."

"You know I can get that easily, Mr. Staunton." The caseworker looked at him with a steady gaze.

"Then do it." David walked ahead of her into Lil's room. The woman followed him.

Sarah leaned against the corridor wall. She was an intruder in the family tragedy being played out here but she needed to hear that Lil was better. Guilt drew her here and guilt kept her here hoping to hear a little girl wake up and say she felt better and was ready to go home now.

Instead, a man in scrubs walked down the hallway, smiled at her absentmindedly, and went into the room. She heard him say something to David; heard David's voice raised in a question, and heard the man apologize. But for what? David began to speak and was loud enough that she (and the gentleman mopping at the far end of the corridor) heard everything.

"That's insane. There's something wrong with your machines. Scissors? How could a four-year-old child swallow scissors?"

He lowered his voice then but continued to speak. She had never heard him truly angry before. The doctor (presumably) said something else in a low voice.

"Again? No! You know, better than I do, how much radiation is received from an MRI and x-ray. Unless you have new equipment down there that you haven't used before, forget it. Scissors? Seashells? You told us before you found rocks and nails. If you can't do any better than this we need a referral and transfer to another hospital."

"Mr. Staunton, I recommend that you follow the hospital's advice. Or are you refusing medical treatment for your child?" The caseworker's voice held a hint of a threat.

"I am requesting better medical treatment for my child. She is not to be used as a guinea pig to test faulty medical equipment. If you force this, don't forget that you and your department are liable too." His voice held more than a hint of a threat.

A brief silence fell. The stair door at the end of the hallway opened and Angela and her husband emerged. Angela wore a loose, linen dress with thin-strapped, gladiator sandals and looked like a tired fertility goddess, ripe with new life ready to spring forth. Her husband, John, kept one arm protectively around her shoulders. Their eyes were down and they didn't see

Sarah until they stopped outside Lil's room. Before anyone could speak, pandemonium erupted in the early afternoon quiet.

The sounds coming from the room were not human. John hurried to the door and stopped just inside, barring Angela and Sarah from the room. Peering over his raised arm they saw that Lil had finally awakened.

Hissing and growling, the child crouched on the floor, looking up through damp, tangled locks of hair. Her arm was bloody where she had ripped out the IV line and her eyes, cunning and feral, gleamed. She lunged at the doctor, who held her off and began shouting for an orderly. Lil bit down on his hand and pulled away a chunk of skin and flesh, spitting it on the floor. The doctor screamed and she grinned, white, baby teeth awash in a mouthful of blood.

David came at her from behind, pinning her arms to her sides and shouting for help. John ripped the top sheet from the bed and together they wrapped it around the struggling child, immobilizing her. She bucked and screamed until they placed her on the bed where her eyes rolled back in her head and she suddenly went limp and quiet. Blood trickled down from the corners of her mouth. David sat beside her and gathered her into his arms.

The doctor walked to a sink, grabbed several paper towels and wrapped his hand while the child services caseworker stood in shock in a corner of the room. The orderlies arrived, a large man in scrubs and a muscular woman sporting a she-mullet. They looked around; the woman went to the bed and had David put Lil back in the bed, lying on her side. A nurse entered and approached the doctor who waved her off. She exclaimed over Lil, demanding to know what happened. When no one answered, she snapped on latex gloves and began to gently clean the blood from the child's mouth.

Angela walked to the bed and touched her niece on the shoulder. Lil's eyes snapped open and she muttered in deep guttural sounds. She retched, her little body convulsed in spasms and she vomited onto the floor. The dark gray mass burned and smoked. Everyone stared in disbelief at the smoldering embers and ash on the shiny, tiled floor. Lil stopped retching and seemed to lose consciousness. Angry red blisters covered her mouth. David held her while Angela soaked a paper towel in cool water and held it to her lips.

"Get her moved to a secure room and find a straightjacket. I'm referring her to the staff psychiatrist and I want her on Thorazine immediately." The doctor spoke to the nurse and the orderlies. He didn't look at David.

"What does psychiatry have to do with an illness causing a little girl to vomit burning ash? What is going on here? Are you trying to tell me you don't see this?" He gestured at the floor.

"She is dangerous, Mr. Staunton, to others and possibly herself. As for her symptoms- I don't know what could cause this. It's beyond my experience. That's one reason we need a fresh perspective."

"She has been in your care for over twenty-four hours. What have you done to her to cause something like this?" Angela demanded tearfully.

Sarah stood by the door, horrified and knowing she was the only one here who knew what was happening; the only one who knew that something evil was in this room. She had released it back into this world and she had to find a way to stop it. She needed to find Liddy right away.

As Sarah backed out the door, Lil struggled in David's arms and sat up. Her eyes were still rolled back, showing the whites. She spoke but had difficulty forming words around her blistered tongue and lips.

"You will not banish me. I will not go back into the Abyss." The voice was deep and resonant. She collapsed back in David's arms. Everyone in the room turned pale when that impossible voice came out of her mouth. Angela swayed and almost fell before John caught her and got her to a chair. The doctor, writing orders on a sheet, tensed when he heard it but did not speak.

The orderlies worked efficiently and soon had Lil strapped down to the bed, preparing to move her. The nurse spread a white cream on her scorched lips. She didn't try to put the saline drip line back in.

Angela, John, and Sarah walked behind the rolling bed until they got to the elevator. David kept one hand on Lil the whole time and went in with the orderlies. The doors closed and they were gone.

Chapter Twenty-Six

Sarah drove through the white swirling mist that still filled the streets. No stores or restaurants that she passed were open and none of the traffic lights were operational.

Her phone was not completely charged so she continued driving, hoping to escape the fog at some point and not wanting to go home yet anyway.

She knew those last words were meant for her and that the thing was challenging her. She didn't know how to fight it but she was going to try. Making her way across the bridge out of town, she was soon heading south on Maybank Highway. The fog still hovered but was thinner out here.

Liddy had mentioned living in a house not far from the Bohicket marina. Sarah didn't know exactly where that was. She kept dialing her but went straight to voicemail again. No matter. If she had to she would stop at every house and ask if anyone knew where Liddy Carmody lived.

Again, she drove through a ghostly world. Road signs made last-minute appearances and were quickly gone from view. The roadside stands offering shrimp for sale were closed. A plank shack selling boiled peanuts was open and she stopped, ready to beg for information.

As far as she could see, her car was the only one here. Her boots crunched on the loose gravel as she walked past a picnic table covered with a plastic red-and-white checkered tablecloth. No one was in the shack so she walked around behind it. Seated at another picnic table was an elderly woman, plaiting long, coarse strands of grass together.

"Hi, I'm trying to find a woman I believe lives close by. The last name is Carmody?"

The woman shook her head and went back to her weaving. Sarah tried again.

"The first name is Liddy, Lydia really. She has an architectural business and lives near her parents somewhere near here. I believe they run a chain of grocery stores."

The woman looked at her and said, "Lydia Beauchamp and her mama and daddy used to come up here when they went to church. She marry that Carmody boy?"

"Yes ma'am, I believe she did."

"Go on up another mile to Fontaine road. Turn to the right and you'll see it. Big, old place past the church. Nice folk, the Beauchamps."

"Thank you so much."

She found Fontaine road fast enough but there were several, tiny churches along the road. They were almost all Baptist and she wondered idly why they didn't join together to create one, big church. The fog was much thinner out here. She didn't see any big houses until she drove across a cattle gate and rounded a sharp curve.

A house crowned the slight crest in front of her. Tall, with a columned front porch, it nestled among the green fields and mossy oaks surrounding it. A horse grazed in a paddock close to a gable-front barn. The area could have been the archetype for almost every pastoral primitive ever put on canvas.

Sarah pulled into the crescent driveway and walked to the front door. At her knock, she heard slow footsteps coming closer. A man, slightly stooped with gray in his otherwise black hair and wearing khakis with a polo shirt, opened the door.

"May I help you?"

"Hi, I'm Sarah Faust. I'm trying to find Liddy Carmody. She is one of my customers and she was looking for some information for me..." she trailed off, not sure how to continue.

The man suddenly looked extremely interested. "Oh, of course. She told me a little about you and your- problem. Come in." He ushered her in and led her down a hallway to a small room with a coffered ceiling.

Shiny, polished dark floors were the perfect background for the white, upholstered chairs and warm, honey-colored wooden furniture. Light poured in from floor-to-ceiling windows and filmy curtains billowed in the slight breeze.

"Please, have a seat. Liddy had to go out of town unexpectedly. Her husband's mother fell ill and they are trying to arrange for a rehab facility for a few weeks. A slight stroke, I believe."

Sarah's hopes sank. "I'm so sorry to hear that. I hope she gets well soon. I don't want to take up any more of your time so I'll be on my way."

"There's no hurry for you to go. I think I know what you're here for."

"Oh." She didn't know if she felt embarrassed or relieved. Perhaps a little of both.

"The way Liddy told it, you bought the old Grayhame place in town. That house should have burned to the ground a long time ago but as they say, the devil protects his own." He pursed his lips and shook his head.

Sarah was stung. "It's my family home. I just want to get rid of whatever is causing the problem."

"That can't always be done. Some things have power beyond our understanding." He shook his head again. "I should introduce myself. I'm Liddy's uncle, Vernon Beauchamp. Lydia's father and mother live a little farther up the road and Liddy and her husband live just past that."

She was surprised. She had assumed he was Liddy's father. "It's nice to meet you, Mr. Beauchamp. I understand that you may feel the house is better off destroyed and if that will make all of this go away, I'll do it somehow. Are you sure that burning it down would get rid of everything?"

"No, I'm not sure of that at all. Can you tell me everything that's happened?"

An hour later she felt drained but somehow better. He didn't say much, only frowned deeply when she told him about the fireplace communications and looked concerned when she told him about Lil. He was especially interested in the fog that rolled in and the small people she had seen in the tree. He sat for a few minutes before speaking.

"You should never have communicated with it. You made it stronger and now you have released it. The creature won't leave voluntarily. These things thrive on hate and fear and they're very good at frightening and hurting their victims."

"But it's not trapped anymore. It's free to go as it pleases."

Mr. Beauchamp shook his head. "If I'm on the right track with this, the creature can only go one other place when it leaves this world. The Abyss."

"That's where it said it wouldn't go when it spoke through Lil in the hospital. I've heard of it but what exactly is the Abyss?"

"The Abyss is the place of outer darkness to which the highest ranking rebellious angels were banished after The Fall. You see, when God created mankind, he gave us immortal souls and free will much like the angels. The angels were commanded to serve and care for these new beings but some angels considered this beneath them and rebelled. Their own pride destroyed them but they blamed their fall on mankind and God. They couldn't understand that serving one another in love is the noblest calling of all."

"So they hate us and want us to suffer?"

"More than suffer. They want us to lose the thing they have no chance of anymore."

"Which is?"

"Salvation. They are damned for eternity."

"Do you know what those things in the tree were?"

"Most likely they were 'little people' or the 'Good Folk' you hear about in folklore. Some think they are really lesser angels that were banished here during The Fall."

"Can you help me get rid of it?"

He leaned forward and put his head in his hands. The skin on his hands was dark brown, papery-thin and wrinkled. Sarah realized that he was older than he had looked at first glance. She might be asking too much of him. Lost in thoughts of trying to do this on her own, she jumped when he spoke.

"I can try but ideally you are the proper one to deal with it. Have you ever tried your hand at conjuring before?"

She thought guiltily of the herbs she had burned and scattered as a lark and that mistake with the napkin. They had worked though, and beautifully.

"Just a little. I found Elizabeth's *grimoire* and took a couple of spells for kind of a test drive. They worked."

"Good, you have a spark of the little magic in your blood. That's always helpful." He seemed pleased.

"How soon do you want to get started? I know I'm being presumptuous but would tomorrow be too soon?"

"Tomorrow? No, that won't work. The little girl is close to death. This fog is hiding more than you realize. This creature can break down the barriers of time and bring all sorts of evil into the present. It is free right now but it knows that it can be forced back into the Abyss and it will do everything in its power to keep that from happening. We need to end this tonight."

~

The Piggly Wiggly on the eastern end of Bohicket had almost everything on the list Mr. Beauchamp had written down. He was coming over at nine tonight and had given her very explicit instructions on how to prepare for the ritual and she had a lot to do. Boxes of salt, a bottle of olive oil, and a new, very sharp knife were in a bag in the trunk. She had also picked up a newspaper with a chilling headline.

FIVE MISSING IN FOG

CHARLESTON- Two more children, both under the age of ten, have been reported missing, bringing the total now missing to five. Cara Grant and Samantha Holmes, both of Charleston were last seen near the IMAX on Wharf Road. In both instances, the children strayed from sight of their parents and were lost in the dense fog blanketing the city.

Foul play has not been ruled out in any of the cases.

"We just want her back," said the mother of seven-year-old Michelle Bryan, in a tearful plea for the return of her daughter, missing since Sunday.

A six-month-old infant boy was snatched from a stroller the same day. His mother, struck by a passing motorist when she ran into the street looking for him, remains in critical condition.

South Carolina's agency for missing and endangered children says the families are not suspects in the disappearances.

Driving along Bohicket Road she passed in and out of the shade of the giant oaks lining and towering over the road. Dense copses of tangled palmetto and scrub pines alternated with clearings of saw grass. A deer leapt out of a thicket, coming briefly into view before disappearing again in the thick scrub. She hit her brakes, expecting it to dash into the road but it continued running alongside the road, finally turning and running across a sandy field into deeper woodland.

Following impossibly fast was a group of small people, dressed completely in green and brandishing long, machete-like knives and wooden clubs. They too, flashed in and out of view in the shaded undergrowth and finally took the deer down in a patch of open grass. She heard screams of fierce exultation and the high pitched squeals of the deer as it died.

Sarah sat for just a moment, not believing what she had seen. What were these things?

The fog closed in again once she hit Maybank and she slowed to a crawl. The few other motorists she saw were driving just as slowly but still she felt a sense of relief when she crossed the bridge to the city. Almost home. Suddenly a large tractor-trailer truck shot into her lane as it came up the on-ramp, forcing her off the road and into the small municipal greenway sandwiched between the road and the aquarium. She felt the car's wheels sink into the drenched, soggy ground and it stopped, slamming her head hard into the driver's window. The already cracked windshield splintered and glass slivers were everywhere.

Dazed, she sat for a few moments. She patted her head gingerly and felt a lump and saw blood on her fingers. Nothing serious, I just need to get home. Her right leg started to shake and she realized she was still pressing the brake with her foot. Easing off the brake she pressed the accelerator, steering the car toward the road. The wheels spun in the wet mud. She tried backing up but the car would not go.

She was running out of time. Grabbing the bag of supplies from the trunk she stepped into the mist and started walking. The fog swallowed the car behind her. The air was so full of moisture that beads of water formed on her leather jacket and the paper grocery bag felt immediately damp.

The sounds of her footsteps on the sidewalk were muted. Darkened streetlamps came and went. The street signs were impossible to read until she was right in front of them. Images glimmered just on the edge of her peripheral vision, small, darting creatures that disappeared when she turned her head to look at them directly. She heard a series of whistles that came closer to her then moved away. She started to run.

Whatever stalked her, it knew where she was going. At times she heard it behind her, other times it seemed to be ahead of her. Dead animals were all along the sidewalks and gutters. Most were birds and squirrels but two were dogs, their bodies torn and mutilated. She looked desperately for an open store or a passing pedestrian but the storefronts were dark and she was alone in the city streets. The whole town felt deserted.

She turned right onto Rue, stumbling on the cobbles and wrenching her ankle. Limping on painfully, she heard heavy steps behind her. The bottom of the damp grocery bag fell apart in her arms. She caught the bottle of olive oil just before it hit the street and she scrunched the bag together at the bottom. The footsteps now sounded ahead of her and she stopped. She didn't know which way to go.

A chainsaw roared to life in the murk off to her left and she walked toward the incredibly welcome sound. She heard raised voices and smelled the sharp, fresh scent of newly sawn wood. Two men were bent over a large limb, one of them sawing and the other stacking the logs to one side. She had to stop herself from running into their arms. They saw her and put the saw aside.

"Hey, where did you find the groceries?" Both men zeroed in on the grocery bag.

"The Piggly Wiggly out on Maybank." She felt a sense of heady relief at the mere sight of a human being.

"Thanks! We went out earlier, looking for something open but didn't find anything."

"No problem. Have you heard anything about when the power will come back on?"

"I heard tomorrow afternoon but I wouldn't hold my breath. You take care now, ma'am."

"I will, you too." She walked away and the mist again surrounded her and she felt alone and frightened.

The gateposts to her house were now in sight. She limped around to the back of the house, deliberately not looking at the freshly disturbed earth near the yews. As far as she could tell, whatever followed her was gone. Relieved, she made for the porch.

Her mother stood near the steps. She was dressed as if for a summer's day, hair perfectly in place, feet in thin sandals hovering slightly above the grass. The fog swirled around her in ghostly ribbons.

"Mom?" Her voice trembled.

"Yes, darling, I'm here."

"You're not here; you're not real."

Her mother smiled at her. "I am here, can't you see me? If you stop this now, I can stay, always." Something seemed to be crawling underneath the skin on her face and the smile became a sneer.

"You- this isn't real. Whatever you are, stop it." She felt tears forming in her throat and swallowed hard.

"I miss you, baby. The other side is not what they tell you. It's cold- so cold. Don't let me go back there." Her mother's feet made contact with the ground and she walked forward, lurching and twisting painfully with each step. The left side of her face was burned, the skin blackened and peeling.

Sarah set the torn paper bag down and pulled out one of the salt containers. She punctured the seal with the knife and poured a handful of the white grains into her palm.

"Go away, I know what you are." Her heart twisted when she spoke.

Her mother raised her arms imploringly. Sarah closed her eyes and threw the salt. When she opened her eyes the figure was gone. She went inside.

~

Mr. Beauchamp's instructions had been very clear. Clothing had to be loose and simple and preferably of natural fibers. They would need a room or enclosure with a fireplace. He mentioned the necessity of a sin offering but said he would bring that with him. She had no idea what a sin offering was. He also told her not to eat anything because fasting was an important part of preparing for any religious ritual.

    She swept the parlor and the fireplace hearth. Apparently the location of the casting-out had to be very, very clean, almost like a surgical theater. The house had an air of anticipation, as if it were holding its breath. A soft pattering of raindrops sounded on the roof.

    Upstairs the sweet scent of cherries was so strong it made her dizzy. She showered and dressed in a white linen, summer dress. Her hair was down and loose and she wore no shoes. The old wood flooring felt like cool, smooth satin to her feet. Someone knocked on the door and she went downstairs.

Chapter Twenty-Seven

Dr. Bickerstaff, accompanied by Mrs. Hawks and Mrs. Short, all looking slightly wilted in the rain, stood on her front stoop. Bemused, she invited them in, wondering what could have brought them here. It was an odd time for a social call. Tendrils of fog drifted after them through the doorway, slowly dissipating only after she closed the door.

"It's lovely to see you again. I hope you are still enjoying the Hessian andirons."

"Oh yes, they were a very nice addition to our collection."

Both women held canvas bags that they set down next to the fireplace. Dr. Bickerstaff carried a leather rucksack that he lowered to the floor while he smiled at her.

"It's so nice to see you again, my dear Ms. Faust."

He grabbed her arms, pinning them behind her back while Mrs. Short wrapped a rope around her wrists.

In shock, she barely resisted when they forced her to the floor and tied her ankles together. She began screaming then and Dr. Bickerstaff hit her hard in the mouth. She ran her tongue over her split lip and tasted blood. She screamed again and they tied more rope around her head, forcing her mouth open, the rope gagging her so she could only moan. She bucked and struggled to get free to no avail. They ignored her.

They pushed her few pieces of furniture aside, clearing the center of the room. Dr. Bickerstaff removed a knife and boxes of salt from a bag. Taking the knife, he traced a good-sized circle in the floor then went outside briefly and returned with a basket from which he drew a white dove. Even under the circumstances, Sarah could not help but notice how pristine and pure it appeared. It cooed softly.

Mrs. Hawks started a small fire with kindling from one of the bags. Dr. Bickerstaff held the dove and traced something on its breast with his finger. Taking the knife, he slit its chest and drew out the heart which he threw on the fire. A sizzling sound and the smell of burnt flesh filled the room. He opened the front door and threw the torn, white body into the yard. Sarah felt nauseated.

He reached inside the basket and with bloodied hands pulled out a length of wrought-iron chain. He looked down at her.

"The first time we met I could tell that you didn't believe. I have to say it surprised me. I assumed you knew the history of your house and family. I thought I might have mistaken your identity until I compared the portrait of Mistress Grayhame to you. Genetics are amazing, aren't they? Even after hundreds of years the same features turn up." He bent down and caressed her face. Sarah jerked away.

"Stop it, Reginald. This is neither the time nor the place. Our time is short," Mrs. Hawks said in a reproving tone. She reached into a bag and threw something into the flames that flared briefly and emitted a sharp resinous odor.

She looked down at Sarah. "It's not personal, dear. You have something vastly powerful here, something we did not understand until recently. We want that power. We have watched you for months now and you obviously have no idea how to use what you had before you released it. We will make better use of it."

Dr. Bickerstaff spoke. "Can you imagine tapping into the power and knowledge of a being that has existed since before time began? The answers it could provide to age-old questions? Think about it. It existed before The Flood. This creature may have seen the face of God."

He paced the little room, almost bouncing in his excitement.

"Until now we have tried to call it without success. We thought that perhaps one of your blood would have more luck."

He untied the rope that gagged her and she coughed for several moments before she had breath to scream again. He hit her once more and held the knife to her throat, pricking her just enough to make her bleed. Helping her to a seated position up against the paneled wall, he placed a book on her lap. It was her *grimoire*.

"You do understand what you are trying to control is very evil as well as intelligent? It can kill you if it wants to. And if the stories are true it *will* want to." Her voice was raspy and her mouth felt torn.

"We'll take the risk. A demon will often be drawn to familiar surroundings and objects which is why I brought this." He reached into the rucksack and removed a square object wrapped in brown paper, opened it and propped it against the fireplace wall. It was the portrait of Elizabeth Grayhame.

"We want you to call the demon to come and reside in this. Once it comes, you will wrap it with this chain. We will then be on our way."

"It's a being utterly separated from God, from any sort of goodness at all and you-"

"Just read this paragraph aloud." He pointed with his finger.

She was shaking so hard that the book kept falling out of her lap. Mrs. Short sighed impatiently and cut the ropes binding her hands.

"Now, read it." The older woman pressed the book into her hands.

She looked down at the page. *"I conjure ye, O spirit of fire by Him who removes the earth and maketh it tremble that ye come without delay. Be ye accursed, damned and eternally reproved and tormented with pain that ye may find no repose night or day-"*

She stopped and listened but heard only rain and wind. Mrs. Short told her sharply to continue but began walking through the house, looking out windows into the obscuring mist.

"...unless ye come into this dwelling and submit unto our will-"

There was a loud bang as the kitchen door crashed open. They heard Mrs. Short scream. Dr. Bickerstaff and Mrs. Hawks stepped hastily into the circle on the floor and poured salt all around it. Footsteps shook the little house like thunder. Mrs. Short screamed again then was silent. Sulfur fumes drifted into the room.

A nightmare figure, fully eight-feet tall stood just outside the room. Bright eyes full of an evil intelligence peered from a bulbous head sporting short, thick horns. Long moustaches, clotted with blood, hung down to its naked chest. A man above the waist, it had the hindquarters of a goat with black-furred legs that terminated in black hooves.

Power radiated from him in almost visible waves and he gave an impression of being in this world and another at the same time. Looking directly at him was difficult and she saw him better if she turned her head so that she used her peripheral vision. The fear that washed over the faces of Dr. Bickerstaff and Mrs. Hawks confirmed that they had not known what they were dealing with and Sarah felt disgusted with them. They were cowards, hiding inside their salt-protected circle, foolishly thinking they could influence and gain control of anything this ancient and this evil.

For some reason her contempt cleared her mind and she felt cool-headed. She watched as the thing tried and failed to enter the circle on the floor. Dr. Bickerstaff appeared to take heart from this and looked slightly less pale. He shouted.

"Keep reading! It's your only chance of surviving this."

The conjuration she had been told to read was rubbish. This thing only came here because it wanted to. She had called it but not compelled it. Being threatened with damnation and torment meant nothing to such a creature. It had been damned a long time ago. Searching desperately through the *grimoire* she found the only passage that seemed to offer any hope.

"O God, the Father, all powerful and all merciful, who hast created all things, I entreat thy grace for me, because thou knowest well that I perform not this work to tempt thy power but be unto me a tower of strength against the appearance and assault of all evil spirits and by thy grace to banish-"

The thing suddenly focused on her and she shook under that blazing glare. With a voice incredibly deep and guttural it spoke, "Jaboles haboran Eloy elit nigit garbelon semition…"

She had no idea what it was saying; she only knew it was now coming for her, skirting the salt, those hooves burning prints into the floor. A long, forked tongue, wagging obscenely, flickered in and out of its mouth. Pressing back against the wall, she dropped the book and, reaching for it, accidentally knocked it across the room. The heat and the sulfur fumes coming from the creature burned her eyes and she could barely see.

Reaching behind her she pressed the hidden panel on the wall and groped blindly for the linen napkin inside. She held it in front of her and, fumbling, untied a knot then hung on to the side of the mantel as a roaring maelstrom of wind filled the little room.

Her sofa was blown end over end into the staircase where it smashed the spindles like matchsticks. Dr. Bickerstaff and Mrs. Hawks clawed desperately at the floor before they too were snatched by the wind and flung against the wall, no longer protected by their salt circle. The demon, virtually unaffected by the wind's force, casually stepped on their heads, crushing them like eggshells before it moved on toward Sarah. She wiped her streaming eyes and untied the last knot in the napkin.

The demon roared in outrage as it was knocked over and sent sliding out into the hallway. The wind was now so strong the windows in the room exploded sending daggers of glass into the sinewy flesh. It roared again. Obviously it could feel pain and she took heart, letting go of the jutting mantel and allowing the wind to blow her across the room to where her book was pressed against the wall.

Her hands were covered in writhing streams of red. Blood poured into her eyes. She blinked hard and wiped her face, trying to find her place in the book. Glittering slivers of glass were embedded in the backs of her hands.

"...and by thy grace to banish this spirit and give it license to depart and to trouble us no more. In the name of the most High God, world without end, Amen."

The wind still rushed past her ears but she couldn't see the demon from here. Pulling herself along the wall she eased over to look into the foyer. It was gone. The mutilated bodies of Dr. Bickerstaff and Mrs. Hawks were blown against the wall like detritus washed up on a beach. Mrs. Short's broken body lay just down the hallway and her blood pooled thickly on the floor.

A jagged glass shard protruded from her shoulder. She pulled it out, feeling the warm blood pour down her arm. The wind inside was subsiding but she heard it begin to gust outside. Rain blew in through the shattered windows. There was a sudden, loud *crack* and a gigantic, leaf-covered oak branch plunged through the ceiling, slamming down hard on the floor where Dr. Bickerstaff and Mrs. Hawks lay, covering the bodies with a leafy shroud. It missed her by mere inches. There was a knock on the front door.

Slowly, like a very old, very tired woman, she eased gingerly across the floor. The glass pierced her bare feet. Mr. Beauchamp stood on her front stoop.

"Sarah? What happened here?"

~

She told him most of it as he drove her to the hospital. He checked the three bodies for signs of possible life but they were indisputably dead. Calling 911 he reported the deaths then took Sarah, who was bleeding profusely, to the ER. The storm increased and the fog was all but dispersed, replaced by mounting winds and rain that appeared to be coming down sideways at times. The streets around the hospital were flooding but Mr. Beauchamp finally pulled into the ER parking lot and helped her inside.

She told admissions she had been standing under her windows when they were shattered by a tree branch. It took over an hour for a nurse and an intern to pick all the glass from her skin and another hour to answer questions from a police officer who seemed suspicious about her story. After she was swabbed with antiseptic and bandaged with gauze they let Mr. Beauchamp sit with her while she waited for her paperwork to be processed.

"It's finally gone," she said, feeling relaxed and a little euphoric from the painkillers. The wind howled outside and the building shook with booming bursts of thunder. The power flickered briefly then came back on.

"Sarah, this may not be over. It's not that easy to get rid of something like this. You probably at least frightened it away but

I'm not sure it's banished." Mr. Beauchamp rubbed his chin in reflection.

Trying to recount the whole scene for him was difficult. She tried to remember the exact wording of the passages she had read from the book but couldn't.

"But I used the banishing spell and a sacrifice was offered."

"Yes, but you didn't offer it. I don't know what will result from whatever was performed at your house. That man and the two women did not have the right intentions. When something like this has been called into the world, it has lasting repercussions."

The nurse came in just then and gave her a questioning glance before taking her temperature.

"I thought so. You're running a fever, Ms. Faust. I'm going to tell the doctor. He may want you admitted. When was your last tetanus shot?"

Sarah had no idea. The doctor came back in, told her he wanted to keep her overnight for observation and had the nurse give her a tetanus shot. Mr. Beauchamp said he would try to contact her tomorrow and left. She spent the rest of the night in a feverish, confused daze, hearing the thunder rumble and imagining the demon pursued her as she ran down the shiny-floored corridors.

The next morning her fever had broken and she felt hungry and ready to go home. She fretted impatiently while waiting for her discharge. The nurse was kind enough to give her flip-flops to wear home since she had come in without shoes and tried to get her to call someone to drive her home but she didn't want to bother anyone. She called a cab for the short trip. Most stores and restaurants she passed had electricity again and were open for business.

The house wasn't as bad as it could have been. The big branch still lay on the floor and Sarah hoped the police had concluded that was what killed Dr. Bickerstaff and both women. The bodies had been removed but the blood remained on the floor and walls. She called the police department and spoke to one of the detectives.

"No, Ms. Faust, the forensics team has all they need. You're free to make any repairs and do any cleaning needed. There are several professional cleaning companies in town. Do you want their numbers?"

So despite an overwhelming need to go to bed and sleep, she wiped everything down and scrubbed the floors with oil soap. The hoof marks were still there and she suspected they were too deep to sand out. Her sofa was damp and scuffed but otherwise okay and she simply pushed it back in place. The lamps were a total loss.

Mr. Beauchamp had been kind enough to put plastic over the windows after the police left last night and had even swept up most of the glass. He left a note letting her know what he had done and even left the name of a window replacement and a roof repair company. She called both right away. By late afternoon her roof had been patched but the windows had to be ordered from out of town. A towing company delivered her car, windshield replaced.

Walking around her garden, she noticed that the herbs in the parterres were brown and wilted and the wisteria vine near it had lost all of its leaves. She avoided looking at the hideous little satyr.

She called Angela. Lil was much better and excited about going home. David had her transferred to another hospital where the staff had repeated the tests from the previous hospital and found nothing unusual internally.

Sarah rang off then her phone immediately buzzed in her hand.

"Hello?"

"Sarah? It's David. Just wanted to let you know Lil is getting out this afternoon."

"David, I'm so relieved. So she's better then?"

"Right as rain. The other thing is- would you like to come over for supper on Saturday? The girls will be there but I want you to know- I am asking you out on a date." He sounded adorably nervous.

"Love to. Let me know what I can bring."

"Just yourself." He hung up.

Well, she thought. I didn't know that was coming. She felt a little tingle of excitement and thought about what she would wear. Maybe life could get back to normal now. She suspected the police would have more questions about the deaths of Dr. Bickerstaff and Mrs. Hawks and Mrs. Short and she wasn't sure what to say. Tell the truth about how they just stopped by to capture a demon to make it do their bidding? She couldn't see that conversation going well at all.

Her best bet would probably be to stick to the story she told the officer in the hospital; that the three of them were antique collectors who had found a portrait of her supposed ancestor and brought it over to show her. The portrait was still here, water-stained now but otherwise okay. She would return it to the city at the first opportunity.

A door slammed somewhere in the house and she jumped. The windows were open; of course things would blow around. She laughed shakily, and then noticed a humming sound coming from the kitchen. Walking slowly down the hallway she realized what it was. The electricity was finally on and the refrigerator had started up.

Relieved, but annoyed with her own jumpiness she went down to the basement to do the laundry. She waited until the tub filled then added bleach and closed the lid. That's when she heard the footsteps overhead. Light steps were followed by the heavy stomping of hooves. A strong smell of sulfur drifted down. A child screamed.

Filled with dread, she climbed the stairs. At the top she heard a child scream again and it chilled her. Looking around the corner she caught just a glimpse of long, dark hair and gray mottled skin before it disappeared. A foul miasma of decay hung in the air. She heard a rustle of cloth to her left. Brightly-colored skirts whisked around the entrance to the parlor. She followed.

Elizabeth knelt by the fireplace, arms protectively around the four little bodies in sacking. She was crying, holding the children who could not or would not respond to her. The sorrow in her expression was so deep that it hurt Sarah just to see it.

Elizabeth looked up and for the first time seemed really aware of Sarah's presence. Reaching behind her she picked up the *grimoire* from the mantel, searching through it until she found the passage she wanted. She placed the open book on the floor, looked imploringly at Sarah and began to fade and flicker from sight. The children faded with her.

Taking up the book she found the pages damp with spectral tears. A paragraph, very faded and barely legible, was handwritten in the margin. She read,

"I implore by the name of EL, powerful and wonderful, in Heaven where the angels neither cease nor rest in their praise of thee, bind me this creature that it may no more trouble thy creations here on Earth. Let thy children pass on to their new home with thee in glory and no more linger here in earthly pain."

Picking up the iron chain Dr. Bickerstaff brought the night before and still holding the book she walked, feet hurting with every step, outside to the horned statue.

"I bid thee, demon, come unto this place, resist me not, wherever ye be. I name thee, Malkuth (as soon as she said the name she heard a roar of anger) *and invoke thee to enter this abode and dwell herein at my express command. Hear me and know that I am of the blood that did compel thee before."*

The little statue glowed and she heard a ringing sound. Quickly she wrapped the iron chain around the neck and let it hang there. The glow flickered out.

The light gradually faded and night birds called in the darkness. She sat down in the cool, damp grass. She had failed and she suspected that Elizabeth had had the same problem hundreds of years ago. She heard a motor coming down the street. A car door opened and shut and she heard someone knock on her front door. Too tired to move she sat still and eventually footsteps rustled through the grass and around the side of the house.

"Sarah?" Liddy walked into view. "Are you okay?"

"It didn't work. I couldn't banish it. I may have released the children's spirits but I'm not sure." Exhausted, she dropped her head and closed her eyes

"My uncle called me. He wasn't sure you had gotten rid of it."

"Things got out of control."

"Where is it?"

She pointed tiredly toward the chained statue. Liddy took a look but didn't get too close.

"I've got an idea. You have it contained for now, right?"

"It can still affect anyone in or near this house. My neighbor's daughters will be back soon. It's been using the spirits of the dead children here to hurt the youngest daughter. I have to fix this, Liddy."

"Go to bed. I'll be here early tomorrow with my landscaping crew."

"Why would-"

"I'll explain tomorrow."

~

True to her word, Liddy was outside the house the next morning at seven. Two men, neither of whom seemed to be able to speak English, accompanied her. The taller one had already secured the base of the statue with a chain and was attaching it to a hitch on a long-bed pickup.

Sarah dressed hurriedly and ran downstairs just in time to see her statue toppled into the truck bed, chain clanking as it fell face first, just missing the rear window and coming to rest at an angle. Liddy stood to one side, watching.

"Where are you taking it? It can infest any place it inhabits. I can't release this on anyone else. It's too dangerous." She twisted her hair up in a bun as she walked out to the sidewalk.

"Get in." Liddy climbed into her Mercedes as the truck pulled away. "I told you I have an idea."

They followed the truck out of the city to the Bohicket Marina and Liddy outlined her plan along the way finishing with, "… then we just dump it. With any luck it will sink to the seafloor and never trouble anyone again."

"Why did no one ever try this before?"

"Remember that it was more or less buried in the garden for years. It's possible no one knew it was there. I know I didn't."

I think you moving in stirred it up somehow. You are the first family member to actually live in the house in the last two hundred years."

"How far out do we need to go? How deep is the water here?"

"Not deep enough. We need to go out past the Intra Coastal waterway and into the Atlantic. We'll take it out until we're out of sight of land."

It was a beautiful morning with a white mist hovering low over the calm surface of the water. With the exception of an older couple breakfasting at one of the cafes, the place was deserted.

A cabin cruiser rocked gently at the end of dock B and the two men wrestled the statue on board. They left, one of the men wiping his hands repeatedly on his shirt with an expression of disgust on his face. Even though they didn't know exactly what they were handling they still picked up on the unwholesomeness. Sarah gave them each thirty dollars.

Liddy was an old hand when it came to boating and she ordered Sarah around like a sea-captain. She ran through a checklist and finally they were cruising smoothly out of the slip, past brooding pelicans sitting atop old pier pilings dotting Bohicket Creek then into the Edisto River.

The Atlantic eventually came into view, sparkling in the early morning sun. Liddy opened up the throttle then and they soon lost sight of land. Even so, she kept going, cresting the gentle waves and sending up foamy white splashes of water. The statue bounced and rolled slightly since they hadn't bothered to tie it down.

Finally stopping but not trying to drop anchor, Liddy took out a heavy-duty lock and secured the iron chain with it.

"Ready?" Sarah nodded and they raised the statue to an upright position before toppling it over the side where it sank beneath the waves.

Sarah stood watching but it was gone from view in seconds. "That was somewhat anti-climactic after all the-"

The boat began to rock from side to side almost pitching them out. Sarah grabbed the railing and Liddy hung on to a seat while they tossed violently in the waves. The sun disappeared as a dark fog surrounded them and the waves grew taller and more violent. They managed to get into the seats and Liddy started the engine. It sputtered and died. All they could do was try to ride it out. The boat jerked so violently Sarah feared it would break in two.

A wave splashed over the railing, knocking Sarah from her seat and onto the floor. The water stank and she saw fish, or parts of them, eddying about in the wash. She pulled herself back up and saw another wave approaching, a terrifying dark wall of water.

Liddy was again attempting to start the engine. She saw the wave too and knew it could capsize them unless she could angle the bow to meet it. The motor coughed then sputtered to life. The boat was turning but the wave came on too fast. Instead of capsized they were swamped and began to sink as the waves continued to wash over them.

Sarah found a bucket and started bailing. Her hands were numb from the cold and she couldn't feel her feet but she frantically kept dipping and tossing the water out. Liddy managed to get the boat going forward and slowly, slowly they pulled away and into calmer waters.

They limped along, Sarah still bailing as the boat gradually rose a little higher. Now the waters around them were nearly smooth but behind a mini storm raged where they had sunk the statue. It slowly subsided as they watched. Hundreds of dead fish rose to the surface around them, floating back and forth, thumping against the sides of the boat.

Back at the marina they docked and walked slowly out to Liddy's car. Sarah had lost one shoe and she dropped the remaining one in a trashcan as they walked by. They were both soaked and Liddy turned the heater on as they drove back into town, neither one of them saying much until they pulled up in front of the house.

"Whatever happens after this, no one can say you didn't do your best to get rid of it."

"I couldn't have done it without you. I don't know how to thank you."

Liddy laughed a little. "Always warn me in future if you think you have possessed statuary. We came a little too close to drowning today."

Sarah couldn't laugh. "I promise. Always."

Liddy drove away and Sarah opened her front door and went inside.

Was it over? She heard nothing, sensed nothing at all supernatural in the house. Her bedroom still smelled faintly of cherries but that had nothing to do with the demon surely. The hot water in the shower stung her many cuts and she had to blot away blood with the towel. She spent the rest of the day cleaning up, finally pulling the big branch in the hallway outside to the curb. The window glass company called to let her know her windows were in and they could install them the day after tomorrow.

The next morning dawned cool with clear skies. Pouring a cup of coffee she walked out onto her back porch and sat on the steps, listening to the hum of distant traffic, watching the eastern sky brighten. Shoots of pale green were already beginning to grow over the little mound of earth near the yews and soon it would blend with the rest of the yard.

Her feet were sore and walking made it worse but she continued to get ready for the day. Work was exactly what she needed to take her mind off everything.

Sales at the warehouse were brisk. Everyone was catching up on projects put on hold over the last few days and almost all had a story to tell about what happened to them during the storm. A few people were still without power but expected it to be restored today.

Michael called to see how she had weathered the storm and they agreed to meet for lunch tomorrow. His apartment hadn't been hit by the hail and stones but most of his court cases had to be deferred because downtown had been without electricity. The rest of his family had escaped damage except for Cooper who had found her dog dead and literally in pieces in her backyard.

"The children didn't see it but Cooper was hysterical. My dad said it was partially eaten. I'm guessing an alligator is responsible but dad said the bite marks were too small for an alligator and looked more human than anything else."

Law enforcement still searched frantically for the missing children but clues were non-existent and Michael was stumped. He had helped compile a list of known area pedophiles but they all had pretty solid alibis for the times in question. There was no sign of foul play in any of the disappearances and he held out hope the children would still turn up. Sarah felt sick inside and prayed they would be found.

She stayed late to catch up on paperwork. Throughout the day random flashbacks played in her mind and she knew she was lucky to be alive. Driving home she saw downed branches still stacked on the sidewalks awaiting chippers but the streets were clear.

Her little street was getting back to normal. A few live oaks were gone leaving obvious gaps in the landscaping since they had been so huge. It was a shame. Most had been well over one hundred years old. She walked around to the back of the house, looking at her own damaged tree. The branch that had held the old rope swing had gone down and the swing lay in a tangled, splintered mess against the side of the house.

Inside she gingerly unwrapped the sheet from the chandelier in the dining room. Only her reflection stared back at her from the dangling crystals. She released a breath she didn't know she had been holding and smiled.

Epilogue

The currents along the Atlantic coast follow a generally predictable pattern, a course that fishermen and pleasure cruisers know well. The Gulf Stream which sweeps around Florida on its way north is one of the most powerful currents. It slows down once it reaches the colder waters of Cape Hatteras and often breaks into littler streams that are heavily influenced by tidal currents all the way up the East coast.

Vacationers often stroll the beaches near the Chesapeake Bay at night, especially on a night like this one with a full moon hanging over the eastern sky. The tide was especially high and due to that and the heavy storms over the past few days the beaches were a treasure trove of seashells and other washed-up debris.

Kevin and Laura Bryant, out for an after supper walk on the last night of their vacation, had already filled multiple bags with "treasures" discovered by their three and five-year-old sons. When they heard excited shouts and saw the boys begin digging in the sand, they braced themselves against the whines they were going to get when they refused to allow anything else in the minivan.

"It's a giant shell!" Both boys were ecstatic and Kevin, a little excited too, grinned apologetically at his wife and began to dig. They soon uncovered what looked like a bronze head with horns. Laura became interested now.

"I think it will fit in the back if we lay the seats down."

Laura nodded. It would go perfectly in the middle of the herb garden. She couldn't wait to see how it looked without that chain around its neck.

The End

L.I. Albemont is the author of the best-selling, *Contagion, A Novel of The Living Dead, World Without End,* and

Dead Coast, the latest installment in the Living Dead series. She has recently released ***The Kirk,*** a horror thriller. You can find her blog at http://lialbemont.blogspot.com/

From the author

Enjoy *A Haunting*? If you did, posting a review here or at Barnes and Noble.com is a great way to help other readers find it for themselves.

I love, love to get emails from my readers. Contact me anytime at lialbemont@gmail.com.

Please enjoy this excerpt from *The Kirk*, now available from Amazon.com and BarnesandNoble.com.

Prologue

Couriers carried back the glad tidings of peace and safety, and a glowing account of rich lands, fine forests, great water courses- rivers, creeks, brooks, and bubbling springs. In short, the land of milk and honey had been found.
M.V. Ingram

Land. Acreage. Daring wanderers left the misty folds of the British Isles in search of it. A small spot in the world where a man could plant crops, pasture his livestock and live free, answerable to no lord and master save God.

The Piedmont region of North America is a lush land of hills and valleys comprising vast, dense forests and fertile meadows ascending gradually to the ancient Appalachian Mountains. Born during the Ordovician period the mountains first rose when the North American plate collided with an ocean plate, folding vast layers of rock and thrusting them upward to dizzying heights.

In the late seventeen hundreds much of the land was still considered the western frontier, a rugged region known well only to explorers, traders, and the natives.

When the first families of European immigrants arrived they were delighted to find that the tales of prime farmland and woodland sent back by explorers were no lie. They entered a land of tumbling streams and sparkling waterfalls that led to deep, slow-moving rivers ideal for transport and irrigation.

At the same time they were surprised at the lack of cultivation. Despite the existence of large populations of the Catawba and Cherokee people above and below the area the soil lay unbroken except by trees and wild plants.

The natives referred to the land as the "dark and bloody ground" and some related rumors and old tales of human sacrifice made by a mongrel, degenerate tribe, who delivered up their children to "pass through the fire" to appease an ancient and powerful being. Fierce battles were fought there between warring tribes but none settled on the blood-drenched soil. To the Catawba the land was, and always would be, cursed, and they did not want to wake what they believed slumbered there.

Undaunted by the Catawba tales and bringing with them their culture and their faith, the intrepid settlers negotiated sales of the territory with the natives claiming ownership and, with their growing families, began to fell trees to create pastures and build their rude log homes. It was then that they came upon the enormous earthen mounds scattered throughout the forests. Being from the British Isles they were not unfamiliar with such phenomena and in general knew better than to disturb the ancient mounds. Mounds that were already thousands of years old when Columbus landed on Caribbean shores.

It was the Robard family who laid claim to the mound dotted acres. One of the original settlers, Mr. James Robard soon built his log cabin and sent to Baltimore for the rest of his family. They arrived in July of 1777. By spring of the next year they would all be dead, victims of an arcane horror acted out during the cold and snowy winter of 1777-78.

By most accounts Mrs. Robard was found first. Neighbors discovered her desiccated body staked to the ground of the spring house, razor cuts crisscrossed her arms and throat, deep, narrow wounds that must have taken some time to drain the body. Her daughters were close by in the smokehouse, hanging upside down from open rafters, small bodies gutted and trussed, revolving slowly in the sweet hickory smoke. The family's two slaves hung alongside them.

James Robard was still alive when three men forced the door of the cabin but were only in time to watch as he slit his own throat.

The Robards were not the only victims of that winter, just the most well-known. The fledgling town closed ranks and kept its secrets.

For a time the land fell into disuse, locals occasionally using it as common grazing pasture.

Game near the mounds was plentiful but often inedible. Hunters sometimes found malformed prey with extra hooves or even vestigial legs. One memorable kill involved a deer with two heads, one of which was capable of a sort of piteous speech before it was silenced. It was burned rather than eaten. Blackberries there, no matter how plump and sweet, were left for the birds.

Farmers soon learned that cattle grazing in certain fields either perished of a wasting disease and/or yielded poor quality milk and beef. Such areas were soon fenced off and in little more than a generation trees soared again into the gentle blue sky, vast canopies creating shaded microclimates lush with ferns and vines that sometimes quivered when no wind blew.

The ground here was seismically active and occasional mild tremors caused the mounds to dislodge rotting, stained bones which the settlers quietly reinterred with appropriate prayers as they had done in the dark water peat bogs of the Old Country. The dead were best never disrespected.

Printed in Great Britain
by Amazon